AMBER ALERT

Ron Vergona

Copyright 2016 © Ron Vergona

Published by:

Coeur d'Alene, Idaho

To my wife Addie, and children Jessica and Michael, for their love and support.

Prologue

PALE, YELLOW EYES PIERCED THE sparkling lake waters.

Perched in an ancient black cottonwood, the bald eagle's white, feathered neck ratcheted in robotic fashion, cataloguing both prey and the all but nonexistent predator.

About two-thirds up the tree's broad, open crown, this fearless predator rested in a gnarled branch that resembled the flexed bicep of an overactive weightlifter. The cottonwood's grayish-brown bark partially obscured its nest, while the buttery leaves foretold an early start to the impending winter along the southern Canadian border.

The eagle's keen vision dismissed any threats from the massive stone dwelling a hundred yards to the south. The huge bird had grown accustomed to the heightened human activity.

In an air of defiance, it unleashed a shrill, high-pitched chirp. The sound reverberated across the lake and the nearby foothills that punctuated the western outreaches of Creston Valley.

This mighty creature had ruled the heavens and earth since the beginning of time and had no reason to suspect a new order struggled to be born.

The crosshairs of the riflescope on the Knights Armament dual purpose weapon outlined the eagle. An easy target, but the young man's finger remained indexed.

Bartholomew didn't like easy.

That's because his whole life had been comfortable. Not stress-free but choreographed. He reflected the stature and tenacity of his grandfather's youth—cloaked by an inner drive to take matters into his own hands and ignore the consequences.

Bartholomew waited. He'd been playing this game throughout the spring and summer months, and now he grew weary of the sport.

The eagle took a final glance at its dynasty and launched itself up and out of the nest, its stately white head and black body shrinking in contrast to its pumping six-foot wingspan. In a matter of seconds, the magnificent bird soared a thousand feet above the lake. It began a slow and downward spiraling pattern, eyes fixed on the translucent water, searching for unsuspecting prey.

Bartholomew flinched at the light touch on his shoulder. Without shifting his eye from the scope, he said, "What do you think, Grandpa?"

A resignation belied his grandfather's words. "Do it, Bartholomew." The tall, frail-looking old man released his grip on Bartholomew's shoulder and turned to his guest, Aamir Rahaman.

Three loud reports disrupted the harmony in the isolated valley, and the spent cartridges clanked across the cantilevered deck and bounced into the lake. Seconds later, following a harrowing scream, the morbidly wounded bald eagle fell into the same chilly waters.

The dwindling flock would soon migrate on a southerly path to the shores of Lake Pend Oreille in the Idaho panhandle with at least one less member.

Aamir Rahaman looked at the spectacle and shrugged. He did not attain the same pleasure out of this kind of hunt as he did for human prey. He watched the huge bird fall close to the sleek aluminum boat dock attached to the lower level of the deck. With the breeze blowing toward the house, Rahaman caught a faint metallic scent as the eagle's body dropped. The spreading pool of blood swirled in the gentle waves lapping against the shore.

He focused his attention on the words coming from the old man, whom he knew only by the name: Mr. Clean.

Rahaman and his colleagues had performed a thorough investigation but found no evidence of the man's real identity. Just a chain of paperwork linking this property to Consolidated Canadian Mills, a corporation headquartered in a neighboring valley. The stone mansion behind him sat in the middle of over six hundred acres, overlooking a two-hundred-seventy-five-acre private lake. A significant portion of the acreage had been cleared for a small airfield. This site purportedly served as a retreat to entertain the company's growing list of clients.

"Aamir. Please excuse my grandson's indiscretions. It is not easy to discipline one so young, whose belly is filled with fire." A cloud of darkness shadowed Mr. Clean's face, but the moment passed. "Our journey has lasted far too long, and I find it hard to believe we are approaching this final phase."

Mr. Clean waved a hand toward Bartholomew, who placed the weapon on a bench along the deck's railing. Bartholomew pulled a white cap from his back pocket and snugged it over a head of close-cropped light blond hair. He bounded down the steps to the lower deck and then onto the boat dock.

Not for a closer look at his kill, but to greet the submerged craft breaking through the surface a little farther out on the lake.

Mr. Clean continued, "This younger generation finds it exciting to do things their own way. But Bartholomew is a worthy soldier. A true believer in our mission."

Rahaman caught the slight hesitation in Mr. Clean's voice. With the stakes this high, he fretted every detail.

Both men walked to the edge of the deck and leaned against the railing. The vessel had now completely surfaced, and with sheets of water cascading down the gleaming curved hull, it headed for the dock.

This was Aamir Rahaman's first glimpse of the new craft.

He stared at this strange vessel and then looked back to Mr. Clean. "Do you not think the American government will be suspicious? Such unusual activities occurring under their very noses?"

Mr. Clean waved to the man emerging from the center hatch of the sleek vessel as it bobbed in the tranquil waters. He then turned to Rahaman, who detected an edge in his voice. "My friend, there is no need for concern about those bureaucratic imbeciles. You must know this from experience, as an attorney serving your— *brethren*—at the ICCA in San Francisco."

Rahaman bristled at the man's choice of such a word. Any member of the new Islamic Center for Cultural Affairs complex in San Francisco held only contempt for the infidels and abhorred any veiled references to Christianity.

Pointing a crooked finger to his own chest, Mr. Clean said, "I am now a government contractor paid by the United States military to perform underwater experiments in their homeland—from where this craft has journeyed. There will be no problems or interference, only facilitation. And perhaps, even periodic bonuses for meeting our deadlines."

A smile added more wrinkles to his face, and he waved a finger at Rahaman. "If anything, you should be more wary of the ordinary citizens on the American side of the border. Since we are affiliated with their federal government, they may think we are working as a team to conspire against the local population."

Mr. Clean gazed out across the lake and raised his head. A booming laughter escaped his lips and resounded throughout the valley, echoing from the hillsides.

As if in response, the sharp cries of a lone bald eagle blanketed the human mirth.

Aamir Rahaman stood in silence, not knowing which to fear most.

CHAPTER 1

(one year later)

THE TORRENTIAL RAINS HAD SLOWED; the persistent drizzle and the howling winds of the dissipating storm lingered. Through the rhythmic thumping of the windshield wipers, the flashing lights cast ghostlike reflections off the wet asphalt and eerily danced across the rain-soaked walls and windows of the buildings lining the path of the emergency response vehicles.

The blaring sirens shook the sleeping neighborhood as the hazmat crew from the Dogpatch fire station trucked toward its destination.

The department's new white Suburban took the lead with Parkinson at the wheel. Steve Casella, hazmat coordinator, sat in the passenger seat. Amber, a white German Shepherd, paced, barked, and whined in the rear cargo area. She was not only Casella's personal companion, but one of the most highly trained canines in the San Francisco Fire Department.

The rest of the crew drove right on the heels of the Suburban in the department's latest high-tech custom rig. Not one of the largest hazmat vehicles manufactured by Ferrara but custom-built to Casella's specifications to match the team's unique responsibilities.

Parkinson glanced at Casella, watching him end the phone call. Parkinson's curly red hair, cherub face, and short stature contradicted his strength. A reliable, steadfast partner, Steve knew no one better to have his back.

"How'd Edie catch on to this?"

Steve shrugged. "Guess she heard the alert signal from the portable monitor."

"It's three o'clock in the morning. Don't tell me she sits at home waiting for that pesky alarm to start ringing; just to see what the hell you're up to? Jesus. It'd be damn hard for you to get a little action on the side."

Steve shook his head, running a hand through his scattered, dark brown hair. "You want me to mention that to Edie?"

"Hell, no. She's probably pissed enough getting jolted awake by this new interagency alert system."

"She was already up, changing Rosa." He looked over at Parkinson. "By the way, Parky, remind me I need to stop and pick up diapers when our shift ends."

Amber stopped pacing and stared at Steve, making a low chuffing sound.

Parkinson cringed and changed the subject. "Whatever happened to boring me with your handyman skills? All the work you're doing on that used-to-be man-cave in the mountains?"

A smile spread across Steve's face. He had lived for years—comfortably—in a modest one bedroom, one bath, A-frame house in the hills above the Sonoma Valley, about an hour north of San Francisco. Things got cozier when Edie moved in. Then six months ago, along came Rosa.

They had recently embarked on a major reconstruction project. When completed, the remodeled residence would have a total of four bedrooms, three and a half baths, and approximately three times the current square footage.

Steve and Edie hassled daily with the building contractor; each from their own perspective, offering advice to the beleaguered construction crew.

"This new project is moving along... maybe a little slower than....." Steve shook his head, but then nodded. "But right now, I'm leaving all the details to the professionals."

After saying this, he pulled out a tiny notepad and jotted down a few ideas to present to the contractor when he got off shift. More than likely leading to additional change-orders and translating into added cost overruns.

Parkinson swung the Suburban off Market Street as uniformed officers pulled aside the perimeter blockades to the side street and waved them through. The rain had now stopped, and he switched off the wipers. A full complement of police vehicles, fire rigs, and at least three bomb squad trucks lined the street across from the Islamic Center for Cultural Affairs, or ICCA. Parkinson pulled over and Steve jumped out, signaling to his crew where the rig should be parked.

Casella commanded a specialized hazmat team trained to deal with potential terrorist activities in the San Francisco Bay Area. They assisted local and federal law enforcement agencies in identifying risks and coordinating manpower.

As first responders to many dicey situations, it made sense to have these guys trained to assess the threat potential from any given incident and be prepared to take action before the situation got out of control. Steve also held a unique consulting position as a sworn federal agent in the Department of Homeland Security.

Tonight, the city's bomb squad unit had been first on scene. Once the location was verified as the site of the ICCA, they notified the Department of Homeland Security, triggering the new standard DHS alert protocols. It appeared the initial call had been a false alarm, but as a precaution they called in Casella's hazmat team to check out the scene. Other officials from DHS were advised to stand down.

Although part of a specialized program where select firefighters now carried firearms, Casella was informed that the situation was under control; no signs of any imminent threats. They left the heavy artillery in the rig, but his crew still carried department-issued lightweight handguns holstered onto their utility belts.

The hazmat team scrambled from the rig and got to work prepping their equipment. After grabbing Amber from the back of the Suburban and attaching her harness and lead, Steve headed to the scene unfolding outside the main entrance to the ICCA. He inhaled the residual dampness in the air that mixed with the grimy fragrances drifting up from the pavement after the earlier storm failed to clean away the lasting odors of the urban environment.

Surrounded by a full complement of city officials, a tall, thin man with a full beard stood near the entrance to the ICCA. He pounded a fist against his palm. A ruddy hue splotched across the exposed protrusions of his pitted olive cheeks. "Who called you people? This harassment must end. I have allowed your bomb experts access to our building, and they have found nothing."

One of the detectives frowned and spoke to the man. "Mr. Zakaria, I would think you'd be relieved to know there is no threat to your center."

Maajidah Zakaria's eyes dug into the detective, and he wiped a bead of sweat from his forehead. He took a step forward and jabbed a finger at the man. "I would not put it past you people to have called in this bomb scare yourselves as an excuse to snoop around inside our mosque."

Zakaria, the director of the ICCA, waved his arms toward the heavy doors. "Since we opened this sacred building, we have been met with constant harassment by the city, the state, and the federal agencies. We have complied with every last one of your inane ordinances and restrictions. Our imam believes our religious freedoms have been under attack." As he continued to list his specific complaints, his voice grew more strident.

Zakaria glanced over and spotted Steve Casella, with his armed crew set to enter the building. His eyes became narrow slits. "And now you expect me to let these additional spies inside our building? We are prepared to sue the city for violating both our civil rights and our rights to religious freedom. Our attorney has been working on this case since the first episode in April."

Capt. Jordan, the shift commander at the Dogpatch fire station, stepped forward. "Mr. Zakaria, you've got every right to consult with your lawyer on these matters, but right now we need to complete our investigation and inspection. It's a matter of public safety. It's our responsibility to make certain no dangerous substances are found inside."

Pushing his jaw out, Zakaria offered one final argument. "The police bomb squad has not found anything even remotely suspicious. This imposition is nothing more than—"

Capt. Jordan ignored Zakaria and nodded to Casella. Steve motioned for his crew to head inside. He whispered to Capt. Jordan, who shrugged and patted Steve's shoulder before walking away. Steve smiled at Maajidah Zakaria and strode up the steps to the entrance of the building. He signaled Amber to sit at his side and opened the door for Zakaria. Zakaria took a guarded look at the white German Shepherd and marched inside. Steve followed, with Amber at his side.

Outside the air hung thick, as a blanket of fog rolled over the coastal hills, spreading dank fingers up and down the peninsula. The first responders wound down the operations, leaving a small crew to maintain a safe perimeter around the building and surrounding structures of the Islamic Center for Cultural Affairs. No one expected any further developments as the city struggled to fight off another early morning intrusion on its nightly respite.

In the ICCA's stark reception area, Maajidah Zakaria glared at Steve Casella, his bravado muted by frequent eye shifts to the large white dog. Amber's tenseness coursed up the lead to Steve's hand, and he gave her a command to rest in place. He wanted his full attention centered on Zakaria. Amber obeyed and settled down by his side, folding her hips underneath and resting her head on outstretched front paws.

"I meant what I stated outside," Zakaria said, his eyes blinking in an erratic rhythm. "My community is tired of these pretentious attempts at harassment. Our attorney is gathering evidence that our civil rights and religious freedoms have been violated. You people have no right to barge into this mosque." His voice faltered as he kept a watchful eye on the dog.

Steve smiled and reached into his pocket. They'd started calling this place a mosque last April. He thumbed through a slim leather case and pulled out two business cards: stepping forward and offering them to Zakaria. To make sure Zakaria got the point, he then flashed two sets of credentials in front of the man's face.

After a slight hesitation, Zakaria accepted the cards and held them both out to read. A fleeting change flashed across his face, and he lifted his eyebrows. He waved one of the cards and said, "The leaders of your department explained about the need for your hazmat unit to inspect the premises. For the record, I am not allowing this without submitting a formal protest."

When Zakaria's eyes shifted to the other card, his hand gave a slight tremble. "But what is the significance of this? What does it mean, you work for the Department of Homeland Security?"

Amber's head popped up and her ears pricked. Steve grasped the lead tighter and gestured to Amber again, but the dog stayed on full alert.

With the dog's change in demeanor, Zakaria took a step backwards, his back stiffening. With a little less authority, he continued, "You are a consultant, working on an anti-terrorist task force?"

While maintaining a firm grip on Amber, Steve smiled. "So if you'd like to file a formal complaint, Mr. Zakaria, you can say I'm with the government,t and I'm here to help."

"This is an outrage. You cannot get away with this kind of intimidation. First thing in the morning I will have our attorney look into the legality of your intrusion. This is a clear violation of our rights. You have no probable cause to search these premises. You can be assured our attorney will contact your superiors."

"I'd be glad to speak with your lawyer. I can contact him as soon as we're done. If I recall, his name is Aamir Rahaman. And if I'm not mistaken, we've dealt with him on other occasions. His file is back in the Suburban, and I'm sure I have his phone number."

Amber sprang to her feet and strained against the lead, low growling sounds escaping from closed jaws. Her left foot pawed the white marble floor; the irritating scrapes echoing in the reception area. Amber's snout arched upward, coaxing out any hidden smells floating in the atmosphere.

Although she wasn't focused on Zakaria, he took several more steps back, a sheen of sweat covering his exposed facial features. The pits on his cheeks trapping the salty pools. He attempted another round of protest, but the words appeared to catch in his throat as he watched Steve lean over Amber, release her lead, and then give her a sharp command.

Zakaria retreated behind the reception desk in the corner of the room; not much of an impediment to Amber. Fortunately for Zakaria, Amber showed him little interest as she circled the room, checking the air, the floor, and other surfaces; homing in on specific molecular particles as per her training. She ignored the fear-provoked pheromones spiraling from Zakaria's venting pores.

Amber's head shifted to the right, and she let loose with several high-pitched yelps. Her feet slipped against the polished floor as she found something of interest and charged toward an open door in the middle of the right side of the room. She skidded through the doorway and disappeared to the left.

With an increasing distance between him and the dog, Zakaria's voice returned, and he yelled, "You cannot let your dog run freely. Now you have gone too far."

Steve glanced over his shoulder at Zakaria and said, "Sure looks like probable cause to me." He dashed after Amber. Once through the door, Steve found himself in a dark, narrow corridor. About two-thirds down on the right he saw Amber sitting in front of a closed steel door, incessant barks racking her body. A bright emergency exit sign hung above on the wall.

Steve jogged up to Amber. "What'd you find, girl?"

Amber didn't answer but backed up several steps. She crouched and launched herself against the horizontal locking bar across the door.

The door crashed open and Zakaria screamed, "No! No! You must stop that animal. You are not permitted to go through there. It is still part of our community center—and private property."

Amber was gone before the door slammed shut.

Steve needed no further encouragement to follow Amber's lead, and he pushed against the bar on the door, stepping into an alleyway outside the ICCA building. Wisps of fog shrouded the sole source of illumination, darkening the gloomy strip.

This time Zakaria did not follow Casella or shout any other complaints. He turned and retreated down the corridor. His left hand reached inside his coat and pulled out a cell phone. The words he spoke were not in

English. Not that it mattered. Steve's focus remained on Amber as the door slammed shut behind him.

Filled with purpose, Amber clawed her way around and over piles of trash in the alleyway. Cupped between the towering walls, the air reeked of strong, foul odors, and Steve couldn't believe Amber remained on task. Near the end of the alley, Amber jumped onto a closed green dumpster. From there she climbed to an open metal fire escape landing. Without hesitating, she scampered up to a third-story open window, her nails clicking off the ladder rungs. After a quick turn to bark at Steve, she leapt inside.

"Son of a bitch," Steve muttered, but kept moving. With less dexterity, and more grunts and groans than Amber, he hefted himself onto the dumpster and up the fire escape. He stared at the same open window. He grabbed his handheld, shouting commands to Parkinson as he twisted his body through the window.

Steve stood at one end of a central hallway with closed doors lining both sides. Several low wattage bare light bulbs hung from the ceiling and cast a grim light down the hall. Faded gray paint peeled off the walls. A faint, acrid odor permeated the stale air. This ratcheted up his alert level. Amber bounded back and forth, not stopping for any length of time in front of any one door.

Her barking escalated and her movements became more animated.

About halfway down the hall, Steve stopped in front of one of the closed doors. He listened to muffled noises coming from inside. Amber remained unfocused and scurried about in a frenzy. Steve reached his hand out to grasp the doorknob. He was about to turn it when Amber dove at him from behind.

Steve crashed to the floor as a deafening blast filled the hall and splintering fragments of the door panel flew across the narrow space and rained down the opposite wall. Amber's body spiraled away from the force of the shotgun blast.

Steve recovered, shook off the ringing in his ears, and pushed himself to a kneeling position, facing the direction of the riddled door. As he did this, he unsnapped his holster and reached for his .40 caliber Glock 22.

The residual section of the door flew aside, and a man sprinted across the hall and pulled open a door on the opposite wall. He almost made it inside, but Amber scrambled toward the fleeing figure, grasping a kicking foot that wedged partway in the closing door.

Steve climbed to his feet, readying his Glock when another man entered the hall from the left, about twenty feet past Amber's struggling efforts to incapacitate her prey. The man aimed an assault weapon at Amber, but Steve brought the Glock around and fired off two shots, eliminating the threat.

Distracted, Amber lost the battle to pull the man back into the hall, settling on his left running shoe. Steve heard the distinctive slide of a pump action shotgun and grabbed Amber's collar. From inside the room two shots disintegrated the door as Steve and Amber hit the floor below the devastating pellets.

All at once it sounded like the entire building had jumped to life.

Frantic shouts and more menacing noises filled the space. Steve's eyes darted around, coming to rest on the exit sign above the door at the far end of the hall. He called to Amber, and they took off, vaulting over the fallen body of the man Steve just shot. He shoved open the door and entered a stairwell. Emergency lighting blinked incessantly, interrupting his concentration. Steve glanced down over the steel railing and was rewarded by a burst of automatic rounds from below, ricocheting about the cramped space. His ears rang again from the sharp blasts echoing in the stairwell.

"Come on, Amber, looks like we're going up." He fired several blind rounds in the direction of his assailants and spun about, taking the steps two at a time, hugging the wall. Amber barked and growled but followed Steve up the stairs. Besides the periodic sprays of bullets, the stairs beneath his feet shuddered; the movements bracketed by a number of concussive discharges.

And now he smelled smoke infiltrating and rising from below.

After passing the sixth floor, he climbed the final set of steps that led to the roof entrance. The door was locked, but Steve stepped back and drove a raised boot directly into the locking mechanism. With a sickening crunch, the rotted wooden jamb fragmented, and the door crashed open.

"Another damn code violation," Steve said.

As Steve and Amber made their way out of the stairwell and onto the roof, the smoke thickened and, thanks to Steve's last action, rose in vigorous response to the unfettered opening at the top. He envisioned standing over a chimney with a bonfire raging below.

The rising temperature of the escaping air was a harbinger of what would come next. The gunfire stopped, but the roof structure shook and rattled as the number of explosions increased.

The entire building was ready to implode.

Steve encouraged Amber to stay close and headed toward the brick parapet at the north end of the roof. The distance wasn't great, but the footing became almost impossible. Time was running out and, in a matter of seconds, the roof would cave in. There was a good chance the outer walls of the building could buckle too.

With no other viable choices, Steve radioed in his situation and climbed onto the parapet. Several bricks had already loosened, dropping six stories and crashing to the pavement.

They inched their way along, heading for the northeast corner of the building. The smoke thickened and Steve coughed. His eyes stung from the fumes, and he had trouble judging the distance to the roof of the adjacent building. It looked to be a five-story unit, with a ten-to-twelve-foot gap between the two structures.

He got hold of Amber's harness, trying to figure out a way to make Amber jump. He finally decided that if he jumped first, Amber would most likely follow.

But what if she didn't?

Steve never got the chance to find out. Amber looked up at Steve and barked twice. She grabbed one of his wrists with her jaws and gave it a slight tug. After a final bark, she galloped toward the end of the parapet and launched herself over the edge, disappearing from Steve's line of vision.

A second later Amber let loose with a series of rapid barks.

"Well, that looked easy. Damn show-off dog."

As the building shifted beneath him, he ran forward and jumped across the open space. He landed hard and rolled onto his shoulder, the momentum pulling him through, and he wound up on his back. Steve blinked several times and his vision filled with the looming head of a white dog and a wet tongue.

A deafening explosion sent shockwaves across the rooftop. Billowing plumes of thick, black smoke obscured the night. Oxygen sucked from the sulfurous clouds washing over them while debris rained all around.

Steve's radio crackled with an urgent, but measured voice. "Not bad, Casella. A little bit slow compared to your partner. I'm guessing you're conscious and didn't damage anything of importance?"

"Roger that, Parky. I landed on my head."

"Lucky guy. Nothing critical to damage there. But here's the thing. In case you haven't noticed, the building you chose to jump to is also engulfed in flames. Get your ass moving and head to the southeast corner. The boys got a surprise for you. And Casella? Don't be late."

Steve could tell by Parkinson's voice; the situation was serious. He blinked away the smoke and ash from his eyes and made it halfway to his destination by the time Parkinson signed off.

As he approached the edge of the roof, he saw the flashing lights reflecting from the windows of the building across the street. Pressing, yet ordered voices blasted up from below. The ladder was fully extended and swinging into position.

Parkinson helped Steve and Amber onto the platform. Glancing down, Steve watched the flames licking out of the shattered windows from the lower floors. The ladder shifted away from the building and began to retract and pivot.

Steve anticipated what would come next, but it still unnerved him.

Long before they reached the ground, the huge ladder truck began a harrowing maneuver. With the stabilizers still extended, the monstrous rig scraped back from the raging inferno. It sounded like a dinosaur in its final death throes.

Another blast drowned out those noises as the second building crumbled.

Steve patted Amber, whose fur was no longer anything close to white. He looked at Parkinson. Parkinson's grimy features relaxed and turned into a smile as his finger pointed down to the ladder truck.

"You guessed it, Steve. It's your old buddy, Ziggy, at the controls. Try not to embarrass yourself. If you gotta hug him, please wait till after we put out the damn fire."

CHAPTER 2

ALTHOUGH PRESIDENT TYLER GRIFFIN'S DEEP-SET eyes were virtually black, the man seated across from him couldn't help but compare their intensity to the second eye—pale yellow—unmoving and burning into him from over the president's shoulder.

The American bald eagle, centerpiece of the presidential seal framed on the paneled wall, represented Tyler Griffin's personal tenacity and dedication to the nation.

As Agent Mike Finley looked closer, behind Griffin's trademark stare, he noticed a slight crack in the president's resolve, and this image frightened him more than the normal ferocity of the leader of the free world.

Mike Finley had been around D.C. for most of his long career. In his early fifties, clean-shaved head, and carrying only a few extra pounds, he tried to stay in top physical shape. He could deal with impatience, anger, and threats, but if this president gave up the fight, then Finley's dreams of an early retirement would be moot.

The formal meeting ended thirty minutes ago, and the other participants were dismissed. President Griffin and Mike Finley had moved to one of the smaller conference rooms located in the White House Situation Room complex on the ground floor of the West Wing. This room, devoid of the standard recording devices, remained off limits to the watch-staff personnel.

Finley finished briefing the president on the latest findings of a covert project.

Although, technically, Finley's credentials indicated he worked for the Department of Homeland Security, in reality, the DHS agent reported directly to the president.

The president had code-named the project, *Amber Alert.* At the time, Finley laughed at the president's attempt at humor, but right now that damn dog probably had as much insight as to what the hell was going on as anyone else did.

Finley watched Griffin struggle to maintain focus.

"I'll take care of it right away, sir," Finley said.

He jotted down a few notes, grateful for the opportunity to look away from the haunted expression fixed on the president. He clicked his pen closed and took a final gulp of tepid coffee.

"Let's keep this information close, Mike. Ever since the former president filled me in on a few particular items, I've gotten a bit paranoid. I'm not sure she fully understood the history of those documents, let alone the potential implications." The president shook his head and let out a long breath. "Christ, I'm not sure anybody does. But what you got here is starting to make it all sound real."

Pulling a memo marked urgent from a crowded folder, Griffin handed it to Finley. "The Israeli ambassador has been begging for another meeting. Before I see him, can you get me a head's up on what's got his panties in a bunch? See if you can feel out our intel guys or lean on the prime minister's office. Everything's a major issue with the ambassador. But if it's something important, I don't like being blindsided."

The president paused, his face relaxing. "By the way, Mike. That little incident in San Francisco?"

Finley stopped shoving papers in his briefcase and looked up. He thought he caught a fleeting return of the old Tyler Griffin from the slight smile on the president's face, but it quickly faded.

"Yes?"

"Can I assume we were not too surprised at what the Islamic Center for Cultural Affairs had been up to?"

Finley shrugged and bit his lower lip. "Gotta love how Amber peeled away those layers and sniffed things out."

"So, do you think the dog called in the bomb threat too?"

"Who's to say, Mr. President?"

"Tell Casella he did one hell of a job keeping a low profile on the situation." He raised his eyebrows and tapped the folded newspaper sitting next to the documents in front of him. "I see the press chronicled the story in explicit detail like every other news outlet in the nation. Our actions at the supposed community center should keep the DOJ lawyers busy for the foreseeable future."

Finley opened his palms and raised his brows. His lips spread into a slight smile. Then he turned serious. "Sir, the media only gave you a temporary pass after the previous attempted terrorist bombing in San Francisco. They're no longer on board with the added surveillances on certain mosques."

Griffin shook his head. "Fun while it lasted. One of these days Baghdad by the Bay is going to run out of near misses." He shrugged. "For a while, congress even tabled most of the impeachment threats too."

"But now they're starting to beat the same old drums again," Finley said. "The threats of legal action against DHS are on the rise. The damn lawyers are back to circling us like a bunch of hungry sharks. Every Muslim organization in the country is screaming bloody murder. They've stepped up the usual rhetoric about intolerance and profiling. If word about the Amber Alert project got out, there'd be real hell to pay. And I think certain members of congress might get a little nervous too."

Griffin placed a hand over the latest report from Finley. "If I'm not mistaken, Mike, we're only seeing the tip of the iceberg on what's going on right in our own backyard. I want you to put more pressure on whoever is doing the most complaining. Let's see if we can squeeze out anything else. I'm getting a bad feeling about this. Worrying about overt threats of terror is one thing, but in truth, could we have been this stupid to ignore these signs of subversive activity within our own borders?"

The president looked back up at Finley. "One other thing. Arrange for Casella to meet with me next week. It's been a while since we've gone over these details in person, and with the latest info you gave me, I want to be sure we're all on the same page. And make sure he brings his wife with him. Edie's last report has got my skin crawling."

As Finley finished gathering up his papers, the president's mind wandered back to a conversation with his predecessor, Alice Andersen. She'd given him information relating to a potential catastrophic scheme. He would've liked to dismiss it as a ridiculous urban legend, but he knew Andersen didn't buy into tall tales. This was the kind of conspiracy theory Edie could sink her teeth into. He'd presented a key part of the Amber Alert project to her for that particular reason.

"I want a briefing from Edie too. Besides, it's been too long since we've seen their little one. The first lady thinks we need more distractions in the White House. As if Brianna and Sean aren't enough."

"I guess with your two older boys away in college, the first lady must be getting a little lonely with only the younger kids around." Finley coughed and then continued. "On my way over, I stopped by the secret service office to say hello to the guys. And I saw Brianna hanging out there, along with Sean. I guess at sixteen, it's time Brianna started working, but at six, don't you think Sean is a bit young?"

The president chuffed and shook his head. "Sean, I can deal with—just be glad you aren't working for Brianna."

After Finley left, Tyler Griffin didn't stand up right away. He folded his hands and stared across the empty room. At just past five o'clock in the afternoon, it wasn't even close to the president's usual long day at the office, but he'd made up his mind. He gathered up his papers and placed them in his briefcase. It had been a gift from his wife right after he took the plunge into the political waters in the Garden State.

Like the president, the old leather briefcase showed distinct signs of aging. The number of creases compounded on an almost daily basis, and the left buckle took extra care to close properly. The president wasn't about to trade it in for a new one. Like this nation, he considered it worth hanging on to.

Following a quick stop in the Oval Office to sign a critical document, Tyler Griffin headed home.

With security detail in tow, the president departed the West Wing onto the ground floor of the White House's main residence. He paused a moment by the elevator and then turned back to the secret service office off the north side of the center hall.

The evening shift hadn't been aware of Brianna or Sean's earlier presence, and he discovered that the first lady was still holed up in her upstairs office. The president headed back to the elevator and decided to go see the first lady on the third floor, bypassing their private residence.

As he exited the elevator, the sounds of muffled laughter drifted from inside the first lady's office suite.

"Well," he murmured to himself, "I guess Alison's day is going better than mine. At least it doesn't sound like I'll be interrupting anything too important."

The president entered the outer reception area, tossed his briefcase on one of the chairs, and knocked on the door to the first lady's office.

"Come on in, Mr. President," a familiar voice responded. He recognized the stifled giggle coming from the first lady's chief of staff, Badiyah Jamail. Before Griffin reached down to turn the knob, the door opened and Jamail scurried out, carrying an armful of papers.

"Good evening, Mr. President," Jamail said in a formal tone, all signs of laughter shut down. She stood aside as Griffin stepped into the room. "I apologize for still being here. Your detail called to inform us you were on your way up, sir."

"Not a problem, Badiyah." He looked at the first lady seated behind her desk. "If you two aren't quite finished, I can wait outside and get some more work done myself."

Alison Griffin cocked her head and narrowed her eyes. Badiyah Jamail jumped in, saying, "I need to take care of those details, ma'am. I'll go organize these folders in the outer office and then be on my way."

Jamail pressed the papers against her chest with one hand and tugged lightly on the door. It swung shut but didn't close all the way. She dropped everything on the desk near the door outside the first lady's office.

Ignoring the papers, she stood next to the door. While listening, her eyes glanced around the room and settled on the president's briefcase that was sitting on the chair in front of the desk. Multitasking was one of her strongpoints. She also had other talents neither the first lady, the president, nor the secret service were aware of.

In the first lady's office, Alison got up from behind the desk and met Tyler as he crossed the room. She replaced most of her concerned look with a broad smile, but he sensed the shadows remaining behind her absorbing, deep blue eyes. At this time of day her scattered freckles cast an alluring glow over her pale complexion. They embraced, Tyler's hand gently diving under the coppery tints of her dark brown hair.

Alison sighed and leaned back. The president sensed her eyes scrutinizing his features.

"From the look on your face, the last thing you need to do is any more work today." She playfully patted his stomach. "You could perhaps use more time in the workout room. Burn off a few pounds while blowing off a little steam."

The president opened his mouth to respond, but the first lady turned away and continued. "Instead, let's go have a seat." As Alison walked to the sofa across from the two south-facing windows, she glanced out at the promenade and the South Lawn.

Tyler watched Alison, in her slender black jeans and cream-colored T-shirt, take a seat, her hair flowing over the low back of the sofa. This same look stole his heart when he was a sophomore in high school. She still fit gracefully into a pair of jeans.

He liked this casual look, although when Alison stepped down the White House staircase in a formal gown for one of those boring state dinners—well, he didn't mind playing second fiddle to the first lady.

At the moment, he considered himself overdressed. Removing his jacket, he tossed it over the back of a chair and walked to the sofa, loosening his tie and sitting down next to Alison. He allowed himself a moment to relax, closing his eyes and inhaling the faint scent of her perfume.

Alison smiled and touched his cheek. "So, Mr. President, I can't remember you wandering up to this old attic space in quite some time. Not to mention I get to see your face while the sun's still shining." She placed a hand over his, and her expression became serious. "Let's get to it, Tyler. What's got you so worried?"

Badiyah Jamail concentrated on two separate tasks. She had recently been made aware of things heating up at a faster pace than expected, and the timetable needed to be moved up as critical events rapidly unfolded. And now, in the last several minutes she concluded her leaders may have underestimated the information-gathering abilities of the present administration and the potential impact it could have on certain aspects of their plans.

Jamail, absorbed in her thoughts, never saw the president's daughter standing in the open doorway.

"Hello, Badiyah," Brianna said in a loud voice.

Badiyah Jamail jumped back from the closed doorway, knocking the stack of folders off the desk and onto the president's briefcase, scattering papers all over the floor. "Oh, Brianna," she said, trying to put a smile on her troubled face. "You startled me."

Brianna's eyes darted around the room. Jamail saw her glance at the president's briefcase and then refocus on the sliver of sunlight seeping through the slight gap in the door to the first lady's office.

Jamail kneeled down and began gathering up the fallen papers, giving her something to focus on other than Brianna's creepy, staring eyes. "The president is meeting with the first lady. I'm finishing up my work before taking care of a few last-minute assignments."

It annoyed her that this pampered little brat made her feel so uneasy and had her trying to explain her actions. After all, she had been a long-time fixture, working in the White House long before the Griffins moved in. She had worked hard to remain on the White House staff, playing important roles in the last several first families.

This was not the time to become unnerved by a know-it-all teenage girl.

"Why don't I help you, Badiyah, then you can get yourself out of here and not have to be distracted by what's going on in my mother's office."

Brianna got to work, helping Jamail.

Jamail almost argued with Brianna but, instead, bit her tongue and thanked her. In a final flurry of activity, she grabbed her papers and rushed out of the room. She glanced over her shoulder and watched the president's daughter pick up her father's briefcase, catching a few mumbled words.

"You're welcome, Badiyah." Brianna turned toward her mother's office. With a sharp knock on the door, Brianna called out, "I hope you guys aren't fooling around on the sofa again."

She nudged the door open a little wider and stood in the doorway. She held out the briefcase in one hand, the other placed over her green eyes. Brianna spread her fingers apart and shook her head, her curly red hair bouncing across her shoulders. "Darn, I thought I'd bust you guys. You're no fun. Here ya go, Dad."

Brianna walked to the sofa and handed over the briefcase. "You left this beat-up old thing out there." She cocked her head to the door.

In a lower voice, she added, "Call me Islamophobic, but I for one don't trust Badiyah Jamail. I don't care how long she's worked at the White House, or how dedicated she pretends to be."

The president stood up, took his briefcase, and coughed. "Yes, Brianna. I'll take it under advisement. Maybe I'll have Agent Finley check her out."

He smiled at his precocious daughter.

Brianna smiled back. "No need, Dad. I'm on the case."

She stepped up on her tippy toes and kissed her father on the cheek and scooted over, plopping down next to her mother. "Mommy, guess what…."

Tyler Griffin beamed as he stepped back and watched Alison and Brianna in an animated mother-daughter conversation. Brianna bounced back and forth between a child and an adult so fast it made his head spin.

He absently glanced at his briefcase, noticing the finicky buckle wasn't quite fastened properly.

Did I leave it like that?

His mouth formed an open circle as he glanced between his daughter and the outer office.

Badiyah Jamail was long gone for the day.

CHAPTER 3

STEVE CASELLA STRUGGLED TO GET the hi-tech infant car seat into the rented Escalade at Spokane International Airport. The two-hour flight from Oakland proved uneventful except for the attention Amber garnered from passengers interested in the white German Shepherd sitting in the main cabin.

Until recently, Amber didn't share the same privileges as service dogs. Unless on duty, trained K9 civilian and military dogs had not been permitted to fly in the cabin. Amber spent many hours crated below in the luggage compartment.

Edie Pauling, holding their six-month-old daughter, Rosa, ended her phone call and said to Steve, "Jack says to tell you to enjoy the trip and not to worry. Everything's under control." Jack Rothstein was the contractor working on remodeling their A-frame house in Sonoma. "I could be wrong, but he might've sounded relieved we'd be gone for a while."

Steve opened his mouth but remained silent.

"At least till I told him about the suggestion list I tacked to the permit packet on the front door."

"I don't recall discussing any—" Steve started.

"Ah, Steve, do you want to hold Rosa, and I'll finish up with the car seat? Doesn't look like you're making much progress."

Steve blew out a deep breath and turned his head. "I can final check the equipment on my hazmat rig a lot quicker than this is taking, but I think the damn car seat is latched in as good as it gets. You want to inspect it? Be my guest."

He stepped back and reached out his arms for Rosa. "Let's go, sweetie, time to buckle up and go for a ride." He gently grasped the baby and kissed her tiny forehead.

Those words got Amber's attention and she jumped up and barked. She'd been patiently waiting by the Escalade's rear hatch.

Satisfied with Steve's handiwork, Edie opened the hatch and Amber jumped in. Edie did her best to find room for the luggage. Rosa required more traveling necessities than Amber, encroaching on her space, but the dog didn't mind. She was eager to take care of another member of the Casella family.

Steve had kept three puppies from Amber's litter: Greta, Sophie, and Max. They weren't along for this trip. Instead, they were being cared for at Steve's dog training facility, recently expanded to board dogs.

Steve got behind the wheel and drove the Escalade out of the airport and onto the interstate, heading toward Coeur d'Alene, Idaho. They owned a house on thirty acres in the mountains east of Lake Coeur d'Alene, about an hour's drive from the Spokane Airport.

"I'm looking forward to spending time at your dad's house," Edie said.

She still referred to their secluded retreat as his dad's, even though Steve's father had been dead for several years. The house brought back intense memories; some good, some not so good.

"You sure you're okay with staying so far away from the convention center?" Edie glanced out the window as they passed the downtown Spokane exit for the convention center complex.

"I can't imagine coming up here and not staying at the house," Steve said. "And it'd be good to stop by the community club too. I'd like to meet up with the guys; grab a few beers and catch up on local gossip."

"Just you and the guys? You don't want me along to slow you down?"

"If I recall, you always managed to keep up with Joe and Jimmy, one brew at a time. By the way, how come Sampson and Beth aren't staying with us at the house?"

"For one thing, my brother's a real city boy. He's never been comfortable with nature closing in all around him. Trees and natural bodies of water make him nervous. I don't think I've ever seen him set foot in a lake. He has this funny need to see where his body's headed and can only barely tolerate clear swimming pool water. Beth probably could've talked him into joining us, but the real reason they're staying in Spokane is because of a particular hotel she's been researching."

"What? Now she's a travel agent? I thought she just started up her own business in cybersecurity?"

Edie shook her head even though she knew he was kidding. "Don't you ever listen to me?"

Steve glanced in both the rearview and side mirrors before signaling a lane change and shifting into the middle lane. He kept his eyes on the road, not looking at Edie.

Amber chuffed several times and peeked her head around the car seat to make sure Rosa was still sleeping.

"To remind you," Edie said, tapping her fingers on Steve's shoulder. "Beth is interested in exploring haunted places. According to Beth, this hotel she picked in Spokane, the Spokane Falls Lodge, has an interesting ghost story tied to it. Something happened there during the first summer it opened. There's supposed to be this ghost of a Russian immigrant roaming the halls. He apparently jumped from a balcony. Sampson and Beth are in the middle of a four-week journey, cruising cross-country and checking out as many haunted spots as they can."

"I can't imagine any ghosts showing up with your brother around. He'd likely scare the hell out of any spirits. Especially Russians. Except maybe Vladimir Putin's ghost. Unfortunately, at this point the world is still dealing with his live image."

"You can discuss that with Sampson yourself. Remember? We're meeting Sampson and Beth tomorrow morning at their hotel for breakfast." She paused and added, "Your workshop starts at 1:00 o'clock?"

"Yep."

"You prepared to speak to a room full of females?"

"Yep." Steve smiled and nodded.

"This is a romance writers convention, isn't it?"

"Yep." Steve's eyes darted to Edie and then back on the road.

"But your books aren't romances. They're suspense novels—thrillers."

"So? They wanted a writer who used romantic elements as part of a larger story. Like character development, plot twists."

"I see." Edie pursed her lips. "Aren't most romance writers… women?"

She pinched his cheek.

"That's a sexist remark," Steve said.

Edie reached into her small carry-on bag and pulled out a copy of Steve's latest novel, looking at the front and back of the book. She pointed to the name of the author. "P.T. Roberts. Good pen name. By any chance, do they even know you're a man? Have you personally talked to anyone in this organization?"

"Of course." He hesitated and then added, "Although we've only communicated by email. The chairman—person—woman, did ask what the 'P' stood for."

"And?"

Steve brushed his hair back. "I told her the 'P" stood for Penny." He shrugged.

"So, you didn't explain—Penny is your mother's name? Or the 'T' stands for Tom, your dad? Never mind 'Roberts' stands for your Uncle Bob?"

"Nope."

"Let me guess. The name, Steve Casella, never worked its way into the conversation?"

"Nope."

"So, they think your name is Penny?"

"Yep." His face remained blank. "Penny isn't necessarily a girl's name. It could· be short for Pennywise—like the clown in Stephen King's novel, *It*."

Steve's eyebrows twitched.

Edie tilted her head and responded, "Arguably, Pennywise, the clown, was an entity and had no gender."

Steve shifted the Escalade back into the right lane and hiked his shoulders. "Well, except when they made the book into a TV movie and Pennywise was played by a male actor."

"What do you think is gonna happen when an audience of passionate, emotionally driven female romance writers finds out P.T. Roberts is a man?"

"Well, I'd need one hell of an excuse to back out of this now." Steve spoke slowly and stared straight ahead.

Edie felt a sudden chill, but remained quiet and stole a quick glance at Rosa.

CHAPTER 4

FACING RIVERFRONT PARK, THE TWENTY-STORY Spokane Falls Lodge dominated the landscape on the north banks of the Spokane River. Across the river, a little to the east, was the Spokane Convention Center. The lodge's top floor signature restaurant offered a magnificent view of downtown Spokane, a series of waterfalls and rapids, and the surrounding valley.

Seated at a quiet table and taking in the scenery through the restaurant's floor-to-ceiling windows, Beth Dawson said to Sampson Pauling, "I'm glad we timed this trip to get the chance to see Steve and Edie again."

After saying those words, Beth's face tensed. She glanced at the candle the waiter had just lit. Her hand pressed against her chest.

Sampson caught a glimpse of her favorite medallion half hidden under the frilly lace fabric of her cream-colored blouse as the dim light of the candle flickered off its silvery surface.

He stayed silent and Beth continued, "I've got something important to talk to Edie about."

Sampson stared into Beth's eyes. "You've been awful quiet about the details. Care to share what you and my sister are up to?"

"I'm not sure." Her lips tightened. "Maybe Edie can make more sense out of the information." She shrugged. "Breakfast should be interesting."

A smile masked the dark shadows Sampson sensed lurking inside.

"Besides," she continued, "I can't wait to see Rosa and rock that beautiful baby in my arms again."

The server finished filling glasses of Fumé Blanc from a bottle of Washington State wine. Sampson gazed down at the upper falls on the Spokane River and chose to keep the conversation light. He turned to Beth, picked up his glass and smiled back. "Don't get any crazy ideas inside that pretty little head of yours."

His stomach fluttered at an image of Rosa as he reached out to clink glasses.

Sampson, an imposing figure with dark chocolate skin, wasn't prone to emotional bouts, but whenever he stared into Beth's large brown eyes, he melted like a hot fudge sundae left on a boardwalk bench at Seaside Heights in August.

Beth ran her fingers through the tight curls on her short black hair. She extended her arm, placing a hand on top of his. Her delicate fingers overshadowed by Sampson's beefy hand but, nevertheless, a perfect match in skin tone.

Sampson Pauling had known Beth Dawson for many years. The two had gotten together from time-to-time, but nothing serious developed until Sampson called on Beth's computer skills. Connections to high-powered D.C. databases helped her dig into a plot aimed at destroying Sampson's brother, as well as any future political ambitions of Tyler Griffin and his family.

Sampson viewed this current trip as the next phase in their relationship. Knowing where he intended it to lead scared the hell out of him. From the sly look on Beth's face, it appeared she was savoring every second of his discomfort.

"I'm counting on you to keep me safe tonight." Beth fluttered her eyelashes. "I loved the way you persuaded the hotel manager to switch our reservation and give us the same room where the unfortunate incident took place."

Sampson didn't believe in ghosts, spirits, or goblins. Nor did he understand Beth's penchant to search out haunted places. But he enjoyed the opportunity to spend all this time with her as he worked up the courage to ask her an important question.

"I consider these ghosts another form of the people I deal with at work. They just need to be clear on one thing. As a bail bondsman, my job is to see they get to where they're supposed to go. Sometimes they need a little encouragement to do the right thing."

Sampson and Beth chatted through their appetizers, main courses, and shared dessert. They headed hand-in-hand to their room; one floor below the restaurant. Neither of them worried about any ghostly apparitions while they slipped under the covers and tuned out the rest of the world.

Spent, they dozed off, oblivious to the setting sun casting fading silhouettes across the quiet room. As darkness stole the shadows, Beth stirred and sat up. She stretched both arms above her head, covers dropping to her waist. Sampson responded to her movements.

His eyes flickered open. "Hold that pose."

With an athletic grace, Beth stripped off the covers and swung her legs to the floor in a playful gesture which outmaneuvered Sampson's reach. Hands on hips, her face broke into a huge smile.

"That pose also works for me." Sampson's returning smile showed a good number of teeth.

Crossing her arms over her breasts, she took a step back.

"I don't think you're covering much with those slender limbs. You need help?"

She nodded, but said, "Keep that thought for when we get back."

"We're we going?"

"Remember? The gondola ride. To see the falls?" Beth turned and walked to the window. "It's a perfect night. Besides, this will probably be the only chance we'll get."

Her body stood outlined by the faint glow seeping through the window, Sampson's eyes glued to her image. Before he spoke, he swallowed and let out a quiet laugh. "I like heights almost as much as the thought of landing in a natural body of water. Not to mention the raging rapids I can hear from the comfort of this bed. But don't let me stop you from going."

Beth shrugged. "You gonna sit around and pine away for me?"

"Nope. I'll be headed to the hotel's gym and work off this tension. That way I'll be gentler with your delicate body when you return."

"Suit yourself, big boy." Beth disappeared into the bathroom.

Sampson listened to the sounds of the shower.

He considered changing his mind and joining Beth. A gondola ride could be a great place to pop the question. *Nah.* He'd probably be too nervous and drop the damn ring into the river.

If he could talk to Steve alone for a few minutes after breakfast tomorrow, he'd shake him down for some suggestions. That thought made him laugh loud enough to worry that Beth would hear him above the noise of the shower. If he took any of Steve's advice on his relationship with Edie, he'd be old and gray before getting the job done.

How the hell did a white dude from California hitch up with the likes of my sister?

He loved his sister, but not many people appreciated her Jersey-girl attitude.

* * * * * *

Alone, but confident, Beth Dawson walked across the hotel grounds and entered Riverside Park. Her hand lingered on her cheek. She stroked the imprint of Sampson's earlier goodbye kiss. His tender words still buzzed in her ear.

Absorbed in thought, she didn't notice the man when he followed her across the hotel lobby and still shadowed her actions as she entered the park and strode over one of the pedestrian suspension bridges.

Beth purchased a ticket for the Spokane Falls Skyride and ambled over to the boarding area. The daytime crowds in the park had thinned; no one waited in line for the gondola ride. The attraction was scheduled to close in thirty minutes.

Beth climbed into the next waiting car, and before the attendant stepped up to close the doors, a man leaned his head inside.

"Mind if I join you?"

He didn't wait for an answer and slipped onto the facing seat. The doors slid shut. With a slight jolt the gondola car began moving. The jarring motion had firmly refocused Beth's attention back to the present.

She rapped at the window and called out to the attendant, but he had receded into the shadows. The car glided away from the safety of the station.

The man sitting across from her raised a hand and, in a casual motion, tugged back his jacket to expose a holstered handgun. Floodlights mounted on the support stanchion for the gondola cable cast a harsh glow, magnifying the size of the weapon and the threatening glower on the man's face.

"Ms. Dawson." The voice sounded deep and menacing. "I'd like to introduce myself. My name is Bartholomew, and I wish to talk with you."

He smiled and glanced outside the gondola as the car rose higher above the ground.

"This gives us the privacy we need. An excellent location for this evening's discussion."

Beth let out a long breath but didn't respond. She slowly recovered from her initial shock and tried to consider her choices, if any existed. She had no idea who this guy was or what he wanted.

Bartholomew continued, "A pity your boyfriend didn't join you, but please be assured he'll be taken care of as well. I suspect he is right now experiencing a similar encounter."

The gondola passed over the parking lot for Spokane's government complex. Beth, facing forward, stole a quick glance over Bartholomew's shoulder as the distant lights of the Monroe Street bridge came into view. The traffic was light in both directions.

Beth found her voice. "What do you want with me and Sampson?"

"Yes, Beth, we should get to the heart of the matter. As you can see, this ride is short." He leaned forward, causing Beth to press back in her seat. "If you are not cooperative, it will be even shorter for you."

"Who the hell are you?"

To her right, the sounds of water cascading over the dam and the lower falls permeated the tiny enclosure like distant thunder from an approaching storm. The grinding vibrations of the moving cable made Beth think of a noose tightening around her neck.

"Yes, that would be the question." Bartholomew nodded. "You've been quite the little busybody."

With snake-like quickness his arm darted out and he squeezed her hand. Just as quickly, he released his grip.

"Those delicate fingers have been industrious, no?" He continued before she could respond. "Perhaps you considered yourself too clever. Didn't think there'd be any traces of your little exploitations?"

Beth tried to veil the sinking sensation in her gut, but her hands began to tremble. Now she knew exactly who she was dealing with. Not this man precisely, but who he represented.

Her words sounded weak and unconvincing.

"I'm a security consultant. I analyze programming infrastructures. My job is to probe databases for clients, looking for potential security holes. Sometimes I—I inadvertently access restricted sites, but if that happens I back right out."

"We've logged at least a half dozen such breaches. On not only one, but several server locations. And every one of those servers is equipped with rigorous encryption firewalls." He hiked his shoulders and added in a low, mumbling voice. "Except maybe the data links with Grandpa's new buddies."

Beth looked down at her hands but didn't reply. She heard a sharp click and her eyes caught Bartholomew inserting an object into the safety locking mechanism above the doors. She slid to the far corner of the car, but the paltry distance gave her no relief. No options came to mind.

From the information she uncovered while hacking into these hidden internet sites and furrowing through the coded messages, it was painfully clear this group was dangerous. That was why she planned on turning the tiny memory card over to Edie Pauling. Edie would make certain it got into the appropriate hands.

Beth's initial fear transitioned into a frustrated anger.

Understanding the enormity of the potential consequences of what she discovered made her realize the futility of any protests, let alone any hopes of escape. Her body tensed, but the shaking ceased as she gathered any remaining courage to face this smug bastard.

Beth Dawson turned toward her captor and stared straight into the eyes of the devil.

"Well now," Bartholomew said, "I see you're starting to appreciate the big picture. So tell me, who have you shared this knowledge with? For now, you can forget lying about what your boyfriend knows. Like I said, we've got that covered."

"He doesn't know a damn thing about any of this." Beth hesitated for a split second. "Besides, it's too late. Killing me won't stop anything. I've made sure the information I uncovered will all get released."

"Nice try. But I don't think so. And not a very original response." Bartholomew pressed the release mechanism and pried at the narrow gap between the doors. They immediately slid back against the outside walls of the gondola. "But I do appreciate your confession."

The intensity of the gushing waters escalated and filled the tiny interior with a thunderous noise. Beth could hear a distinct whooshing as the water foamed and washed over the rocky riverbed.

Bartholomew continued, "If that happens to be true, however, now's your chance to come *clean*."

Beth thought it odd he laughed after saying those last words.

He spread out his hands, indicating the open doors. "Care to tell me how you planned to do that and where you have hidden the evidence?"

The deafening turmoil of the falls reverberated, sending mists of water vapor against her chilled skin. Although it portended her fate, it also brought an invigorating charge to the air. She sensed the environment being cleansed by the ionized atmosphere, clearing her head and leaving her with a determination to act.

Beth made a desperate leap at Bartholomew, her scream drowned out by the roaring waters. Like batting away a troublesome fly, his arm blocked her meager attempt. She bit down hard on the toned muscles of his forearm before he catapulted her across the car.

Falling backwards through the open space, her fingers grasped the edges of the doors and her feet hooked onto the interior walls. The wind buffeted her blouse. The cold air slipped under the light garment and slapped the medallion against her breast.

In disbelief, she watched Bartholomew's tongue lash out and lick up the blood from the torn skin on his arm. His next move looked almost like an afterthought.

With blood dripping down his chin, a tight smile spread across his face. He lifted his boot and squared it against Beth's stomach. His hand reached inside his jacket and pulled out a shiny stainless steel handgun. His boot applied more pressure. At the same time that Beth lost her fight to hold on, Bartholomew fired a single shot into her chest.

Spread-eagled, she first felt suspended in mid-air. Below, the sound of the tumbling falls ratcheted louder. She heard the crashing sounds of water pounding off the jutting rocks. The sprays of mist and foam funneling upwards grasped at her falling body.

At the last second, Beth curled herself into a tight ball. She plunged beneath the surface.

Above, in the gondola, Bartholomew tucked the weapon back in its holster and tore open Beth's purse. Cursing, he tossed it aside.

The gondola car had passed under the Monroe Street bridge and was approaching the turnaround stanchion. Once the gondola reached its lowest level and rounded the last pillar, Bartholomew positioned himself in the open doorway and dropped to the grassy bank.

After dusting himself off, he walked over to the edge of the raging river. He didn't see any sign of Beth Dawson. He shrugged. Her body could either wash up against one of the nearby rocks or continue to float downstream to a more tranquil eddy pool in the flowing river.

He glanced at his arm. The bleeding had almost stopped. The emerging pain gave him pleasure, reminding him of the image of the bitch's body hurtling through the misty night breeze. Most likely she was dead long before bashing against the rocks in the river. He had better things to attend to than standing around and waiting for the bloody body to resurface.

Bartholomew checked his watch and turned away from the river. Time to move on. He sprinted to the chain-link fence and found the spot he had earlier cut open. His large frame squeezed through the steel fabric, and he climbed the steep embankment. He uncovered the small motorbike hidden under the brush and wheeled it up to the narrow Centennial Trail.

The engine sputtered to life and Bartholomew drove back to where his team parked their truck. As he rode, he decided on another course of action for the oversized black man. Assuming they hadn't killed him, Sampson Pauling was about to take a trip.

Bartholomew prided himself on thinking on his feet. Any stupid foot soldier could follow orders.

"Let's put the boyfriend on ice," he muttered to himself. "Doesn't matter what the hell she might've told him, or if he'll talk. This guy might be of further use to us. There should be more than enough space for one more asshole. I'm convinced Grandpa will approve of this."

CHAPTER 5

BADIYAH JAMAIL WAVED TO THE security team in the guardhouse and scurried out to the street. She hailed a taxi and recited the address. As the cab threaded into traffic on Pennsylvania Avenue, the driver glanced in his rearview mirror at his passenger and said in broken English, "You work at White House?"

Jamail nodded, but her closed deportment didn't invite any further conversation. She pulled a hijab from the large canvas bag hanging from her shoulder and adjusted the scarf over her head.

There was no time to make a stop at her apartment and change into more habitual Muslim attire. She was late for this briefing and, with the information she'd just gathered, the timeframe for the next phase might need to be stepped up again.

She had spent many years of her adult life in Washington, D.C. Being in this country sometimes caused her to forget the Muslim cultures and traditions. On the surface, she expected the men to treat her like an equal partner in their operations. Deep down, a cold wave of truth crept through her gut.

Ten minutes later, the taxi pulled to the curb a block north of the Dupont Circle. Jamail handed the driver the fare and a modest tip. She hurried across the street and inserted a key into the door of a boutique bookstore. The store was closed for the day.

She entered and walked past the bookshelves, disappearing through the curtain behind the cash register.

At the end of a short hallway Jamail punched in numbers on a keypad next to the door. After the locking mechanism clicked free, Jamail opened the door and proceeded down the narrow staircase.

Five men sat at a round table in one corner of the basement storage area. Clouds of cigarette smoke hung below a rusted lighting fixture centered over the table. The air reeked of stale tobacco smells, overriding the damp fetid aroma of more deadly hazards.

As she stood at the bottom of the stairs, Jamail caught the shocked expressions on the faces of the men staring at her. Dakheel Noorani looked over his shoulder to see what caused this interruption.

In an instant, Noorani, leader of this cell, pushed away from the table and rose to his feet, closing the gap to where Jamail waited. His chair overturned and crashed against the stained concrete floor.

Noorani's open palm swung at her lowered face. A sharp crack echoed across the room and droplets of blood from Jamail's split lip soaked into her hijab.

Jamail responded by lowering her head further and listening to Noorani's reprimands. Her fantasies had evaporated at her first sight of the men seated at the table. She deserved no less, having entered this sanctum wearing western garb; the hijab being the sole attempt at deference to the warriors in the room.

"I have warned you many times." Noorani spit out the words as he returned to his place at the table. One of the men had already picked up his chair.

Jamail kept her place on the far side of the room, not making eye contact with anyone at the table.

Noorani said, "Get to it, Jamail. We have important matters to discuss. You have disgraced yourself in the eyes of Allah. We will deal with that matter later."

Badiyah Jamail relayed the information she'd learned from the notes and reports in the president's briefcase and the overheard conversation in the first lady's office. She never once looked up, knowing none of the men would even face her. She dared not wipe away the drying blood. In between her words, she tasted the bitter, metallic fluid clinging to the inside of her lower lip.

Noorani and the other men continued discussing the final details of a daring plan. Jamail's new information accentuated their need to act. They had no idea if the recent incident at the ICCA in San Francisco was an unfortunate coincidence, or a sign of a more aggressive approach by the current administration. Either way, when Aamir Rahaman had called and asked them to transfer needed replacement supplies to the West Coast, Noorani jumped into action.

With an air of disdain, he turned to Jamail and told her what she must do next. And then he waved his hand in dismissal and pointed her to the door.

CHAPTER 6

STEVE CASELLA SLIPPED ON A light tweed sport coat and busied himself packing a briefcase. His faded black jeans and scuffed running shoes contrasted with any attempt at formality. They were on their way to meet Edie's brother, Sampson, and his girlfriend, Beth, for breakfast. Later, Steve was scheduled to teach a workshop at a romance writers conference at the Spokane Convention Center. Amber would be joining him at the podium. Steve gave her a quick grooming, but the only thing accomplished was to cover his jeans in Amber's white fur.

He headed to the front door of their house in the eastern hills overlooking Lake Coeur d'Alene. While speaking into her phone, Edie tapped him on the shoulder and handed over one of those roller thingies to remove the excess dog hair from his trousers. He gave her an *'are you kidding me?'* look but rolled the sticky cylinder over his wardrobe before tossing it onto the porch swing on the front deck.

Edie still held the phone to her ear.

"You ready to go?" Steve asked in a low voice. "If we want to meet your brother for breakfast, we'll need to get a move on it. I'll fasten Rosa into her car seat." He paused and raised his eyebrows. "And stop bothering Jack. They're working on the new bedroom wall today. I've spoken to him twice this morning, and he's putting together the change list. Said he'd email it before the end of the day."

Edie pulled the phone away from her ear. "Not talking to Jack now. He doesn't appear to be taking my calls. Texted him last night."

Her lips tightened. "I've called Sampson's cell phone several times. Tried Beth's too. Nobody answers. And I left a message last night—to confirm the time? Never got any response." She punched in a different number. "I'll try the front desk at their hotel."

"Could be the ghosts they're searching for are interfering with the cell signals," Steve said, but swallowed his words as he saw the expression on Edie's face turn dark.

Edie stood up straighter, but then leaned against one of the porch columns. Steve watched her knuckles stiffen as she pressed the phone to her ear. Her eyes opened wide, and she bit hard on her lower lip. She sat down onto the porch swing and nodded her head several times.

Amber shook, sending swirls of white fur into the air. She padded over to Edie, resting a warm, wet snout on her lap.

Steve picked up bits and pieces of the conversation and sprang into action. He tossed his briefcase back inside the house and extracted Rosa from the stroller. With one hand he maneuvered it shut while he carried his daughter to the rented Escalade. After fastening her safely into the car seat, he opened the rear hatch and called Amber. By then Edie had ended the call and was sprinting to the front passenger side of the SUV. Steve shoved down the hatch and jumped behind the wheel. He gunned the engine, and they jolted forward, leaving sprays of dust and gravel in the wake of the oversized SUV.

Steve glanced at Edie.

She wiped a hand across her face. "Beth is in Deaconess Hospital. She's alive, but they wouldn't give out any more information. It's not clear exactly what happened. Sampson's—missing."

* * * * * *

An hour later they stood arguing with the head nurse outside the intensive care unit. Rosa fell asleep as Edie rocked her gently in her arms. A man in a rumpled tan linen suit ambled over and interrupted the exchange.

He placed a hand on Steve's shoulder. "I'm Lt. Atkinson. Detective. Spokane Police Department. Major Crimes Division. Why don't we go into the visitor lounge at the end of the hall." Each word stretched and drawn out like melting string cheese.

Edie placed the sleeping baby in the stroller, and they followed the detective.

By the time they took seats in the empty room, Steve and Edie had explained their relationship to Beth Dawson and tried to override the detective's reluctance to share any facts. The only information they learned from the detective confirmed what the head nurse had told them. Beth Dawson's vital signs were stable, but she had lapsed into unconsciousness while the doctors in the E.R. worked on her.

Atkinson parked his lanky frame on the sofa across from Steve and Edie. His suit jacket hung loosely, exaggerating the sharp hanger tip impressions on the shoulder material. He grabbed a notepad and a chewed-up pencil from his coat pocket, ready to fire questions. His pasty complexion matched the curled, white spiraled pages in his hand.

Edie nodded at Steve, and he pulled out his credentials.

Atkinson scrutinized Steve's Department of Homeland Security ID, handed it back, and gave him a long, hard look. The detective shrugged and leaned back, spreading his arms across the sofa's tired cushions. After a brief moment of watching the baby sleeping in the stroller tucked next to Edie, Atkinson let out a breath.

"First, Casella, your position with DHS has no bearing on my case." He coughed twice and relaxed. "As a courtesy, and seeing you are acquainted with the victim, this is what I can tell you. Ms. Dawson's body was spotted in the Spokane River, floating about a quarter mile west of the Monroe Street bridge. Two bikers riding along the path at the edge of the river dove in and pulled her out. Luckily, they did a good job resuscitating her until the paramedics arrived and took over. Ms. Dawson woke up briefly while in the ambulance. The paramedics comprehended only part of what she muttered. They did get her name and that she was staying at the Spokane Falls Lodge with her boyfriend."

The detective paused, unwrapped a cough drop, and popped it in his mouth. The honey-colored candy disappeared behind a coffee-stained row of teeth. He thumbed through several more pages of the notepad. "From what we gathered, she was riding on the Spokane Falls Skyride. That's a tourist attraction in Riverside Park. It gives people a bird's eye view of the falls."

He looked up as if expecting a question. "Could've been involved in a struggle—then shoved or fell from the gondola." Atkinson hesitated again, appeared to make a decision, and picked up his attaché case, placing it on his lap.

As he rifled through it, Edie asked, "Who was with her in the gondola?" Steve knew she was desperate to find out what happened to Sampson.

Atkinson looked up and nodded as he closed the lid and placed an evidence bag on top. "We got a partial description from the attendant working at the Skyride." He picked up his notepad again, giving it his full attention.

Edie leaned forward and Steve put a hand on her shoulder, giving her a quick head shake. He feared that any second she would grab the notepad or seize the detective by the neck and help him spit it all out.

"Ah... here it is." Another pronounced silence. He mouthed the next words as if studying his lines for a play. "The second passenger—male. White. Fair-skinned—possibly tall. Either bald or close-cropped hair."

Edie let out a deep sigh.

Steve asked, "They walked up to the gondola together?"

"The attendant couldn't say for sure. He didn't see them again after they got on board." The detective stared out the window. "The gondola returned empty."

"Did you secure the gondola car?" Steve asked.

That got a menacing glare from Atkinson. Steve raised his hands and apologized. "I'm not trying to tell you how to do your job." He grabbed hold of Edie's hand. "We're just anxious to find out what's going on."

Atkinson's eyes burned into Steve for several more seconds, and he gave a slight nod. "The evidence found in the gondola is being examined. We found a small purse. The contents strewn about the car. There was also a single .40 caliber casing found behind a seat cushion."

"Are you saying Beth was shot too?" Edie blurted out.

Atkinson's face shifted into a subtle smile. He pointed at the evidence bag on top of his attaché case. "The paramedics discovered this after they got the victim into the ambulance."

Steve and Edie stared at the large, bent and misshaped silver medallion.

"Yeah," Atkinson said, "they believe this saved her life. The medallion hung around her neck and took the bullet dead center. Right into the head of the eagle. The flattened piece of lead is still embedded there. Ms. Dawson wound up with two broken ribs and a bruised sternum, but—" He shrugged.

"May I?" Steve asked, pointing to the evidence bag. Atkinson handed it to him.

Edie checked Rosa and then turned to the detective. "What about my brother? Sampson Pauling. He was traveling with Beth Dawson, but he seems to have disappeared."

"As of now, he's no longer a suspect." He swallowed the remaining fragment of the cough drop. "There's no evidence placing him anywhere near the incident. But we're interested in speaking with him."

Edie rubbed her hands over her face. "Sampson would never walk away. If he could, he would've been in touch with me by now. I've left him at least a half dozen voice mails and texts since last night."

"We did a quick look-see in Ms. Dawson's hotel room but found no evidence of any kind of struggle. A cell phone and a man's wallet were sitting in plain sight on the desk. The room is now sealed off while we wait for a warrant. We'll have our investigators do a thorough search—see if they come up with any leads. As of now, we got nothing."

Reading from his notes, Atkinson continued, "There is a record of Sampson Pauling entering the hotel's gym. He was reported to be alone. Worked out for thirty minutes and left. Alone. No one remembers him talking to anyone."

"What are you doing to find him?" Edie asked.

"Under ordinary circumstances, with no evidence of foul play, it would be too early to even consider him missing. But like I said, we'd like to question him about the attack on Ms. Dawson. He's considered a person of interest, so we've got officers canvassing the area. We'll probably alert the local media. I'm confident something will turn up."

While Steve listened to this exchange, he'd placed an arm around Edie's shoulder. He still held the evidence bag containing the damaged medallion. "Detective," he said, holding out the bag. "The medallion itself appears to be relatively intact, except where it's indented from the bullet lodged in the front. But what do you make of those particles in the bottom of the bag? They don't look metallic."

Atkinson took back the bag and examined the contents again. "Too early to tell." He stood up and shook hands with Steve and Edie. "I'm heading over to the lab. You can be assured they'll do a thorough job checking it out." He glanced at the sleeping baby and his mouth formed a hint of a smile that quickly faded. "We'll be in touch. And don't worry, I'm positive we'll find your brother."

His words sounded rote and didn't instill much confidence. The detective's lanky frame disappeared through the doorway. They listened to the echo of his footsteps fade down the hall.

Edie wiped a tear from her eye. "I'm not about to wait for Atkinson or anyone else to determine what's going on. Something bad has happened to Sampson. There's no way his disappearance isn't related to the attack on Beth."

"No argument there."

"Remember I told you Beth wanted to give me some important information?"

Steve nodded.

"She's never one to exaggerate. She sounded scared about whatever she found. But didn't want to discuss any details over the phone. I got the impression she stumbled onto something while scanning through a number of secure servers. Said what she found was frightening. Wanted to turn it over to me."

Edie paused, hesitating. "When I spoke to Beth last month, I asked her for a few pointers on digging into identity links and tracing key individuals based on patterns of money transfers. I was getting nowhere on my own. This profiling Tyler asked me to investigate was complicated enough."

"You think Beth might've dug a little too deep and opened the wrong door?"

"I didn't expect her to get involved with any actual snooping herself. I only wanted advice from her expertise." Edie slapped both hands over her face and rubbed her eyes. "I guess I was naïve thinking she wouldn't try this on her own."

"Maybe you're jumping to conclusions." After getting no response from Edie, Steve grabbed his phone.

Seeing the building resolve on Edie's face, Steve decided on a move. He trusted her instincts.

"Atkinson isn't going to like this, but I'm calling in the cavalry. It's time to use the national security trump card. Let's get the feds involved in this investigation. I also want to make sure we bring in more security to keep an eye on Beth. When she's fit to travel, we can transfer her to a more secure facility."

"Good thinking, Steve. Now let's go see Beth."

CHAPTER 7

MR. CLEAN STOOD AT THE window overlooking his private lake in the Creston Valley of British Columbia. He couldn't place what was different. The sun rose as usual above the mountain peaks, sending shimmering rays across the water's surface. He watched the slight undulations of the lighter branches on the nearby trees responding to the stirring of the morning breeze.

Then it hit him. Those majestic raptors were absent. He now recalled this year's appearance had been fleeting. He couldn't remember the last time he'd seen a bald eagle soar over the waters and swoop down to catch its prey. Perhaps the increased activities surrounding this stone dwelling caused them to find a more tranquil setting.

He had forgotten watching Bartholomew target shooting at the birds.

On the exact same grounds, but in a different era, the original inhabitants of this land heralded the prodigious eagle as a messenger, or even the persona, of the Great Spirit. A symbol of power and strength overriding the trifling dominions of the human essence. Its massive wings opening to bring forth the light of day and closing to embrace the darkness of night. The earth's weather borne from the powerful movements of its beating wings.

To the original inhabitants of this land, the human form was thought to have materialized when this soaring bird of prey spiraled downward and pressed a clawed foot upon the ground.

In every culture from the beginning of time, the eagle has played a symbolic role. Legend warns that to kill one of these creatures would instantly turn the perpetrator into a monster, one to be shunned by all mankind.

More likely the monster had always existed, awaiting the opportunity to reveal itself.

Mr. Clean had been careful and avoided drawing attention to this isolated property near the U.S. border. The increased air traffic to his tiny airfield could be observed, but also explained and justified to nearby residents. Not unusual for the growing business at Consolidated Canadian Mills. The jobs and money flowing into the area's economy provided a means for overlooking such annoyances.

But perhaps the bald eagle now sensed a deeper, underlying threat. The magnificent birds of prey had existed for eons. Could they survive the forthcoming dangers from the new humanity?

Mr. Clean listened to the faint droning of an incoming flight and checked his watch. The private air strip lay about a hundred yards to the east, adjacent to the tree line bordering the manicured grounds of his estate. Once the passengers arriving on the single engine prop airplane disembarked, Mr. Clean's current guest would board the aircraft.

"Aamir," Mr. Clean said, turning to the man seated in the leather armchair. "I see your associates are arriving. We must finish our business before you depart. I have instructed the pilot as to your next destination. Your men will be transported to our Bayview facility in plenty of time to prepare for their expected guests."

Aamir Rahaman gave a slight nod. "We are moving more quickly than originally planned, but from our sources in D.C. I have learned it is necessary to escalate these final steps. The mass turmoil at the borders of all western nations, and the escalating acts of terror, should keep Washington distracted from the dangers they will soon face in their own backyard. As of now, President Griffin and his intelligence assets have only an inkling of what will come next."

"And we must keep it like that, Aamir. If your sources are correct, and the president himself is involved in a covert investigation of our larger threat—this must not be ignored. Our coalition must remain hidden."

Mr. Clean paused before emphasizing his next words. "Not only from the prying eyes in D.C., but from your allies in Iran as well. At present, they hold the key to this important phase."

"That is true, my friend. The Iranian clerics are blinded by ideology and therefore cannot comprehend the inevitable destiny. They see what benefits their goals and reward those who echo their dogma. But once the dust has settled on the holy land, there will be no viable options left. Islam shall reign supreme."

To Mr. Clean, those words represented merely the means to the end. A world where Allah played no role at all. Mr. Clean and his predecessors had learned long ago that the key step was to unite the world under the guise of religious fervor. Without faith there could be no passion. Without passion, no fear could be generated. Without fear, the final conflict could not begin.

Providing the resources for acquiring weapons of mass destruction had been child's play for a man of Mr. Clean's capabilities.

Long after the aircraft departed with Aamir Rahaman on board, Mr. Clean stared out onto the tranquil waters of the lake. Bartholomew would be returning soon. He'd make this journey via one of the submarine transport vehicles after securing their guests inside the underwater module near the southern end of Lake Pend Oreille.

Except for Bartholomew, Mr. Clean's family was all but a distant memory.

To be sure, they still existed and had spread to the four corners of the globe. Unlike the close family structure he remembered as a boy. The tiny fishing village where he was born didn't have a formal name. The locals knew it only as the place belonging to his family.

It had been years since anyone called him by his real name. Now he had many names and identities, each filling a particular need.

Similar individuals from other designated families existed, but over the years the numbers had dwindled. This ancient torch had been carried on by an elite sect known only to a select group. Wild speculations over the centuries made for good conspiracy tales, but barely scratched the surface of the potential consequences.

In the early part of the twentieth century, the power of the torch had ebbed, and fading zeal threatened to obscure the ultimate goal. With the emergence of the Muslim Brotherhood, a political force steeped in religious fanaticism, the remaining leaders of Mr. Clean's ancient sect seized the opportunity to work with them and resurrect the dream.

The years had slipped by. Mr. Clean expanded his father's fortune and chose this path.

No, it had chosen him.

Now the time drew near, but he grew weaker by the day. Not in his belief of the cause, but the years had finally caught up. He sensed that this time the goal was close. But there had been false starts before. He knew he would not be around for many more.

Mr. Clean accepted the fact that Bartholomew might carry the torch for the next generation. If so, he needed to believe in the entire saga. The covenants made.

Yes, he thought. The time has come. But deep in his heart he questioned if his grandson could handle such a challenge.

CHAPTER 8

THE STRIKING SIX STORY ATRIUM in the Spokane Falls Lodge glistened in the late morning sun, providing a bold, welcoming atmosphere. At the moment, the splendor escaped Steve Casella's attention. After spending an eternity on his phone, he dropped it on the square glass table. Edie busied herself entertaining Rosa, and Amber crouched next to the sofa, guarding their perimeter.

Steve leaned back in his seat and let out a long sigh. "Everything's been hashed out on the jurisdiction for Beth's attempted murder. The locals agreed to the feds taking over the investigation on the grounds of national security issues. Well, agreed may not be the exact term."

He arched his brows at Edie. "At this point, we don't have much evidence tying it to national security. This could all blow up in our faces. Jumping the gun might wind up embarrassing the president."

Smiling at her daughter, Edie nodded and turned serious. "I'm positive about this Steve. I can feel it. Whatever Beth uncovered has got to be important." She lowered her head and bounced Rosa on her knee. In a softer voice, she added, "Otherwise none of this would've happened." Her eyes focused on Steve. "And I'm still worried she might not be safe—even in the hospital."

Steve nodded and pressed his lips tight. "The FBI will have their guys at the hospital within the hour. Until then, the locals agreed to station officers outside her door."

Steve and Edie had spent the last half hour at Beth Dawson's bedside in Deaconess Hospital. The doctors were confident she'd make a complete recovery but opted to place Beth in a medically induced coma for several days as a precautionary measure.

Beth had sustained head trauma as a result of her fall from the gondola. Her brain function appeared normal, based on her responses in the ambulance and emergency room, but the additional testing performed at the hospital suggested the presence of cerebral edema. The initial CT scan was inconclusive, but the follow-up MRI convinced the doctors this was the appropriate course of treatment to give the injured tissue a better chance to recover.

For the moment, there was nothing Steve and Edie could do but leave Beth in the hands of her doctors and focus on figuring out what was going on and what happened to Sampson.

Steve reached over and took Rosa. He raised her tiny body in the air.

Edie smiled and waved at Rosa. "While you were straightening things out with the FBI, I got a call from Catori. She's been visiting her mother on the reservation for the last two weeks. She heard what happened to Beth and saw Sampson's picture plastered all over the local news."

Edie paused and looked up at Steve. "I guess Detective Atkinson followed through with getting Sampson's picture to the media a lot quicker than I imagined." She shrugged. "Possibly someone saw something and will come forward. Sampson's not an easy person to forget."

Steve nodded.

"Before hanging up," Edie continued, "Catori talked to her brother, and they're both on their way over. Be here in about ninety minutes. They want to help. And I don't think she means taking care of Rosa."

"Great. Paco's got one of the best investigative minds I've ever come across. Maybe Catori can convince her brother to move on from his job with the tribal police force and take a position with DHS or the FBI."

"I don't think that's going to happen anytime soon. He's dedicated his life to helping the folks on the Kootenecti Reservation, but I'd welcome anything he can add to this. By the time they arrive, we should be cleared to take a look at Sampson and Beth's hotel room."

Rosa's eyes started to droop. Edie took her back from Steve, rocked her a bit in her arms, and then tucked her into the stroller. With one foot, she idly pushed the stroller back and forth while she talked to Steve.

Steve looked around the lobby, trying to piece together his thoughts. He clasped his hands and leaned forward. "So, before the feds come flying through the door, can you clarify something?"

Edie shrugged.

"What you said earlier today in the hospital about asking Beth for help? I assume you were referring to the Amber Alert project?" Amber's ears perked up.

"Right. And you've read those same reports I've been sending to Tyler."

"Yeah, I realize he's interested in more than putting an end to terrorist acts around the globe and expediting DHS's task of hunting down terrorist activities within our own borders. But I'm still not sure how Beth could've helped you with this."

Steve paused, looking for clues on Edie's face. "You said she's a computer expert, but when she worked for the federal government, I thought she was involved with D.C. lobbyist groups and congressional databases. How does that relate to terrorist activities and foreign governments?"

Edie blinked and rubbed a hand down her cheek. "Tyler believes overt terrorist activity merely scratches the surface. You've heard him. The carnage gets all the publicity. He's also concerned with the less obvious threats. Threats to our infrastructure. Those conspiring to end our way of life from within."

Steve spread his hands out. "You should've asked Jimmy Martin for help." He was referring to one of their right-wing, conspiracy-driven friends from the community club in Coeur d'Alene. Steve figured his plans for meeting up with those guys and guzzling down a few beers wouldn't happen anytime soon.

Edie's mouth started to open.

"Never mind," Steve said. "What did you ask Beth to do?"

"Well, I came across lots of holes and missing links in the databases I discovered. I found material on the Muslim Brotherhood, but when I tried looking deeper into their history or dug into their current interactions, my research hit a wall. So, I asked Beth to provide me with other resources to gain access to the information."

Rosa's binky fell to the floor, and she immediately started fussing. Amber beat Edie to it. Edie reached into her bag for a fresh one and stuck it back in Rosa's mouth. Rosa settled right down and closed her eyes.

"I didn't want her to do any hands-on research herself, just point me in the right direction. Looks like she did more than I asked. I should've known better. There's no telling what she got into. This is my fault, Steve. I opened the door. I need to stay close to this investigation. We can't let anything else happen to her." She swallowed. "And we still have no clue as to what happened to Sampson."

Steve slid closer to Edie and looped an arm around her shoulder, feeling the tenseness. He pulled her tight but gazed warily into her eyes. "Remember, Edie. Let's not step on the FBI's investigative guys when they show up. We've already pissed off the locals."

"By the book, Steve. That's what I always say."

Steve kept his stare but didn't bother to comment.

CHAPTER 9

SAMPSON PAULING ATTEMPTED TO OPEN his eyes. His eyelids felt heavy, like wet blankets smothering out the world. His huge frame lay prone, toes jammed against cold, hard steel.

In a reflex motion he sat up, smacking his head against taut metal springs.

His eyes shifted to the torn-up sleeve on his shirt, and his hand rubbed lightly over a crude bandage wrapping around his left biceps. He noticed the blood stains on the shirt.

"Think I would've remembered who the hell did this. Sure like to see what the other guy's condition is."

He shrugged and gradually took in his surroundings through the lens of the dim lighting.

"Jesus." His eyes continued to dart about. "I'm in a damn bunk bed."

Realizing he wasn't restrained, he swung his legs to the floor. He ducked his head below the upper bunk and pulled himself to his feet.

"What is this place?" He took several steps, bending down to keep from banging his head against the jutting objects along the low ceiling. The space was shaped like a cylinder, approximately ten feet wide and thirty feet long. He glanced at a small refrigerator, a three-burner stove, a sink, and a microwave oven.

"It's like I'm in an Airstream, but where's all the damn windows?" Sampson spotted a door at one end of the enclosure and headed for it. He opened it and stared at a toilet and a tiny sink.

"Hot damn!"

After using the facilities, he stepped back into the larger chamber. At the other end he saw a circular steel hatch with a small window in the center. Sampson hurried down the length of the narrow space and peered through the glass. The chamber extended approximately four feet beyond the hatch. There was a similar access door at the other end with another small window.

Sampson glanced around and tried to find a way to open the hatch. Failing, he stared back through the tiny window, focusing on something on the other side of the glass porthole on the outer hatch.

His eyes bulged. "I'm no outdoorsman, but that looks like a fish swimming by."

He turned away from the hatch and looked at his surroundings. Not knowing how he missed it before, he sensed the slow rocking and swaying movements beneath his feet.

"I'm no detective, but this feels like a boat. Don't tell me I'm stuck in a natural body of water."

Then it hit him. "My God! Beth. Son of a bitch. Where the hell could she be?"

Sampson walked slowly back to the bunk beds and sunk down onto the mattress. The springs cried out in protest to the assault. He lowered his head into his hands and tried to understand what happened after his workout at the hotel gym.

* * * * * *

Everything appeared fragmented, like watching an old movie spliced together—key pieces jumbled or missing. In the hotel gym, Sampson first did a five-mile run on the treadmill and then switched to the weight machine, progressing through a short but intense series. He'd finished up on the tread climber and returned to the treadmill for a quick cool-down.

He couldn't recall anyone suspicious hanging around during his workout. Nothing out of place surfaced. The several others he'd noticed were absorbed in their own regimens and hadn't paid him any attention.

Sampson had left the gym with a towel wrapped around his neck. He stepped onto the elevator and punched the button for the nineteenth floor, leaning back against a rear corner. He remembered closing his eyes, slipping into a light catnap.

Something startled him.

Must've been the car stopping and the doors sliding open. Everything after that was a blur. But it made sense—someone else had gotten on board the elevator. Nothing about what occurred afterwards registered with any clarity. He had the vague recollection of a popping noise and a pin prick. Soft voices had unfurled around him, and his world had faded to black.

* * * * * *

Sampson blinked his eyes several times and once again took in his cramped surroundings. A sudden feeling of claustrophobia grabbed him, almost propelling him back against the thin mattress. He took in deep breaths and gripped the frame on the upper bunk. This helped clear his head.

For several moments he tightened his eyes shut and listened. A faint but steady humming sound filled the background, accompanied by a low-pitched vibration under his feet. He still sensed the gentle movements of his new home.

The air, while breathable, had an odd smell, making him think of stale diesel fuel tainted with a hint of rotten eggs. Could be his imagination, but when he swallowed, he swore he could actually taste the air.

His dad had told him stories he'd learned from working in a submarine museum. Sampson hadn't paid much attention. His current situation easily resembled those nebulous memories.

Sampson didn't have a clue as to what was happening, but he was now pissed-off. It ate at him that he didn't know if Beth was okay. She had been anxious to speak to Edie. She'd been vague as to exactly what information she wanted to pass on to his sister. He wished he'd pressed her for more specifics. He recalled Beth and his sister chatting last month about a project Edie was researching for the president.

Did this have anything to do with Beth's concerns?

Or was this a random kidnapping?

That last thought almost made him laugh.

"Only a moron would think that. What the hell has Beth stumbled into?" Sampson stared into every corner of the chamber.

Much louder, he yelled, "I don't know if you bastards can see or hear me, but I'll tell you this. If you hurt one hair on Beth, I'll be coming after you and will tear you all apart—limb by limb."

CHAPTER 10

CAPT. MARIO LORENZINI, DETERMINED TO maintain an upbeat attitude, tried to keep any budding aggravations in check.

He'd spent the last six days with his family—his beautiful wife, Anna, and his two children, Dante and Camila—relaxing in a quiet rented beachfront villa overlooking the sparkling blue Mediterranean waters of the Amalfi coast. Yesterday, heavy traffic extended the long drive home to over four hours, but they still arrived early enough to unwind.

Lorenzini got a good night's sleep, woke up refreshed, and made it to Rome's Leonardo da Vinci International Airport at least fifteen minutes earlier than his required check-in time.

Remnants of the pleasant lapping of the tranquil Mediterranean and the soft lavender fragrance accenting the warm sea breezes swirled in his head as he walked across the asphalt pavement and into the airport terminal.

Lorenzini kept a watchful eye on the man seated to his left in the cramped cockpit of the Airbus A321. He shifted in his seat as Taqhid Kalil completed the pre-flight checklist. This would be Kalil's virgin flight as first officer, piloting the A321. Lorenzini's demeanor continued to waver. He tried to put aside his inherent dislike of Kalil and maintain his objectivity by concentrating on the man's performance.

Kalil came across as a bit stiff and formal. The man had no sense of humor and could be condescending at times. But he had an excellent flight record and Lorenzini considered him to be a competent pilot.

Today, however, Lorenzini noticed a subtle tenseness in Kalil's actions. Kalil's voice during his radio communications with aircraft control sounded awkward. Still, he'd done everything by the book and followed all procedures without any hiccups.

Their aircraft was second in line for take-off on runway 34R. Lorenzini scanned the instrument panel array. Everything appeared normal. He stole a quick glance at Kalil and noticed a sheen forming on the man's forehead. He shrugged to himself, thinking even a stiff-assed, aloof, anti-social—Lorenzini chided himself and put his growing frustrations on hold. The guy's a little nervous on his maiden flight as pilot. Lorenzini decided to lighten up the moment before Kalil began his takeoff run.

"Hey, Taqhid? You hear the story about the German Shepherd and the pilot?" Lorenzini gave Kalil's shoulder a light punch.

Kalil twitched and then froze in place. He turned his head toward Lorenzini, but his mouth remained closed beneath huge staring eyes.

Taken aback, Lorenzini hesitated, then figured—what the hell. "So, it's the pilot's job to keep the German Shepherd well-fed." He paused for the punchline. "And it's the German Shepherd's job to bite the pilot in the ass if he attempts to touch any of the flight controls."

Kalil's eyes narrowed, and his mouth opened, but he remained quiet.

Lorenzini jumped in and attempted to explain the joke. "You see, the Airbus is designed to fly itself. The engineers consider the human component to be... I guess you might say intrusive to the aircraft's performance. Different from the Boeing design where they expect the pilot to have input to...." His words drifted off as he watched Kalil's face turn impassive. Any further discussion was cut off when the radio squawked to life.

"Alitalia flight AZ224. You are cleared for take-off. Runway 34R."

Lorenzini acknowledged the transmission and both men focused on getting the Airbus, loaded with 198 passengers and six crew members, into the air for their three hour and twenty-minute, non-stop flight to Tel Aviv, Israel.

"Nice work, Taqhid." Lorenzini jotted down notes in the log after Kalil executed a textbook take-off and maneuvered the aircraft to its cruising altitude.

Kalil completed entering the necessary data into the flight computer and the autopilot aligned them onto the correct course for the routine medium-haul flight.

Kalil turned to Lorenzini, his head in a slight bow. "Where is this nasty dog you speak of? I have touched these precious instruments, but the dog has not done its job." His mouth almost turned upwards into a smile, and he opened his palms to Lorenzini.

For the first time since getting on board, Lorenzini's posture relaxed.

The two spent the next several hours exchanging small talk. Though amiable, Lorenzini sensed something off in Kalil's behavior. Lorenzini considered himself a good Catholic and a moderately religious person, but Kalil's obsessive narrations about Allah began to give him the creeps. The man spoke of a glorious future, but not in a personal context. Lorenzini was glad when they slipped into silence for the remaining segment of the flight.

Kalil spoke up several minutes prior to preparing for the aircraft's descent into Ben Gurion International Airport outside Tel Aviv.

"Mario, would you mind taking over for a moment? I must make a quick trip to the lavatory." Kalil released his harness and twisted out of the seat.

"Not a problem, Taqhid. Let me call back and get one of the flight attendants up here in the cockpit before you release the door lock. Damn regulations. Can't even take a piss without broadcasting it to the world." He nodded and reached for the intercom.

Before Lorenzini could grasp the handset, Kalil drew a steel garrote from his pocket and spun it around Lorenzini's neck. He yanked back on the tee handle grips, pulling the thin wire taut. At the same time, Kalil kicked at the locking mechanism on Lorenzini's seat, sliding the chair to its rear position. Kalil released a guttural grunting sound as he increased pressure on the garrote.

No sounds emerged from Lorenzini's compressed larynx. His arms thrashed, trying to grasp the garrote. Failing, he stretched forward, but his arms grappled at air.

His efforts were short-lived.

Kalil waited another several moments after Lorenzini's body slackened before releasing his grip on the garrote. He left the wire hanging from Lorenzini's neck, watching rivulets of blood disappear beneath his shirt. The body slumped sideways, held loosely in place by the harness.

Taqhid Kalil climbed back into the left seat and prepared the aircraft for its initial descent into Ben Gurion International Airport.

A similar event would soon unfold on a Boeing 777 aircraft. That particular Alitalia flight had taken off from Leonardo da Vinci International Airport approximately six hours prior to the departure of flight AZ224. It was a non-stop flight headed to Newark Liberty International Airport in New Jersey.

CHAPTER 11

FBI INVESTIGATORS DESCENDED ON THE Spokane Falls Lodge and politely informed Steve Casella that he was free to wait in the lobby. Steve grabbed Edie's shoulder as she prepared to jump to her feet and confront the agents.

"There's an easier way to deal with this," Steve said. Edie relented and Steve punched a number on his phone.

Ten minutes after the brief confrontation with the feds, and still waiting for Steve's phone call to circumvent the bureaucratic ether, Paco and Catori Torrence walked through the lobby entrance.

Paco wore his Kootenecti Tribal Police uniform. His entrance commanded the attention of everyone in the lobby, especially the females. At a height of six foot one and a solid two hundred pounds, Paco's dark, rugged good looks always assured him of more than a passing glance from any number of eligible and, not so eligible, young ladies both on and off the reservation. The uniform was icing on the cake.

When Paco first joined the reservation's police department following a stint as an M.P. in the U.S. Army, he had a huge chip on his shoulder regarding the injustices to the surviving Native American people; encouraged by long-standing, archaic government policies. He'd finally learned how to use this defiant attitude to his advantage.

If the appearance of Paco Torrence's imposing form caused a stir in the lobby, when his sister, Catori, glided to his side and strode across the expansive atrium, her captivating image stole the oxygen from the vast six-story space.

Walking next to her brother, Catori's slight size did nothing to diminish the response to her allure. Just shy of five feet, the tiny creature lit up the room. She had an olive-toned complexion with high cheek bones and slanted, almond-shaped eyes. Her dark brown hair fell almost to her waist.

Behind her beauty, an all-empowering manifestation of tribal legend and power magnetized everything within her grasp, including phenomena from the distant past to the unforeseeable future. Her grandmother, Lomasi, who passed on several years ago, died peacefully, with the understanding Catori would carry on the tribal lore.

When Catori spotted Rosa, she magically transformed, and her own inner child burst forth. She kneeled in front of Edie, stretching out her arms. Her gentle touch coddled the infant close to her breast as she chanted unheard words in the baby's ear.

Catori caught sight of Amber, and she reached out an arm. "Come here you big fur ball." Amber padded over and licked Catori's face while Catori roughed up the back of the dog's neck.

As Steve looked on, the tension drained from his body. He placed a hand on Edie's shoulder and glanced at her. He could see the same response in her eyes.

When they first met Catori, a child of fifteen, she had exuded a similar aura and strength. The fact Steve and Edie now spent many hours with Catori, who helped out with Steve's canine training facility, did nothing to diminish the enormity of her presence.

The resilience in this young girl was amazing. Not long ago she'd been drawn into a dreadful medical nightmare. The unethical and criminal activities at a renowned health clinic had almost cost Catori her life. She had rebounded from those experiences and was even more captivating than ever.

Steve's phone chirped. He listened for several seconds and smiled. "Yeah, I appreciate your help. Better this got handled by the big boys." A little louder, to grab Edie's attention, he added, "Right. Let's do it by a different book. Thanks."

Steve turned to the others. "What say we head up to the room and see how things are going with the feds?"

Paco's stoic image transformed. "Now you're talking, Steve. I'm always ready to help out fellow law enforcement officers. Especially federal agents." Paco brushed unseen lint from his crisp uniform. "And I'm sure they're eager to discuss their investigations with me."

He placed a hand on Steve's back as they all headed to the elevator. "Hey, Steve. You don't look any different to me since the last time I saw you. You sure you're a fed now too?"

Steve looked at Paco and arched his brows. "Be careful with your characterizations, Paco. With the convoluted bureaucracies involved with tribal laws and the Bureau of Indian affairs, there's a strong possibility you're a federal employee too."

A wide grin spread across Paco's face. "That'd scare the crap out of those assholes in D.C."

The elevator doors opened on the nineteenth floor, and four adults, a baby, and a dog exited. They turned down the corridor and approached Room 1909. Two FBI agents stood outside the door. The burly one had a cell phone stuck to his ear. From his expression, the conversation wasn't going his way.

With a frown, he ended the call and shoved the phone in his pocket. He leaned forward and stared at the strange entourage standing in front of him. "Who the hell *are* you people?"

Steve guessed the phone conversation had him rattled. In light of being told to stand down and acquiesce to these people now assembled in front of him, the agent probably needed to save face or at least blow smoke up their asses.

The agent stared at the dog. "And what is Scooby-Doo doing here?"

Edie responded. "In case you haven't noticed, this dog is white, unlike the cherished dog of color and beloved cartoon character you're referring to."

Amber crouched down extending her front paws. Her hind legs poised straight beneath a tense body. Her upper lip curled, and a low throbbing growl rumbled from her throat.

The burly agent backed up against the wall.

"Knock it off, Amber," Steve scolded. Amber inched closer to the burly agent, sat up on her haunches, and raised a paw. This was accompanied by a gentle whimper.

In a reflex action, the burly agent kneeled down and shook hands with the dog.

Amber chuffed loudly and looked over at Steve.

Recovering, the agent stood up and wiped his hand on his pants. His attention turned to Paco Torrence, eyes riveted at the insignia on Paco's uniform. He then glanced at the nameplate on the shirt pocket.

"Deputy Torrence? Isn't this a bit out of your jurisdiction?" The burly agent smirked. "Yeah, I'd say you're way off the reservation."

As little as a year ago, Paco Torrence would've probably pulled out his service weapon and placed a bullet between the asshole's eyes. But the more refined Paco took in several distinct sniffs with his nose and said, "I was slugging down shots in the Plummer saloon when this overwhelming stench grabbed hold of me."

He paused and smiled, tapping the side of his nose. "I followed it right to the source. A bunch of rotting feds trying to do a real cop's job."

"Okay, boys. You win," Catori said, shaking her head. "All this testosterone is way too much for us poor, helpless girls. Right, Edie?"

Edie fanned her face with her free hand as Rosa squirmed against her shoulder.

Catori shrugged and looked at Steve. "Perhaps Mr. Casella—oops—I mean *Agent* Casella has something to add."

The burly agent raised his hands and nodded at Steve. "I don't give a damn who the hell you people are." He tapped the pocket holding his phone. "But seeing my boss informed me he'd ream me a new asshole if I didn't cooperate with you, this is the deal."

One at a time, he counted off the list on his fingers. "Put on the gloves. Don't disturb anything. And there's no way in hell the dog or the baby sets foot in the room."

He looked at Edie.

"You two young ladies can take turns holding the baby and go in one at a time."

"Ouch," Edie said. "That's kind of a sexist remark, don't you think, Catori?"

Steve put a hand on Edie's shoulder. He didn't quite say '*knock it off*', but nevertheless got Edie to back down. He nodded at the agent. "For now, that'll work." He pointed at Amber. "At some point, I'm probably going to need to let my partner do her job."

After a long stare, the burly agent tightened his lips. "The evidence bags from the victim's body and those recovered from the gondola have been retrieved from the locals. They'll be delivered here in the next several minutes. I'm told you wanted another look at the items before sending it to our lab."

Steve nodded and they got to work preparing to enter the room. Edie held onto Rosa, and Catori slipped on a pair of vinyl gloves, standing motionless in the open doorway to Room 1909.

Catori's face turned blank, and she folded her arms across her chest. Edie tightened her grip on Rosa. The baby squirmed and let out a tiny cry while Edie kissed Rosa's forehead and stroked her back.

The burly agent started to open his mouth, but his partner jabbed him in the ribs. They both stood and watched the developing scene.

Edie tapped Steve on the shoulder. His eyes followed Edie's in time to see Catori's whole body shiver. As quickly as it started, Catori's body relaxed and she took several deep breaths. She walked into the room but didn't stop until after passing through the open sliding doors that led to the balcony.

Steve gave Paco and the two agents a look and held up his hand. Alone, he followed Catori across the room and stepped onto the balcony.

He watched Catori's hands grip the railing. Her eyes wide open, staring down nineteen stories, straight into the ground.

CHAPTER 12

THE SUN RODE HIGH IN the clear skies over Creston Valley, reflecting off the shimmering lake waters and masking a portal hidden far beneath the surface.

Seated at the patio table on the deck of his lakefront estate, Mr. Clean scanned the horizon beyond the lake, still waiting for one of the scarce remaining eagles to swoop back down and grab an unsuspecting prey from the depths of the tempting waters.

Bartholomew placed the glass down in front of his grandfather and took a seat across from him. Droplets of water ran down the outside of the chilled tumbler filled with the single malt Scotch.

Mr. Clean hadn't uttered a single word since Bartholomew finished describing his encounter with Beth Dawson or his improvised plans for Sampson Pauling. The old man nodded several times while Bartholomew spoke, but never took his eyes from the tranquil waters of the lake.

From his statements, it was clear Bartholomew did not know how badly he had failed in his mission. Mr. Clean had seen his grandson's sloppiness on prior occasions and grew concerned at this rising impudence. Others had also complained of Bartholomew's lack of judgment.

Something Mr. Clean had thus far chosen to ignore.

At length, Mr. Clean turned his head and stared at Bartholomew. He extended his hand and grasped the tumbler. After taking a protracted sip of the smooth, velvety liquor, a slight smile materialized, but never reached his eyes. He gave his grandson a nod and tempered his first words. "I am no longer in the field, so for now I will not second guess your actions. Nevertheless, you must make certain nothing derails our plans for the first lady. As I explained, we have worked closely with Aamir Rahaman and his men to put this strategy together. The cost of our operation is staggering. It cannot be allowed to fail."

Bartholomew shrugged and his expression remained neutral. "I can assure you, Grandpa, there is no possible chance for this to interfere with the rest of our plans. As I said, we may find another use for Dawson's boyfriend."

Not sure Bartholomew understood the potential consequences of his actions, and growing more impatient, Mr. Clean's next words bit harder. "Apparently, you have not heard the news. Beth Dawson is still alive."

He let this revelation hang in the air.

"The reports have been understandably vague, so I did some checking on my own. She is either unconscious or in a coma. And at this moment surrounded by armed guards. I understand they plan to move her to a more secure location. It appears you have not only missed the opportunity to find out exactly what information this meddling bitch extracted from our databases, but...." His words faded away.

Bartholomew swallowed, and his face blanched. He did not speak and avoided his grandfather's stare.

"Her actions at this particular time cannot be a coincidence. We have learned her boyfriend's family has strong ties to the president, so it is unlikely she simply stumbled into our systems." Mr. Clean raised a shaky finger and pointed it at Bartholomew. "I want whoever oversees our cybersecurity eliminated. Unlike the government, I expect my people to pay for their mistakes. Do I make myself clear?"

Bartholomew flinched at his grandfather's gesture, and a bead of sweat formed on his forehead.

"You were supposed to destroy any evidence and eliminate the threat." The words expressed more of a sadness than a direct admonition.

Bartholomew fumbled for an answer. "She should've died from the fall alone... and I shot her at point blank range. Perhaps I acted too... but the girl refused to talk. I rifled through her purse... and found nothing. We did a thorough search of her hotel room, and it was clean."

In a more forceful tone, he added, "This is one of the reasons why I thought it best to keep her boyfriend alive."

"We shall see," his grandfather replied with a slight quiver in his voice. "In the meantime, I have informed Aamir Rahaman of the potential breach. As you know, our systems are now linked. We both thought it wise to move more quickly. And I am still concerned about those rumors from the White House. According to Rahaman's inside source, the president's own inquiries have had a degree of success."

His hand shook as he placed the glass down, and some of the contents spilled onto the table. "If what's happening in D.C. is in any way related to the hacking of our servers, it is imperative we find out."

Mr. Clean's body sagged, and he said nothing for several seconds. He finally relented and gave his grandson a more reassuring look. "Perhaps you are correct in regard to this Pauling character. Because of his family's ties to the president, we might be able to use this to our advantage."

Mr. Clean pushed tired hands against the armrests of the patio chair and raised his aching frame. The years crushing at him as he shuffled to the railing. Instead of looking out on the lake, he turned and faced Bartholomew, leaning back against the railing for support. His hooded eyes took on a distant look. A wan smile transformed his face. He spoke to his grandson, but in his head a far different image came into focus.

"Bartholomew, you remind me of myself when I was your age." He paused, allowing himself a small chuckle. "Well, perhaps a little younger than you are now."

Mr. Clean's eyes sparkled at an unseen vision, and the spreading smile stretched the wrinkles from his withered face. "My father sat me down and spun an unbelievable tale of power and glory. One of hard-fought victories. Bloody battles. The emergence of a powerful entity destined to rule the world."

Bartholomew let out a deep sigh, but he remained motionless, and his grandfather continued to speak.

"The Sideris family, our family, was one of the chosen... nobility... if you will, to inherit the earth." Mr. Clean's eyes closed, and he nodded to himself, evoking his youth and the dreamlike world of a tiny fishing village.

The scenes of the endless Greek Isles as vivid in his mind today as when he sailed the sparkling seas with his father. A briny scent from the past penetrated his consciousness, causing him to pause and inhale the wispy vapors. When he continued, he spoke in a lyrical character.

"Over the ages our ancestors seized ungodly treasures and accumulated fortunes throughout the world. All in the hands of this unique enclave of power. One day the time would be right for the world to unite under our domain."

All of a sudden, the old man's eyes popped open and riveted into Bartholomew.

The imposing figure returned in all his strength and commitment. In a professorial tone, he said, "Can you tell me, Bartholomew, what will come next? Did you understand the changes at the start of the last century? Those setting the path for this ultimate destination? And do you remember the many trips we took to Georgia? The most recent manifestation of your birthright."

This abrupt change in his grandfather's demeanor caused Bartholomew to suck in a breath.

Mr. Clean waited for Bartholomew to pick up his cue.

After a brief hesitation, Bartholomew responded, assuming the familiar role of student to mentor. As expected, he repeated the facts his grandfather had taught him over the years: How the coalition joined hands with the Muslim Brotherhood rather than fight them. How the Muslim Brotherhood used religious ideology to further their own political goals. And how the Muslim Brotherhood was almost as adept at subverting the populace as slaughtering the innocent in deluges of bloody terrorist activities.

When Bartholomew finished his anticipated rhetoric, Mr. Clean sat back down and said, "Do not forget, one of the last obstacles to achieve irrevocable domination now resides in the Oval Office. This man hangs onto dying principles like a tenacious bulldog. But when all is said and done, there is little President Tyler Griffin can do to stop this inevitable onslaught against the wavering sovereignty of a sinking nation. No single act of terror, no matter how brutal, can do what an insidious attack from within can accomplish. With one final nudge, the strings will soon tighten, and Griffin will become the ultimate puppet."

Mr. Clean pointed to his empty glass and Bartholomew nodded. "And let us not forget, Bartholomew, we shall spit in the face of God—all the gods. We shall once again unite the entire world's population as one. We shall finally finish the ancient project and build to the heavens. The real tower of Babel will soon exist."

While Bartholomew walked to the bar to refresh his grandfather's drink, Mr. Clean spoke the next words almost to himself. "It is time for the curtain to open on the final act."

CHAPTER 13

(Summer of 1933: Creston Valley, British Columbia)

THE TRAIN JOLTED TO A halt; the 4-6-2 Pacific-type locomotive still belching dark, pungent clouds into the clear valley air. Dimitri Gruzinsky's head popped up with a start. It took him several moments to erase the cobwebs from his sleepy brain. He blinked his eyes and stared out the window of the nearly empty passenger car, realizing he had arrived at his destination.

In an unconscious gesture, he patted his shirt pocket one more time to assure himself the papers were still present. He stood and stretched the short muscular arms from his two hundred-twenty-pound barrel-shaped frame. Gruzinsky picked up his worn tweed coat and slid into it before grabbing a lone bag from the overhead storage compartment. The heavy, tattered satchel appeared almost weightless in the grasp of his callused, tobacco-stained hands.

Dimitri Gruzinsky watched from the platform while thick, billowing smoke dimmed the bright rays of sunshine as the locomotive chugged and rattled, gathering momentum for the next leg in its journey.

A lifelong chain smoker, he fidgeted for a smoke and fired up the last one from his pack. For Dimitri, this voyage from his distant home in Russia had ended. The long journey had begun many years ago when he toiled by his father's side and learned the craft of stone masonry.

Over the years, his father talked with reverence of Dimitri's grandfather's odyssey to the untamed inland Pacific wilderness of southern Canada. He had been one of the hordes of Russian fur traders who came to the region in the late 1800s. Around that same time, a rail system was making inroads to open the isolated region, and a thriving commerce became reality.

Before the expeditions of white men nearly a century earlier, the Creston Valley, where Dimitri Gruzinsky stood, was the ancient home to the Ktunaxa people. This Indian nation now comprised a large and diverse tribal network extending across both sides of the Rockies and as far south as Lake Coeur d'Alene in the Idaho panhandle: the current-day reservation home of the Kootenecti tribe.

Dimitri flicked the cigarette butt onto the vacant tracks. He grabbed the satchel and strode over to a bench near the end of the platform. He sat and reached into his shirt pocket, retrieving the prized documents and carefully spreading them out on his lap.

Last spring, Dimitri's father succumbed to a prolonged bout of emphysema, and Dimitri made his decision. Not to run from his tobacco addiction, but to follow through on his father's idle ramblings about returning to the Canadian wilderness and reclaiming his family's inheritance.

Dimitri reread the papers on his lap as he had done hundreds of times before. The land grant, dated 1884, described the claimed property of over six hundred acres surrounding a pristine lake. At last, Dimitri Gruzinsky would build something for himself.

But first, he needed to obtain work. As he walked toward the downtown area of the recently incorporated village of Creston, he noted the bustling activity. This gave him a security of purpose, gauging that a man of his particular skills would do well. His destiny spread out before him.

For the remaining years on this earth, Dimitri kept busy with his work. After surveying his land, he built a temporary cabin to live in while he earned a reasonable living. Recognized as a trustworthy conveyor of his trade, he became widely sought after for his talents. The construction of his permanent personal housing took longer than he imagined. In between jobs, he toiled to build one of the most magnificent stone structures in not only the Creston Valley, but the entire Pacific Northwest.

Dimitri worked with materials at hand, starting with a preponderance of stones piled along the eastern edges of his private lake. He gave little note to the ancient origins of this conflagration of chiseled formations. They made excellent foundation material and served as both literal and figurative cornerstones to his developing masterpiece.

He had no idea that the first white settlers to the area, more than a century ago, had driven the Ktunaxa people away from their ancient burial grounds, fleeing this gorgeous valley they had occupied for more than 11,000 years.

Dimitri, a fixture in Creston Valley for over forty years, had seen incremental growth spurts as fledgling industries took root in the surrounding region. For his entire life he remained a loner. He continued adding, refining, and rebuilding various components of his never-ending project.

The decades looked on as the colossal mansion grew and spread on the picturesque bluff sitting on the eastern shores of the lake. Huge, arched windows framed dazzling sunsets. He never grew tired of the magnificent displays of nature surrounding the loving toils of his labors.

Till his last day on this earth, Dimitri Gruzinsky recalled one of the most breathtaking sights he had ever witnessed. It occurred the first day he set foot on his grandfather's property. Dimitri sat on a rocky outcropping on the bluff that would one day be the site of his magnificent house. The sun was sinking behind the forested hills to the west of the lake. Two bald eagles swept across the sky, leaving elongated shadows in their wake. One of the huge birds dove below the water's surface. The second bird followed. Both successfully snared their prey and soared up and away. One bird apparently latched onto two fish. As it headed to a nest high in a distant black cottonwood, one of the fish fell free and landed on the shore. Dimitri rushed down to the water's edge and picked up the dead creature.

On a whim, he decided to take it back to the boarding house where he was temporarily staying. When he presented the fish as a gift to the innkeeper, the elderly gentleman's face transitioned into a conspiratorial mask.

"Young man," the innkeeper spoke in English, which Dimitri understood quite well having absorbed himself in the language before embarking on this journey. "You have come across a very unusual specimen. At least for these parts."

Dimitri looked puzzled by the man's words. "I do not understand what you mean."

"This particular specimen has never been native to the Creston Valley. But on extremely rare occasions, one is spotted." The man smiled and reached out patting

Dimitri's arm. "And as far as I recall, the only place it has ever been seen is on the eastern shores of your lake."

Dimitri was about to argue the rationale for the man's thinking. If found in these waters, then it must be either native or has been brought here by man or bird. Not much of a mystery. But the haunted look on the innkeeper's face caused him to quell his words.

"Folks believe that the ancient spirits of the Ktunaxa, after driven from their native lands, have summoned up these primeval creatures from the muddy depths of the lake." The man's hand rested on Dimitri's shoulder. "And the coyotes. Have you not seen them in the still of the night? They are especially fond of the full moon and sometimes serenade its journey across the heavens. They are considered another form of a more ancient creature. A guardian of sorts." The innkeeper's hand pressed on Dimitri's broad shoulder, but it was the man's words that made him hold his tongue.

From that day on, although he fished often in the lake, Dimitri never caught one of those strange fish. From time-to-time, however, a magnificent bald eagle would dive deep beneath the surface and return with one, only to disappear into the heavens.

Dimitri spent many hours staring at the invisible depths in his enchanted lake, in awe of the mighty birds hunting their prey. He often wondered what crept beneath. What did those giant birds witness as they dove into the darkness?

He methodically worked to build his house, using the stones along the lake's shore. It wasn't until years later he learned of the origin of those materials—the abandoned gravestones from the Ktunaxa.

During Dimitri's declining years, he entertained the idea of leaving his estate to the town of Creston for use as a museum. It had been his goal to be buried inside the dwelling. To this purpose, he had built an elaborate crypt under the solid concrete floor in the basement.

When he approached the town leaders with his proposals, he was devastated on both counts.

They thanked him for his offer to convert the house into a museum but declined because his property sat too far from the town's main thoroughfare to be of any practical use. If that wasn't disappointing enough to the dying Russian, their decree that it would be illegal according to Canadian law to bury human remains in a house—sent the poor man away in utter despair.

He returned home and toyed with the idea of burning the massive structure down with himself inside. In the end, he pulled out his old satchel from its dusty corner in the basement and simply disappeared from the Creston Valley.

That was in the summer of 1974. Several weeks later his body was found at the site of the Spokane World's Fair.

Dimitri Gruzinsky had plummeted from a nineteenth story balcony of the newly constructed Spokane Falls Lodge.

CHAPTER 14

(present day)

STEVE CASELLA STEPPED BACK AS Catori's body stiffened, her hands gripping the railing on the balcony outside Room 1909 at the Spokane Falls Lodge.

She sensed his presence fading, while her mind took flight. The modern world melted away and she soared higher than her physical anchor on the hotel's balcony.

Catori evoked the words from Lomasi, her grandmother, and the vision of her nomadic ancestors swept into her head. The present dissolved underneath the persistent splashes of the thunderous waters cascading down the rocky precipices.

Salmon leapt above the foaming currents, only to be grasped in the clenched talons of circling eagles. This was the resting place of the tribe's annual journey from the Bitterroot Mountains. From their ancient origins in the Creston Valley to the far north, the Ktunaxa people, driven from their native home, spread to the south, wandering eastward and westward, forming new nations.

While Catori's eyes remained transfixed on the falls, from beyond a distant mountain peak a shrill voice echoed across the valley. Coyott, the ancient god of light, was at work. This cunning trickster bade any straggling tribal members to follow it.

The creature's baying jolted Catori into another time.

The hotel reappeared around her. At first a glittering image dripping like a photographic emulsion, solidifying into a three-dimensional Kodachrome projection. Crowds of people strolled along winding paths on the banks of the river. Colorful arched-roofed pavilions dotted a lush parklike setting. A carnival atmosphere swirled before her eyes. Children's laughter resonated with the beckoning aromas of exotic culinary delights. The roaring vibrations of a roller coaster accompanied the waxing and waning of screaming chants. Music resounded from the depths of an amphitheater perched along the high banks of the flowing river; yards from where the surging waters spilled down the falls.

Catori spotted a gathering of Native Americans—not her nomadic ancestors—performing a mock wedding ceremony amidst an array of touristy enclaves and nearby patrons who panned for fake gold. She caught a glimpse of gently swaying gondolas, inching along an aerial path beyond a backdrop of foaming waters spraying misty patterns at the bottom of the falls.

The Spokane World's Fair—Expo '74—captured in Catori's vision.

With a sudden jarring motion, Catori imagined herself sailing over the railing—plunging toward the gleaming tiled patio surrounding a multi-colored pavilion nineteen stories below the balcony.

An instant before she smashed onto the pavement, Steve's arms grabbed hold of her shaking body. Catori's eyes bolted open, and she saw the body of the Russian immigrant, Dimitri Gruzinsky, splayed on the ground in front of the Iranian pavilion.

A group of stunned fairgoers instinctively fell away from the scene, looking up to the balcony. And then their eyes turned back to the crushed body. Several gaped at the pooling blood running through the white grouted spaces linking the festive tilework together, while most shut their eyes in horror.

Steve held onto Catori and watched her eyes roll upward, and the lids snap shut.

He took a step closer to the railing, trying to guess what the young girl had envisioned. But knew he was way out of his element. At last, he scooped Catori into his arms and turned away from the balcony.

CHAPTER 15

THE THERMOMETER FLIRTED WITH TRIPLE digits, but unlike neighboring Tel Aviv, the humidity in Jerusalem remained bearable. The hot weather did little to deter the crowds drifting through the outer courtyards or those waiting for the opportunity to enter the sacred church.

While this ancient holy site always drew large numbers of people from around the world, many sacrificing their life savings to make the pilgrimage, there had been a marked increase in the number of visitors over the last six months. Many of faith, and even those with only tentative religious convictions, sensed worldwide tensions growing, on the verge of spiraling to a potential apocalyptic confrontation.

Since childhood, Cynthia Rosenburg-Edwards had dreamed of making a trip like this. She grew up in a Jewish family, but to the dismay of Cynthia's grandparents, her mother and father were lax in following their faith. Cynthia felt conflicted, and an outsider to the Hebrew teachings.

In her final year at Dartmouth College, she met and fell in love with a native Bostonian, Richard Edwards. He didn't share his own family's tradition of being devout Catholics. But Cynthia latched on to a missing need and converted to Catholicism, getting married in one of Boston's finer cathedrals.

Today, fulfilling her childhood dream, Cynthia stood gazing up at the magnificent dome dominating the ancient walls of the Church of the Holy Sepulchre, in the heart of the old city of Jerusalem.

She and her two children arrived last evening at Ben Gurion International Airport and traveled by taxi to their hotel in Jerusalem. Her husband chose not to make the journey, but supported Cynthia, and did nothing to dissuade her from this pilgrimage.

Cynthia grasped the tiny hands of Elsie, four, and Richard, Jr., six, and edged her way through the crowds. As they entered the main courtyard and neared the church's current entrance, her heart raced, anticipating how close she was to entering the vast rotunda under the dome—above the location of the Holy Sepulchre—the tomb of Jesus.

The blazing sun reflected off the ancient stones in the courtyard. Through the shimmering waves of heat, she observed the darkened silhouettes behind the twin arches embracing the massive doors. Unaware at first, Cynthia paused at the sight of people looking skyward, shielding the bright sunlight from their eyes. A faraway droning vibration escalated and soon the ground shook as a deafening roar overtook the sanctity of her thoughts.

The sun became blocked and the sky darkened.

Richard, Jr., pulled his hand free and pointed to the sky. "Look, Mommy! It's coming right at us!"

Cynthia hugged both children in her arms and prayed.

* * * * * *

The Iron Dome represents one of Israel's most critical defense systems to protect the tiny nation from attacks emanating from any one of their nearby hostile neighbors.

Each battery consists of a sophisticated radar system, a state-of-the-art fire control structure, and at least three launch arrays, each housing approximately twenty Tamir interceptor missiles.

Once an alert is authenticated, it takes only minutes to launch a defensive attack. Designed as an anti-missile defense unit, it has never been tested as a means to destroy a commercial airliner.

* * * * * *

Alitalia flight AZ224 was on its final approach to Tel Aviv's Ben Gurion International Airport, twenty-five miles northwest of Jerusalem. In the co-pilot seat, the body of Capt. Mario Lorenzini lay slumped over, blood coagulating under the wire garrote. Taqhid Kalil sat to Lorenzini's left, controlling the Airbus. Radio communications with air traffic control had been routine. Up until this point he had followed all pre-landing instructions, except for one item. He failed to deploy the landing gear.

With a tremoring hand Kalil grasped the sidestick and disengaged the autopilot. He flipped the transmit button, and in a practiced voice said, "This is Alitalia flight AZ224 on final approach to runway 26. Reporting an onboard emergency. We are experiencing landing gear problems. Warning lights indicate a failure of main gear to lower. We are aborting landing. I repeat. Flight AZ224 is aborting landing."

Without waiting for a reply, Kalil deactivated all radio communication systems and pushed forward on the thrusters. He set the flaps to zero and eased back on the sidestick as the aircraft's speed increased. Adjusting course on a different heading, Kalil leveled the aircraft at two thousand feet. Within a minute he sighted his destination. It would have been almost impossible to miss the larger dome of the Church of the Holy Sepulchre.

Before the touted Iron Dome could respond, the massive jetliner plunged into the holy site, disintegrating on impact and spewing burning jet fuel over consecrated soil.

Nearly a thousand prayerful souls perished, either burned or buried in the rubble.

CHAPTER 16

PRESIDENT GRIFFIN ENTERED THE SITUATION Room approximately ten minutes after receiving notification that the crashed jetliner in Jerusalem had been deemed a terrorist attack. Key cabinet members continued to rush into the secure conference facility as updated information flowed in at a feverish pace. The president drummed a closed hand on the table and a tense hush fell over the room.

"I just spoke with the Israeli prime minister." The president's eyes scanned the grim faces seated around the table. "Needless to say, our allies are preparing for an all-out countering of this brutal attack. And they are looking for confirmation that the United States is backing them."

The secretary of defense cleared his throat. "Mr. President, exactly who are they going to target?"

"Iran."

"Where in the hell are they getting their intel from?" the CIA director said. "We've been monitoring and sifting through the data, and it's way too early to be sure of anything."

Tyler Griffin shrugged and made a tight smile. "I've convinced them not to do anything for at least forty-eight hours." He turned to Mike Finley. "Guess we should move up our meeting with the Israeli ambassador."

Finley didn't get the chance to respond.

"Jesus Christ," the CIA director said. "It'll take weeks to verify what we've picked up in the few minutes since the attack."

"Tell me what you got so far," the president said.

"Sir, I'd rather wait and confirm—"

"Damn it, George. I don't think we have that kind of luxury right now. I trust our allies, but the Israelis have a lot more to lose than us. They might be a little jumpy. Tell me what you've got. I can't rely on the Israeli intelligence service to steer any decisions I have to make."

The CIA director shuffled through the papers from a thin folder. "The group making the most noise is the PIJ. The Palestinian Islamic Jihad. And if you remember, Mr. President, Iran severed all ties and support when the PIJ decided to remain neutral and not side with the Iranians in Syria."

He looked directly at the president. "The last thing we want now is to have Israel escalate this travesty. You can bet they wouldn't need much verification to act against the Iranians."

"And who the hell could blame them?" The president's words bounced around the quiet room.

The secretary of state chimed in. "Our latest round of negotiations are finally making headway. The stricter sanctions we placed back on Iran are forcing their hand. Once we reinstitute the nuclear site inspections, we'll advise the U.N. to demand a complete dismantling of Iran's nuclear program."

"That's all bullshit, Mr. President," the secretary of defense interrupted. "The U.N. has been ineffective as usual and has tried to appease the leaders of Iran at every step. They may as well deliver the raw materials to expedite the Iranian nuclear program themselves."

He leaned toward the secretary of state and then turned to the president. "The only things that brought those savages back to the negotiating table were your vows to increase our own military forces and replace our aging nuclear arsenal with state-of-the-art weapons and delivery systems. Not to mention our recent step-up in troop numbers in the region." He waved a flattened hand toward the president. "We've got a formidable fleet strategically placed with the ability to launch anything needed at a moment's notice."

The secretary of state challenged the secretary of defense, his face turning a bright red. "You goddamn war mongers are going to destroy any progress we've made at the negotiating tables."

"Make sure you get your asses out of the line of fire before the first missiles start flying," the secretary of defense snorted.

President Griffin raised both arms. "Okay, gentlemen. I'm seeing the big picture, but right now we need to focus on how the Israelis are going to react. Let's save the ideological discussions for another time."

Almost under his breath, the president murmured, "It'd be a damn miracle if the Iranians didn't have at least several nuclear weapons locked, loaded, and aimed at the heart of Israel right now." In a clear voice, he added, "This could be the final trigger for a nuclear confrontation."

He paused and glanced around the table. "Again, gentlemen, we need real evidence as to Iran's role in this terrible attack. And we need it now." His fist pounded the table. "If the missiles start flying in the Middle East, there's only one nation who could put an end to it. So, let's make sure we're up to the task."

Mike Finley walked to the head of the table and placed several documents in front of the president. He returned to his seat.

Griffin peeled back the first page and blew out a breath. He looked up at Finley. "Why don't you give us the short version?"

The CIA director stared at Finley but remained quiet.

"Yes, sir," Finley said. "As you recall, you asked for a fresh look from… ah… consultants outside the cabinet as to how these different terrorist groups were organized. Where they got their funding. Which states sponsored—"

"I've read all the briefs Edie Pauling has been sending us," the president interrupted. "That's one of the reasons I told you to bring her and Steve to D.C."

The secretary of defense stood so quickly his chair rolled back into a junior staff member seated along the wall behind him. His face glowing brighter red by the second. "Did you say outside consultants? Who gave the approval to—"

The look on the president's face had the secretary slinking back into his chair and wiping a handkerchief across his swollen, blotchy face.

After a moment, the president said, "Go on, Mike."

Before continuing, Finley glanced at the secretary. "Well, on top of the pile is one report I think you'll find interesting, Mr. President."

Griffin stared back at Finley, his palms resting on the edge of the table; fingers tapping.

Mike Finley cleared his throat. "That last report from Edie highlights troubling data on a relatively young organization. Al-Saberoon."

Finley's subtle eye contact left the president confident he would leave out all references to the Amber Alert project and would carefully thread his way through the key information needed to be brought to the attention of the cabinet members.

The CIA director interjected. "We've been watching them too, Mr. President. Their recent activities have been summarized in your daily briefs."

Griffin looked back and forth between the CIA director and Finley. A grim smile appeared but faded quickly. "I like good, healthy competition, gentlemen. Makes for a good horse race. Mike? You first. George? If you have anything to add, jump in at any time." To both of them, he added, raising a hand, "I don't want a historical analysis, just what's related to recent events."

"Yes sir, Mr. President," Finley said. "Al-Saberoon's ideology is in complete alignment with Iran. In fact, it appears they were created by a faction of the Iranian government. There is clear evidence Iran is funding their operations. The interesting piece of information," Finley paused with a brief glance at the CIA director, "is the definite link between Al-Saberoon and the PIJ. So, while on the surface Iran claims to have severed ties with the PIJ, they are still sponsoring many of their anti-Israeli actions."

"So, the Israeli intelligence may have gotten this right?" Griffin said.

Finley nodded. "Looks like it, sir. Edie's last report points out troubling gaps in the flow of money between the two organizations. There appears to be missing channels that so far have everybody stumped."

"What in the hell is that supposed to mean?" the secretary of defense asked.

"According to the report, the Muslim Brotherhood appears to be right in the middle—"

The CIA director interrupted. "The Muslim Brotherhood's got their dirty hands on pretty much all terrorist activities—we've warned the past two administrations about this. And even before that, the FBI had uncovered documents linking key leaders in several Islamic centers in the United States to international organizations which sponsor terrorist groups."

He placed his elbows on the table and folded his hands. "Nobody wants to admit they've succeeded in setting up Islamic front organizations across the nation. Not only that, Mr. President, but recent data suggests they could have operatives infiltrating many government organizations in our own country."

He pointed a finger at Finley, but Finley broke in first. "Thanks for the heads-up, George. But if you recall, DHS has been pushing its constitutional limits trying to rout out these groups. Sometimes with the help of the FBI, but in most cases, it's been more efficient to avoid those aspects of the legal system."

Finley turned to the president. "To finish up, this report suggests an even bigger, more obscure organization may be providing funds and support to the Muslim Brotherhood. But who that is remains a dead-end for now. Edie thinks she's close to finding answers, but right now there's nothing else significant to report."

The president thought about his earlier meeting with Finley and the documents they'd discussed. The Amber Alert project. Was there something else priming these Muslim groups? He wasn't ready to go there yet. "Anything to add, George?"

The CIA director shook his head.

CHAPTER 17

THE ALITALIA FLIGHT FROM ROME to Newark had been routine and mind-numbing for the 290 passengers until approximately forty-five minutes before its scheduled landing. Then the onboard entertainment system along with all internet services went dead.

Most passengers, used to these glitches, pulled off their headsets and picked up something to read. Some engaged a fellow traveler in conversation or closed their eyes for a few minutes of sleep.

Howard Marchesi chose a different path.

At age twelve, Howard shied away from the typical pre-teen activities that consumed most of his fellow sixth grade classmates at the Charter Academy in Livingston, New Jersey. He was a complete computer geek in the extreme sense of the word.

His mother, Carol, a widow of three years, worked hard to pull Howard out of his shell. They had been living in a rural area in the western part of the state, but after her husband died following a bitter fight with pancreatic cancer, Carol moved to a more populated neighborhood in Livingston. Close to her childhood hometown of Cedar Knolls.

Howard Marchesi had always been a loner. He became even more withdrawn after his dad died. As a result, his mom gave up the serenity of rural New Jersey to afford Howard a better opportunity to interact with kids his own age in their new home in Livingston.

Six months ago, doctors diagnosed Howard with a severe case of psoriasis. This drove the insecure youth further inside himself; not wanting to attend any of his classes.

At first balking at the long list of potential side effects from the available therapies for the disease, Carol embarked on a litany of natural remedies.

Each night she cried herself to sleep, praying for a miracle. Extreme diets, acupuncture, light treatments, and natural ointments. Nothing worked and Howard became further withdrawn. At the urging and persistence of Carol's own mother, they brought Howard to a specialist at Lenox Hill Hospital in New York City.

Six weeks ago, Howard completed an intravenous therapeutic regimen that finally brought the progressing disease to its knees. Once Howard finished the primary treatment protocol, his condition showed a significant improvement, but he still continued to feel self-conscious about the slow healing of residual lesions. He was given a number of oral and topical medications, along with a two-page list of instructions on how to suppress future outbreaks. The doctor had warned his mother that stress could be a major factor in triggering more acute episodes.

Carol Marchesi, at a loss of what to do, scraped together enough money to take Howard on a trip to Italy: to the city where his father's grandfather was born.

Howard came alive at seeing for himself the reality of his father's ancestral roots. He spent more hours in the town's library studying his family's history than on the internet. He absorbed the local culture like a sponge.

Over the last two weeks, he had the opportunity to live and breathe his heritage beyond the confinements of a fifteen-inch laptop screen. His mom didn't know how this experience would help him open up to potential new friends at school, but at least for now Howard had taken an active interest in the real world. Carol found the miracle she prayed for as the residual lesions melted away in Howard's enthusiasm.

On the long flight home, Howard drifted to familiar ground but incorporated his personal experiences to augment online searches to put together an interactive chronicle of his vacation.

When the flight's internet service crashed, Howard put his other computer skills to work.

Howard sat in the window seat, with his mom in the middle, and a retired Air Force officer taking up the aisle seat. For the first time since the loss of her husband, Carol found herself flirting with this handsome and fascinating stranger.

Howard tugged on his mother's arm. "Mom. Major Hammond. Look at this. It's really scary."

She smiled at the man seated to her right. "Excuse me, Major Hammond."

Major Russell Hammond returned the smile. "Russ. Please, call me Russ." He glanced past Carol at the laptop sitting on Howard's tray table. His face scrunched in confusion.

Howard's voice rose, and he pointed at the screen. "This story just popped up. An Alitalia jetliner—the same airline we're on right now—crashed into a church."

Carol, her mind still absorbed by the handsome passenger at her side, hadn't caught the meaning of his words. She pursed her lips. "Howard? How on earth is it possible to use the internet? They announced that all in-cabin entertainment services would not be functioning for the remainder of the flight."

Howard shrugged off his mother's question. "Piece of cake, Mom. The onboard flight computer services don't offer much in the way of firewall or encryption protection. I got into their system in less than five minutes. It's up and running fine. I think they must've shut it down on purpose."

Again he pointed at the laptop screen, scrolling down through the story. "But forget that. Aren't you listening? An Alitalia plane crashed into an old church in Jerusalem. That's in Israel. They said the airliner took off from Rome—like we did—but it left several hours after our flight."

Carol's hand flew to her mouth. "Oh my God!" She looked on in horror as a live video filled the screen with shocking pictures of the devastation.

Piles of rubble. Raging flames blackening the skies. Bloody bodies scattered about the crumbled church. Terrified people screaming, looking for missing loved ones. Sirens shrieking in the distance. Police and medical personnel descending on the scene.

Major Hammond leaned closer to the screen, and Howard tilted it in his direction. Hammond looked at his watch. He muttered, "According to the timeline, this happened less than fifteen minutes ago, and these pictures are already spread over the internet?"

Howard's face flashed a tentative tight smile. "Ah... not exactly, Major Hammond. I've always found the typical news outlets boring. They don't always tell the whole story."

Hammond's eyes narrowed. "Okay. Then what *are* we looking at?"

"This is an international satellite uplink. It's from one of the major news operations. All these feeds flow into their headquarters. You can see everything as it unfolds. Before some editor picks and chooses what we should see."

Carol looked up in time to see one of the flight attendants walking down the aisle. She pushed the lid on the laptop down as the airline employee reached their row.

"Hi there, young man," the flight attendant said to Howard. "In a few minutes you'll need to stow the laptop under the seat in front of you. We're about to start our initial descent into Newark." She tapped the overhead speaker grill. "The captain will be making the announcement any minute now."

As she walked away, she smiled again, looking at Major Hammond. "Besides. Our internet service won't be working for the remainder of the flight. This type of problem doesn't happen often on Alitalia. We're sorry for your inconvenience. I understand all passengers will be given drink vouchers." She continued down the aisle.

Major Hammond reached over and angled up the screen and continued watching and reading. Updated information appeared by the second. He was so focused on trying to comprehend the information, Carol's words startled him.

"Russ? Did I understand this correctly? There seems to be indications this was a deliberate act."

Hammond cleared his throat. He tried to keep his voice steady. "According to these reports, the flight was bound for Tel Aviv. While on its final approach, the captain radioed an emergency. The landing gear would not lock in the down position. He aborted the landing, but instead of moving the aircraft into a holding pattern, he headed on a new course—Jerusalem, which is approximately twenty-five miles away. People on the ground claimed the aircraft was aimed directly at the large dome on the Church of the Holy Sepulchre."

Hammond paused and watched the horizon shift as he became aware of a subtle change in airspeed and attitude. The cabin intercom crackled, and the captain announced the standard message regarding the flight's initial descent into Newark.

Hammond continued to read the screen. "That's kind of unusual."

"What, Major?" Howard asked. His mother sat and stared at the screen. Her lips locked in a perfect circle.

"Well, most problems with the landing gear stem from a faulty sensor. The pilot gets a false reading and can't be sure if the landing gear has extended. The flight crew then requests a visual verification from the ground. In this case, no request was made. Observers on the ground never saw any of the bays open. They now suspect the pilot used the emergency message as a diversionary tactic."

Howard arched his brows. "Wouldn't the fact he deliberately flew the plane into the church tell you the same thing?"

Major Hammond stared at the young boy. "How old did you say you were, Howard?"

"I'm almost thirteen."

The airspeed changed as the airliner's rate of descent increased.

Howard pressed his hands against his ears. "Remember to swallow. It helps equalize the pressure while the plane descends."

He looked at his mother. Her hands remained on her lap; her face as fixed as granite.

Major Hammond sensed their air speed slow as the flaps extended. The captain announced their final approach to Newark Liberty Airport. Without much enthusiasm, Howard pointed out the window at the Statue of Liberty.

The aircraft began to bank as it crossed over Newark Bay.

The major remained silent and sat motionless in his seat. He waited for the familiar sound and vibration.

Nothing happened.

He gave it another ten seconds, but the sound of the landing gear descending never occurred.

All at once the picture became clear.

"Howard?" Major Hammond reached across Carol's seat and touched Howard's arm. "Can I assume this isn't the first time you've hacked into an airliner's computer system?"

"I've done it on several occasions." His voice quivered. "But this is the first time I've done it while on board. The other times were from home." He shrugged. "It's much easier from here."

Carol's trance finally broke, and she turned toward her son. "Howard, you promised me you would stop—"

"Hold that thought, Carol." Hammond placed a hand on her shoulder. "Howard, right now you're roaming around in the flight entertainment systems. You ever peek at the aircraft control systems?"

Howard's mouth opened wide. He looked from Major Hammond to his mother. "I would never fiddle around with the flight controls." He shook his head. "I've got a flight simulator, but I'm not stupid enough to—"

"Of course you wouldn't... but you must've been curious about those complicated consoles in the cockpit, right?"

Howard's face brightened. "Sure, I pretty much have the main control positions memorized." He tapped the side of his head.

"Exactly what I wanted to hear." He gave Howard a quick smile. "Now this is what I need you to do." Hammond spelled out the steps for Howard to follow. He asked Howard for the spare power cord from his laptop case and glanced around to see if any of the flight attendants were still hovering about. As he got out of his seat, the cabin intercom came back on, and the captain recited a more urgent announcement.

"We are experiencing a slight technical problem, requiring us to abort our landing. I have informed the control tower and have received approval from air traffic control. We are cleared to change course and fly in a holding pattern until we resolve the issue. This is a routine precaution. I assure you we are in no danger, but I do apologize for this inconvenience. We will do our best to get you safely on the ground as soon as possible. Please remain seated with your seatbelts securely fastened."

About ten feet from the cockpit, Major Hammond recognized the increased thrust as the powerful engines throttled back up. The aircraft shook and gained altitude. The ground fell away, and the climbing aircraft began a slow starboard bank.

Hammond stood by the cockpit door. Once the aircraft's attitude stabilized, he raised his arm to signal Howard. The flight attendants shouted at him, and he could see nearby passengers getting concerned.

Howard's fingers tapped away on the keyboard. His mother remained motionless, staring at him, eyes expressionless.

The lights on the keypad next to the cockpit door flashed green and Hammond opened the door. He saw one of the flight crew slumped over in his seat, blood dripping from his neck. The man in the left seat was focused on what lay ahead and didn't notice Hammond standing behind him or the blinking cockpit door alarm lights on the console.

Hammond glanced at the familiar outside terrain and structures in line with the trajectory of the aircraft, and his instincts took over.

CHAPTER 18

THE MEADOWLANDS ARENA, PART OF the New Jersey Sports Complex, had seen better days. Throughout its history, it suffered an identity crisis with its name changing faster than the succession of professional and college sports fans parading through the arena's turnstiles. Operating at significant losses over the last several years, the arena had been scheduled for demolition.

Today the aging structure resembled its glory days. The main parking lot was filled to capacity with vehicles overflowing into the adjacent stadium parking areas. The interior seating was crammed to its full twenty thousand spectator capacity. But this event had nothing to do with sports. And no groupies swayed to a magical rock band, unless one likened the charged atmosphere to the 1970s musical phenomenon, *Jesus Christ Superstar*.

No, the Son of God did not appear on the rotating center floor stage, but to the thousands of cheering patrons, the Holy Spirit filled the auditorium. As in other parts of a troubled world, invocations of religious revivalism fueled a starving populace. This fervor created both a joyous salvation, juxtapositioned to a call to arms as extremists stood fast to their convictions.

As part of a long family tradition of self-avowed evangelists, the Reverend Jesse Walsh strode onto the Meadowlands Arena stage and commanded the full attention of the cheering crowd. Riding the current wave of religious growth, countering decades of secular dominance, Reverend Jesse Walsh was as close to a modern-day disciple as any rock star who had ever made an appearance in this same venue.

The chanting and thunderous applause gathered momentum as the spotlight shadowed the reverend's deliberate stride across the stage. His accompanying choir added to the escalating cacophony filling the arena.

All this zeal also served another purpose.

Whatever was happening outside became obliterated.

* * * * * *

Major Russell Hammond paused for a fraction of a second. As the New Jersey Sports Complex grew larger in the Alitalia airliner's front cockpit glass, his mind recorded the jam-packed parking lots and envisioned the unsuspecting spectators inside the arena. Hammond had no clue as to the nature of the event. His next moves stemmed from training and instinct. He erased all other considerations from his head.

Using Howard's laptop power cord would take too long. He leapt at the man sitting in the pilot's seat and executed a difficult move most warriors have never mastered. Before the man reacted, Hammond twisted himself around the front of the captain's chair and straddled the startled hijacker.

Without warning, Hammond pushed his right hand under the man's chin. At the same time, his left hand ratcheted down on top of his head. Following a simultaneous pushing and twisting motion, he heard a sharp cracking of vertebrae. Before the man slumped over, Hammond yanked the inert body out of the seat and shoved it on the floor.

As he slipped into the vacant pilot's chair, the aircraft began a slow bank, and the loss of altitude became critical. Hammond pushed forward on the thrusters and adjusted the yoke. The aircraft stuttered and the stall warning alarms blared.

Slowly at first, the huge, lumbering aircraft shifted back, its left wing leveling. But not before the aircraft jolted as the wingtip clipped the top of a broadcast radio tower. The local AM radio station instantly dropped twenty decibels in signal strength when the broadcast power was cut from its primary antenna system.

It had been a while since Hammond piloted a similar aircraft. Most of his missions in the Middle East, inserting PJs, or pararescue jumpers, into the battlefield had relied on flying CV-22 Ospreys. A more maneuverable, short take-off and short landing aircraft.

Hammond's eyes scanned the flight console while the looming outside structures filled the cockpit windows. As he worked the controls, his heart rate spiked up several beats, but his palms remained dry. One tiny bead of perspiration formed on his left temple but went unnoticed.

He stabilized the aircraft and cleared the roof of the aging Meadowlands Arena by less than ten feet.

Without any further information as to what threats he could still be facing, his first priority was to get this airliner on the ground as soon as possible. He kept his current heading, knowing exactly what to do next. The reflection in the cockpit glass captured the slight upturn of his closed lips.

Russell Hammond, a local New Jersey boy, grew up in one of the small towns a couple of miles to the west of the airliner's current position. From his home in Hasbrouck Heights, he'd ridden his bike down the long, steep hill more frequently than he'd ever admitted to his parents. He spent countless hours hanging out in the commercial operations buildings, chatting with the mechanics and pilots working out of Teterboro Airport.

Right now, he sat at the controls of the Alitalia Boeing 777. Both hands gripping the yoke. Unlike the Airbus that minutes before had crashed into the Church of the Holy Sepulchre in Jerusalem, this Boeing aircraft didn't have a joystick.

Hammond observed the familiar approach to runway one: seconds away. No time to alert tower control. He pulled back on the landing gear lever. All wheels descended and locked. Flaps fully extended, spoilers engaged. Fuel levels just under ten percent. Airspeed holding at 157 knots.

He'd need every inch of Teterboro's 7000-foot runway to bring this fully loaded aircraft to a safe stop. Trying to catch the first piece of tarmac, he eased the Boeing down much sooner than protocol dictated. As the jumbo airliner flared, the left main landing gear carriage kissed the top of a power pole.

Sparks flew out.

A severed power line twisting about like a demonic serpent caught a nearby street sign, scorching the first three letters from the green and white metal *Redneck Avenue* placard.

At the edge of the tarmac, the main wheels hit and bounced twice before sticking. The smell of hot, burning rubber filled the air. The one blown tire caused Hammond some concern, but when the nose gear pressed against the tarmac and the reverse thrusters kicked in, he breathed again.

Although the jumbo jet rapidly lost ground speed, the end of the airstrip approached at a lightning rate. Smoke billowed from the overheating brakes. The airliner rolled past the end of the runway. It continued to slow, but the nose gear chewed through the perimeter fence, tires bursting before the huge Boeing came to a stop in the eastbound lanes of Route 46.

Horns blared from passing motorists and a hardened New Jersey driver opened his window, extending his arm and middle finger. "Hey, moron! Where the fuck did you learn how to drive? Move that damn thing outta my way. Go back to New York where ya belong. New York drivers think they own the goddamn road."

CHAPTER 19

THE NATIONAL MALL BUSTLED WITH more activity than normal, although most visitors couldn't have guessed the reason. The secret service detail prided itself on keeping a low profile, but an earlier sweep of the National Museum of Natural History had museum employees and patrons buzzing.

No official announcements appeared on anyone's calendar.

After a brief trip from the White House, the black armored limousine pulled to a stop on Madison Drive NW in front of the museum. The secret service detail cleared a path, and First Lady Alison Griffin, her daughter, Brianna, and the first lady's chief of staff, Badiyah Jamail, walked up the two flights of stairs into the museum's rotunda.

Jamail had spent a good part of the early morning hours coordinating the first lady's appearance, making it known to the secret service detail that the first lady insisted on a minimal intrusion of the museum's activities. Thus, the first lady traveled with only a fraction of the usual security personnel.

Before she arrived, the secret service thoroughly swept the entire museum, and agents remained at all entrances and exits to the vast complex.

The appearance of the first lady had been organized at the last possible minute. Badiyah Jamail rearranged the first lady's busy agenda and reserved the museum's Baird Auditorium. Alison Griffin was to make an unscheduled visit and speak to a large student group that ranged from the gifted and talented to the disabled and special needs children.

Since President Griffin's inauguration, Alison Griffin had campaigned for improved education in the natural sciences as one of the goals for her tenure as first lady. Like her husband, she didn't believe it was the federal government's role to advocate a one-size-fits-all mentality to education. Her main goal was to pique public interest in the sciences and let the local schools implement programs to reflect their individual community needs.

It didn't take much prodding for her to agree to Jamail's plan to address this group of children. Brianna Griffin, at sixteen, had not been eager to accompany her mother to the event, but knew when to pick her battles. Sean would have been a better choice, but the youngest member of the Griffin family woke up this morning with a sore throat and a runny nose.

As the first lady's small entourage descended the stairway to the ground floor and entered the Baird Auditorium, an uneasy sensation swept over Brianna. As usual, her mother remained preoccupied, greeting the children and trying to make everyone feel at home. Brianna focused her attention on Badiyah Jamail.

Under normal circumstances, Brianna was suspicious of the woman's motives. Today she sensed something more strained in Jamail's actions. It could be she stressed over putting this event together at the last minute, but Brianna wasn't ready to give her the benefit of the doubt.

When the opportunity arose, Brianna walked over to Jamail. "Badiyah, why are Mom's agents being kept so far away?"

Turning to Brianna, Jamail wiped the annoyance from her face, but not before Brianna caught the act. "The secret service has searched and cleared the auditorium, not to mention the whole museum. They have positioned agents at all entry and exit points." Her mouth widened with an insincere smile. "Besides, Brianna, your mother insisted she be allowed to interact with the children without any big, frightening agents hovering around her." Jamail patted Brianna on the shoulder and guided her away. "Why don't you go talk to these kids yourself? You probably have a lot in common."

Dismissed, Brianna watched Jamail head over to several museum workers. She heard her order the men to add additional chairs to the stage. Rows of children in wheelchairs formed a tight circle in front of the podium. She saw her mother working her way to the stage. Checking her watch, Brianna realized her mother's speech would start in several minutes. She took one last look around. All the entry and exit points to the auditorium did appear to be manned by at least two agents. She shrugged and took her place near the rear of the stage.

A museum official, all smiles, stepped up to the podium. "Welcome, everyone. As you can see, we are privileged to have a very special guest here today. Some of you kids have already gotten the chance to meet her. I'd like you all to join me in welcoming First Lady Alison Griffin. We are honored to have her speak to us today."

The official turned to the first lady and clapped.

The rows of chairs on the crowded stage made it difficult for the first lady to negotiate her way to the podium. She took the opportunity to greet as many children as she could while squeezing forward.

Standing near the back of the stage in one of the curved alcoves, Brianna strained to get a better glimpse of her mother. She noticed Jamail glued to her mother's side, checking her watch and fielding phone calls at the same time.

Alison Griffin reached the podium and Brianna imagined the genuine smile spreading across her mother's face. Standing behind her, Brianna didn't actually see this, but she knew from experience about the warmth radiating from her mother's presence. She found herself getting caught up in the moment.

The first lady waved at the children and waited for the auditorium to settle down.

As the first lady placed both hands on the lectern and began to speak, a blaring siren screeched through the cavernous auditorium, sounding like the woolly mammoths in the first-floor rotunda had sprung to life.

Children began screaming and crying out in horror. The PA system spewed the urgent message—this was not a drill, and everyone needed to exit the auditorium in a safe and orderly fashion. The children on the stage nearest the first lady panicked, pressing in closer. Alison raised her arms and used her most soothing voice to calm the room.

Jamail grasped the first lady's shoulders and shoved her toward the rear center of the stage. Her efforts bolstered by the throngs of children pushing in all directions. Jamail pulled the backstage center curtains apart and guided the first lady through as Brianna reached her mother's side.

Jamail turned and grabbed the recessed sliding door panels that separated the rear storage room from the main stage. She wrenched them closed before the panicked mob burst through.

Jamail, Brianna, and the first lady stood alone in the darkened space. The heavy paneled doors muffled the frantic shouts of the kids. The first lady yanked at the closed doors. They would not budge.

Jamail had locked them with a key hidden in her pocket.

Not positioned to see the first lady hustled to the rear of the stage, the agents at the nearest stage exits attempted to clear a path for the first lady. They coordinated a safe exit route to the outside of the museum. The closest agents turned to escort her off the stage but had trouble fighting the crush of terrified children and adults.

As they broke through the crowd, they could no longer see the first lady. Several minutes later the stage was empty, and First Lady Alison Griffin was nowhere to be found.

The senior agent closed his eyes and punched the button on his mike, uttering the words no secret service agent ever wanted to say.

CHAPTER 20

AS THE REAR STAGE DOORS in the Baird Auditorium had slid shut, Badiyah Jamail's shouts drowned out the fading noises of the crowd stampeding across the stage. She, along with the first lady and Brianna, had been plunged into darkness.

Jamail steered them away from the locked doors and further back into the room. Before either the first lady or Brianna could speak, a section of the carpeted floor under their feet vibrated and dropped down.

They fell onto a thick padded surface twelve feet below the level of the stage. Jamail landed on top of the first lady. Brianna stumbled her way over the loose padded blocks and tried to push the flailing chief of staff off her mother. Above them, the stage floor swung back in place.

Brianna adjusted her eyes to the dim light and tried to comprehend the situation. From behind, thick arms reached out to grasp her shoulders. She spun around, pulled both legs to her chest and kicked them out. Although impossible to gain much leverage pressed against the padded surfaces, she scored a direct groin hit to her assailant.

"You little whore," the man gasped, rolling away and grabbing his crotch.

Before Brianna twisted herself into a position to do more damage, another pair of hands grabbed her by the feet and dragged her away from the loose padding. Her head bounced against solid flooring, taking most of the fight from her. The man bounded her hands and feet. A third man working with Jamail performed the same task on the first lady.

The first assailant recovered from Brianna's kick. Breathing hard, he grasped Brianna's hair, latching on to a fist full of red tresses. "You are going to pay for that little stunt." He grabbed her breast and squeezed.

Brianna tried to twist free. "Give me another shot and I'll make sure your fucking hand's the only thing left still working. Then neither one of us will have any balls."

The first lady screamed, "Get your filthy hands away from my daughter."

Brianna's head turned in time to see an odd expression on her mother's face. She realized her mother had probably never heard that kind of language coming from her mouth. Maybe she could convince her she learned it in school and avoid getting her older brothers in trouble.

Dirty rags were pressed over their mouths and duct tape stretched around their heads. One of the men shouted, "Come on. We need to move out. They must be sealed inside in less than five minutes."

With Jamail's help, the three men tossed the first lady and Brianna onto a pushcart. They negotiated a path between the labyrinth of steel supporting structures under the angled seating beneath the auditorium. Reaching the far corner, they stepped into a dark alcove and pushed aside a heavy wooden panel that blocked a crude opening in the back wall. They wheeled the cart through the opening. Flashlights flicked on and they piled heaps of boxes and other debris into the space they'd just walked through.

They slipped a wooden panel in place and hastily nailed it against the rough wood frame of the opening before proceeding down a long, narrow corridor, about five feet in height. Electrical conduits and plumbing pipes jutted from the walls and ceiling. After several sharp turns, the tunnel sloped downward, leveled for about a hundred feet, and then sloped back up. The flooring, damp and slippery, made the trek more difficult.

Brianna sucked in a breath and musky odors overpowered the stale smells impregnating the dirty rag taped over her mouth. At the end of the tunnel, one of the men tapped the bottom of his flashlight against a circular metal hatch in the low ceiling. It opened, rusting hinges protesting with an agonizing screech. Fresher air tumbled through the opening and battled with the dank atmosphere.

Hands reached down and roughly pulled the first lady and Brianna through the hatch. By the time Jamail and the other three men climbed out of the tunnel, mother and daughter had been given injections and their sedated bodies were zipped into large, wheeled canvas duffels. The bags were rolled across the dusty concrete floor and through a doorway. They proceeded across the large warehouse space to a box truck parked against the loading dock.

The rear panel of the truck rolled up. The men removed the first lady and Brianna from the canvas bags and dumped them through the hatch of a large cylindrical-shaped vessel strapped to the inside. On the truck's floor, two bodies lay alongside the vessel, blood pooling beneath their chests.

The rear panel slid down. Jamail, with two of her accomplices, climbed into the cab. The engine started and the truck pulled away from the loading dock and onto the delivery entrance road. It threaded its way into the slow-moving traffic and escaped down Twelfth Street, seconds before security barriers swung into place in response to the fire alarms. Patrons were still streaming out of the Museum of Natural History.

The first lady's security detail discovered she had vanished from the Baird Auditorium. Resolute agents standing on the empty stage sounded the alert and began searching the entire museum complex. They determined that smoke devices had been set at key places throughout the museum, triggering the alarms.

There never was a real fire threat.

By the time they sealed off all entrances and exits and abandoned the evacuation, the truck carrying the first lady and Brianna was barreling toward the Capital Beltway.

CHAPTER 21

THE MEETING IN THE SITUATION Room had made little headway into any official position sanctioning Israel's stated vows to launch an attack against Iran. After a brief discussion with the Israeli ambassador, the president initiated another conversation with the Israeli prime minister. He reaffirmed their agreement to stand down for at least forty-eight hours.

In private, Griffin assured the prime minister that the United States would assist Israel in dealing with this horrific terrorist attack. A fact he didn't share with the majority of his cabinet. Both leaders facilitated the opening of communications between intelligence organizations to share information and expedite the investigation into the hijacking of the Alitalia airliner.

The president remained silent for several minutes after ending his last call to the prime minister. He looked over at Mike Finley and pointed to the documents summarizing the background of the terrorist organization, Al-Saberoon. "Mike, I don't care if it's incomplete; make sure Israeli intelligence gets this information."

"Yes, sir, Mr. President. But frankly, I'd be surprised if they didn't already have a more complete dossier than we do."

The president nodded. "Then squeeze whatever the hell you can from them. We need to be looking at the same data. Can't afford to get this one wrong. I want everything on my desk before the end of the day. If things escalate, I may be forced to act without the luxury of discussing the details with my cabinet, let alone going through the motions with congress."

He glanced up at the remaining staff and cabinet members seated at the far end of the table. No one had been paying any attention to the president's conversation with Finley.

The meeting had wound down earlier without reaching any consensus. A handful of stragglers were still present when the report of another hijacked Alitalia airliner interrupted the lingering discussions. This incident had ended on a positive note with the Boeing 777 making an emergency landing at a small airfield in New Jersey. All passengers on board were safe. One crew member and the hijacker appeared to be the only casualties.

The preliminary data confirmed what everyone in the room suspected: this was a second coordinated attack. Once again, the enemy had taken its fight to American soil. For the first time since September 11, 2001, all aircraft flying over the United States were immediately grounded. This time the decision came directly from the White House, preempting the FAA's national operations manager.

The secret service's recommendation to evacuate the president from the White House fell on deaf ears.

The tense atmosphere in the Situation Room continued to escalate when a shaken official burst in with another message: the first lady and the president's daughter were missing.

Agents on scene at the National Museum of Natural History reported that they had simply disappeared in the commotion following a fire alarm in the vast complex.

President Griffin stood up so fast the messenger staggered back, blanched, and couldn't find his breath. "Disappeared?" The president's voice reverberated through the large conference room, making the messenger cringe even more. "She's supposed to be surrounded by the best of the best, and only blocks from the White House—they turn around and my wife and daughter disappear?"

The president paused when he saw the ashen face on the young man targeted by his outrage. He reached out his arm and grasped a shaking shoulder. "Sorry," the president mumbled.

Griffin turned and leaned against the table, at last glancing over at Finley. His face scrunched in confusion. "What the hell was she doing at the museum? And with Brianna? I wasn't aware of any planned appearances."

Finley hung up the secure landline, poised to spring into action. "I just confirmed that a last-minute change made by Badiyah Jamail had the first lady speaking to a group of children at the Baird Auditorium in the museum. The service was informed just prior to her appearance, but they insisted the entire complex had been cleared, and all avenues of entry and exit covered. Once the first lady got on the stage, they were asked to back off and keep a low profile so as not to frighten the kids."

"*Alison* gave the order?" the president asked, eyes narrowing.

"Well, that's what Jamail told them." Finley stared at the president. "Badiyah Jamail appears to be missing as well. I'm on my way there now." Finley grabbed the rest of his papers and prepared to head to the museum.

President Griffin held up a hand for Finley to wait. His body heaved and he wrung his hands in frustration; his face remained flushed, a mixture of worry and fury. Those still seated at the table busied themselves with anything to avoid looking at the president.

Griffin picked up his handset and spoke to the on-duty commander in the White House security office. After a brief conversation, he said, "Thanks Walter. I needed to be sure you have someone pick up my older boys at the university. Right. You'll bring them back to D.C. as soon as possible? Good. And please make sure Sean is safe upstairs." He paused, thinking of the potential implications surrounding the first lady's chief of staff. "I want an agent positioned inside the private living quarters until further notice."

He placed the handset back in the cradle. Then he got up and walked across the room, staring at the multitude of monitors still playing gruesome scenes of the burning church in Jerusalem. The image of his wife and daughter kept flashing in his head. The earlier words of Brianna slammed him hard:

"Call me Islamophobic, but I for one don't trust Badiyah Jamail. I don't care how long she's worked at the White House, or how dedicated she pretends to be."

At this point, he didn't know what to think. To himself, but loud enough to startle the others in the room, the president said, "Those sons of bitches are going to pay for this. They're looking for a fight? Well, if they think the Israelis are pissed…."

Tyler Griffin reeled in his emotions and walked back to the head of the table. He took several deep breaths. His color shifted gradually back to normal. He remained standing. Grasping the back of his chair with both hands, the president lifted his eyes and made sure he'd connected with the remaining individuals in the room.

His voice resonated in a calm, resolved manner; his white knuckles compressing the tufted leather on the chair were the only visible indication of the enduring fury churning within him. "I realize keeping a lid on the first lady's disappearance will be difficult, but until we get a handle on this situation, I am ordering everyone in this room to remain silent. If any leaks come from you or your staff—you'll be held personally responsible. And unlike previous administrations occupying this office, that doesn't translate into a promotion."

The president's eyes completed a final scan of the silent occupants in the room, and he then directed his attention to Finley.

"Mike. Get the word out to those in the field. This investigation is going to be thorough, but on a need-to-know basis. The story is that the first lady is okay but shaken up after the false alarm at the museum. I'll have her secretary cancel all appearances until further notice. Any press releases will give no other details."

Finley gave a terse nod and dashed out the door. As he exited the secured area, he retrieved his cell phone and began a series of calls, barking orders.

The president continued talking.

"We're potentially in the middle of the most dangerous crisis the world could face in our lifetime. If any of the opposition starts screaming that my thinking is compromised and my judgment clouded by personal matters—we'll have a damn panic on our hands. I didn't take this job to be sidelined when the entire world is set to implode. Now keep this news under your belt. We've got work to do."

After the participants filed out of the Situation Room, Tyler Griffin stared back up at the continuing turmoil flashing across the monitors.

He occasionally believed in coincidences, but this wasn't one of those times.

CHAPTER 22

WITH CATORI'S RIGID BODY CRADLED in his arms, Steve Casella spun away from the balcony. He carried her through the empty nineteenth floor hotel room in the Spokane Falls Lodge and back into the corridor.

Catori's body went limp as Steve eased her onto a nearby sofa. Edie and Paco rushed to her side, while the two agents remained ramrod straight on either side of the door to Room 1909.

Amber padded forward and rested her muzzle on Catori's stomach. An almost inaudible high-pitched whining preceded Amber raising her head and stretching it up to Catori's chin. The dog licked her neck. When Catori stirred, Amber sat back on her haunches and turned to Steve.

"What the hell happened?" Edie said, her eyes darting between Steve and Catori.

Steve didn't take his eyes off Catori. Unable to answer the question, he raised his hands, head shaking.

Catori's eyelids fluttered open. With great effort, she pulled herself to a sitting position, shrugging off any assistance. After several slow, deep breaths she raised her head and gazed at the stunned group hovering over her. "Thanks, Steve." She tweaked out a weak smile. "I'm fine. Guess I got a little dizzy on the balcony."

Amber's head tilted; ears pulled back. Catori reached out and scruffed the dog's neck. "Hello again, fur ball." Amber barked twice in response.

Catori took a large gulp from the bottled water Paco offered her. She stretched her arms and sat up straighter. Her smile looked more like a grimace. "Guess I'm done for now. Edie? I'm fine. Let me take Rosa. You guys should get to work inside." She glanced at the two wide-eyed agents at the door. "Unless you want one of those high-T male specimens putting their hands on your daughter."

Edie hesitated, and Catori repeated her reassurances. Rosa chortled as Edie handed her over to Catori.

Paco shrugged. "Spend enough time around my little sister, you get used to these things." After leaning over and kissing Catori on the cheek, he turned and tapped Steve's shoulder. "You heard the young lady. Let's get to work."

In a louder voice, he added, "We can show Heckle and Jeckle how real cops investigate a potential crime scene."

Steve pointed a finger at Paco. "Don't get all wobbly legged in there, because I damn sure won't be carrying you out."

"Then it's a good thing your wife's here." Paco offered an outstretched elbow to Edie. She ignored it and finished putting on the vinyl gloves. They walked past the two speechless agents and into the room. Amber parked herself near the doorway, her peripheral vision keeping the door guardians in view.

At first glance after entering the room, they didn't notice anything out of the ordinary. Two large suitcases sat open on one of the queen beds, and several smaller travel bags were piled on the dressing table.

Paco stared at the disheveled bundle of sheets and blankets on the second bed. "I'll bet even a federal agent could deduce what happened there."

They busied themselves examining every aspect of the room. Edie scanned the contents of the luggage while Paco and Steve searched drawers and checked out the bathroom. Steve and Edie then headed out on the balcony. They surveyed the entire area beyond the hotel but got no clue as to what triggered Catori's bizarre response.

"Not a real surprise. I was with Catori when it happened, and I didn't see anything unusual," Steve said.

Edie nodded. "Give her time. When she sorts it all out, I'm sure it'll be significant. And whatever she saw probably didn't originate outside her head."

They turned back into the room and worked alongside Paco.

Before rejoining the others in the corridor, Paco paused, resting his chin against a closed fist, elbow supported by an arm across his chest. "They were good, Steve. A real professional job. But I've got no doubt every personal item in this room was examined. That means they didn't find what they wanted on Beth."

"You sure the locals or the feds didn't do this?"

Paco stared hard at Steve and then let out something between a laugh and a cough. "You can't be serious. That's not how it's done. If the cops did this, the place would've looked like my bedroom when I was a teenager."

Edie swallowed. "What do you think happened to Sampson?"

Neither Steve nor Paco answered her question.

When they reached the corridor, the burly agent was seated on the sofa lightly bouncing Rosa on his knee and singing softly while Rosa cooed and giggled. Seeing Edie approach, his face reddened and he offered the baby back to her mother. Edie winked at him. He shrugged and walked over to his partner.

Catori looked up from the evidence bag that held Beth's damaged, but life-saving medallion and glanced at the two agents. "This stuff just got dropped off. They said I could take a peek. Steve... I think it's important."

Steve's face tightened and Edie stepped to his side, grasping his arm. They looked at each other and Steve asked, "You getting vibrations... signals... ah...."

Edie finished his sentence. "Is it a Native American symbol? Does the eagle have any significance? Are you getting another vision?"

Catori's face scrunched up. Her eyes opened wide, and she smiled, waving the sealed bag in front of her. "Nope." She rapped the top of her head with her other hand. "All clear. And I don't think this is a Native American artifact. According to the imprint on the back of the medallion—made in China." Catori pointed to the broken pieces at the bottom of the bag. "You guys saw this, right?"

Steve and Edie nodded.

"I'm pretty sure these are pieces of a memory card," Catori said. "Or a computer chip. If this was what they were after, they're gonna be awfully pissed to have missed it."

Steve's phone rang. He checked the caller ID screen. "I don't think this is going to be good news." He turned and walked away. "Yeah, Mike. What's up?"

When Steve returned, he filled them in on the phone call from Agent Mike Finley.

After an intense discussion, he focused on Edie and added, "Our meeting with the president has been pushed up because of the hijackings—"

Edie interrupted. "But what about—"

Steve placed his hands on her shoulders, looking into bright, amber eyes. "I've read through all the reports you forwarded to the White House and can answer most of the questions the president might have. I explained this to Finley. And also the possible links with Beth's assault to the Amber Alert project. He agreed that one of us should remain and talk to Beth—whenever that's possible. And I figured you'd want to stay close till we get more information about what happened to Sampson."

Edie nodded.

"Finley wants me to accompany him to the site of the hijacking in New Jersey. So, I'm taking Amber. We may need her to check out the airliner or the hijacker's body. They're both still at that little airport in Teterboro. There's evidence the hijacker had ties to the destroyed Islamic Center in San Francisco, so Amber's nosework might come in handy."

Steve paused and shook his head, the muscles in his jaw tensing.

"What is it, Steve?" Edie asked.

"I—I'm not sure. Something in Mike's voice... sounded... maybe he's just got too much on his plate. What else could've possibly gone wrong?"

Both Steve and Edie turned to Catori, but she just shrugged.

Steve checked his watch and looked at Paco. "There's a military jet waiting for me at Fairchild Air Force Base. Can you give me a lift?"

Steve kissed Edie and Rosa, called Amber, and headed for the elevator.

CHAPTER 23

FOLLOWING THEIR CROSS-COUNTRY FLIGHT FROM Fairchild Air Force Base near Spokane to Joint Base Andrews twelve miles southeast of D.C., a helicopter whisked Steve Casella and his canine sidekick to the South Lawn of the White House. He jogged under the spinning blades of the VH-60 Blackhawk, with Amber leaving a spiraling trail of white fur in their wake.

Steve's feet squished in the lush grass still spongy and damp from an earlier shower. Clearing the area, he heard the president's Irish Wolfhound barking from inside the Rose Garden but didn't see any signs of the first family. Amber changed direction to confront a potential rival or playmate. A sharp command from Steve had her back on track.

As they approached the promenade to the West Wing, Steve saw Agent Mike Finley rushing toward them from the West Basement entrance to the White House. Finley's face dripped with sweat. No suit jacket. Shoulder holster in plain sight. His shirtsleeves loose and haphazardly rolled. Deep, wet stains under his arms.

With no preamble, Finley grabbed Steve's arm. "Different plans. Couldn't talk on an open phone line. Follow me." He dashed back in the direction of a black SUV parked under the West Wing portico. Over his shoulder, he shouted, "Let's go. I'll fill you in on the way."

Two agents sat in the front seat. The driver gunned the engine before Finley pulled the rear door shut. The

SUV surged across the White House grounds and through the west gate exit. During the short drive to the museum, Steve absorbed most of the details pouring from Finley's abbreviated summary of the incident.

After barreling down the wrong direction on Madison Drive, the SUV screeched to a halt in front of the rotunda entrance to the National Museum of Natural History. Not a problem, since the entire area had been locked down. Vehicular traffic was diverted for several blocks in either direction, and the entire northwest D.C. quadrant was snarled and gridlocked.

Distracted by the charged atmosphere as he entered the rotunda, Steve neglected to secure a lead on Amber. Finley and Steve stopped and listened to the latest update from the head of the first lady's security detail.

Sprinting ahead of Steve, Amber's paws scraped to a stop in front of the centerpiece of the rotunda: a giant wooly mammoth frozen in an aggressive stance. Amber slowly stalked the beast, growling in an attempt to challenge this prehistoric enemy. She circled the creature several times. Her attention then shifted to the west archway of the rotunda.

Steve turned to the sounds of clattering claws as they tried to grip the slippery surface. He watched Amber gain traction and disappear into the mammal exhibit room. Still preoccupied about the disappearance of the first lady and her daughter, Brianna, along with the first lady's chief of staff, Steve paid little attention to Amber's antics.

A little exercise after the long flight would help settle her down for when she needed to work. He didn't think she could get into too much trouble. If she headed into the fossil hall exhibit looking for a bone to bury, well... then he'd have to step in.

After several brief exchanges, Finley said, "Okay guys. Why don't we head down to the auditorium so Steve can check things out?" He looked around. "Steve? Where the hell is your partner?"

Steve gave a whistle and Amber shot back into the rotunda, stopping at his side. The group headed to the stairway. While passing the entrance to the fossil exhibit, Amber's nose tilted upward, and her body spun around in a quick sweeping arc. Steve issued a stern command, and she slipped back to his side.

As they hurried to catch up with the other agents, he did his best to ignore a series of distinct chuffs and whining coming from Amber. He leaned over and whispered, "Do your job, and I'll take you to the museum's gift store."

Amber responded with two quick barks.

Standing in the top aisle of the Baird Auditorium, Steve listened to another agent describe the events leading up to the sounding of the fire alarm, the attempts of the security detail to clear a safe exit path for the first lady, and the shocking discovery of her abrupt disappearance.

Steve got a better feel for the situation as they checked out the different exits. They reaffirmed the specifics of where each agent in the first lady's detail had been stationed and what actions they took after the fire alarms had triggered. They stopped at all the exit points and scanned the auditorium from every vantage point.

Steve and Agent Finley now stood in the middle of the stage in the lower part of the auditorium. Steve walked back and forth several times, scanning the entire room. He sketched out more details on a notepad and turned to Finley. "Even if the first lady's detail kept their distance like ordered, they were all strategically placed. The main part of the stage is in clear view from every one of those positions." He paused, shaking his head.

Finley said, "They described the scene as mass confusion and panic. Scared kids running in every direction. The stage was jam-packed. Once the alarms sounded, more people stormed the stage. But still, even when they attempted to clear an escape route for the first lady, all exits were still covered."

Steve hesitated before responding. "Any chance someone didn't follow protocol, or may have been distracted, even for a second?"

"No way, Steve. I've worked with each and every one of these guys. They're the best, and they take their jobs seriously. If one of them screwed up, he'd be the first to come forward."

Steve raised his arms and nodded. "Let's see if Amber can give us something."

Finley stuck a hand in his briefcase and pulled out two clear plastic bags. He tossed them to Steve. Steve stared at the contents. His jaw opened and closed several times before the words came out. "You *really* are prepared for anything."

"The guys retrieved them from the laundry hampers in the first lady's and Brianna's dressing rooms." Finley coughed. "How you gonna do this? Let Amber sniff 'em both, or one at a time?"

"Amber's a big girl. She can handle both panties at once."

Finley placed the briefcase on the floor and wiped his hands over his face, shaking his head and letting out a deep sigh while Steve scented Amber and got her ready to work. The other agents backed away from the stage and watched in silence as the white German Shepherd downed in front of the two open bags and waited for a command.

After getting the go ahead from Steve, Amber worked the stage with her nose close to the carpeted platform. She circled the immediate area around the podium, pausing to jump up and place both front paws on the slanted edge of the oak lectern.

Following a tracking pattern known only to the trained canine senses, Amber resumed searching and stopped at the rear of the stage. Her head popped up and pushed aside the heavy curtain. She sat facing the center of two closed sliding doors. Her claws scraped the carpet, and she crouched down. Turning her head, she barked twice at Steve.

Steve and Finley looked at Fred Hanson, the head of the first lady's security detail, who stepped forward.

Agent Hanson responded. "Leads to a storage area behind the stage. Go ahead, open it up. One of the first places we looked after realizing the first lady wasn't on the stage. This is the only way in or out. It's a dead-end."

Steve grabbed the left door panel and slid it back into the wall. Amber charged in, paying no attention to the grinding protests from the retracting door. The chamber measured less than twenty feet square. She searched the perimeter, keeping her nose glued to the carpeted floor. The side and back walls were solid plaster; no indications of any secondary exit points.

With a sudden change in behavior, Amber targeted a small area in the center of the room. She turned more aggressive and scratched her paws vigorously at a particular part of the carpet.

Steve knelt down and ran his hands along the section of carpet where Amber had focused. At first he didn't notice anything unusual, but then his fingers paused at a slight mismatch in the carpet's herringbone pattern. He followed the faint outline, tracing an approximate four by eight-foot rectangle. Using a closed fist, he banged in different spots. There might've been slight disparities, but he couldn't be sure if the area within the rectangle vibrated more. He shrugged at Finley, while giving a command for Amber to rest in place.

"Hey, Fred," Finley called. "You guys have any idea what's underneath this floor?"

Hanson grabbed the architectural drawings from one of the other agents and flipped through the pages. He walked closer and placed the papers on the floor. With considerable effort, he squatted his bulky frame in front, while Steve and Finley leaned over his shoulder and scanned the complex schematics.

"According to this," Hanson said, pointing to an exploded diagram of the stage platform, "the entire stage structure sits on top of the main subflooring for the lower base of the auditorium. As you can see, the space is only about three feet high." He looked up. "A bunch of support beams and joists. After our guys got desperate, we checked all the perimeter stem wall panels enclosing the stage platform, but they're fastened tight. No way to open anything."

Steve straightened up and glanced around. He walked back to the main stage area. His head lifted and his eyes scanned the rows of seats angling up from the front of the amphitheater-like auditorium.

"Any way to access the area below the seating?" Steve asked Hanson.

"Not from inside the auditorium, so we didn't follow up right away since all the exits were manned by our agents." Hanson shuffled through the pages again and tapped a finger. "Here, outside the auditorium in the lower service passageway, we located a small access panel. The door was sealed. We asked the museum officials, and they told us that as far as they could remember, the door hadn't been operable for years. No way to open it, other than ripping it apart with a crowbar. And it didn't look like it'd been tampered with."

Amber barked. Steve turned to see her pawing the carpet in the center of the storage area. His head twisted left and right. He then trotted through the left side stage door and into the corridor.

In the wake of a booming crash, glass fragments sprinkled to the floor. Steve reappeared on the stage, a heavy axe slung over his shoulder. He glanced at Finley and shrugged. "I've always wanted to do that. By the time my crew arrives on scene, some amateur's already beat us to it."

Without waiting for comments or permission, using a practiced grip on the molded handle, Steve hefted the fire axe over his head and hacked away at the center section of flooring in the storage area.

As soon as Steve had gotten in position, Amber backed into a corner and sat on her haunches. She barked out periodic encouragements.

Finley and the other agents kept their distance as Steve pounded at the thick, stubborn flooring. Sweat poured down his face, soaking his shirt. Rhythmic grunts accompanied his exertion. Taking a breather, he leaned over, hands on bended knees.

He took several deep breaths and gasped, "Ah, Mike... if you don't mind helping... there's probably another axe enclosure... go check... the other stage door."

After the last words left his lips, he used the axe to help push himself up by planting it straight down hard onto the floor.

Everyone watched as a sharp, splintering noise crackled through the room. A section of flooring crumbled beneath Steve, and he disappeared through the opening.

"Sonofabitch."

Steve's words followed him as he plummeted into the darkness.

Amber padded over to the hole. Her ears twisted forward, head tilted. The stunned agents joined Amber and peered into the abyss. Heavy-duty flashlight beams then bathed the darkened space.

Staring back up at his audience, Steve picked himself up and struggled to stay balanced. He waded through large chunks of foam blocks covering the floor, thankful for remembering to throw the heavy axe away from his body before hitting bottom.

"You okay, Steve?" Finley's voice echoed around Steve.

"Yeah, I'm good." He tried to hide any embarrassment from his voice. "Did somebody say the stage was only three feet high? Damn builders never follow the architect's plans."

Finley said, "Stand back. I'll throw down one of the flashlights."

Steve dug through layers of foam and recovered it. He cast the beam in all directions, slicing through the darkness. A moldy odor hung around him. "I'd like to get Amber down here and see if she can pick up the scent. And could one of you grab a ladder in case there's no other way out?"

"Fred sent two guys to track down a ladder," Finley said, and turned to look at Amber.

The dog hunkered down at the edge of the jagged opening.

"Ready, Amber? Let's go girl. Jump." Steve's voice bounced up through the opening.

Amber stood and took several steps back. She barked three times.

"Come on, girl. Jump. Don't worry. I know you can climb back up the ladder if we get stuck." He paused. "Or I can carry you up."

Amber whimpered and remained still.

"I can have Mike push you through the damn floor."

Amber's head twisted toward Finley, and a smile spread across his face. She growled through curled lips and, after a slight hesitation, jumped down to Steve.

She landed with all four legs extended, and then rolled over, paddling against flying pieces of foam. Steve helped her to the edge of the pile, and she shook herself back on her feet.

Without waiting for the others, Steve reissued his search command to Amber. "Go find Spirit and Pixie. Go get them, girl." He was denoting the secret service's code names for the first lady and Brianna. He remembered that the president, or Leprechaun, as he was referred to, concurred with those designations.

Amber's hesitation lasted less than a second and she scooted in a straight line along the left side of the chamber. There was a narrow path between the wall and the vast steel supporting infrastructure to the right. Amber reached the far end of the space and turned left, disappearing out of the path of the flashlight's beam.

As Steve hustled to catch up with Amber, he heard a clanking sound from behind. The agents lowered a ladder into position and climbed down into the lower basement. Additional beams of light crisscrossed through the space.

Steve turned the corner and almost stumbled on heaps of boxes and other debris strewn in the narrow pathway. Amber wiggled and swam her way over and around the rubble. She didn't have far to go because the trail ended about twenty feet from the start.

The others caught up and pitched in, clearing the obstacles out of their way. Barking, Amber pushed ahead and jumped against a wooden barrier blocking their path. Steve rewarded Amber for her efforts with a quick pat and uttered her favorite success cue.

From behind Steve, Finley said, "I'll bet you say that to all the girls."

Steve stood and turned abruptly—right into the fire axe held in Finley's hands. Finley offered him the tool. He grabbed it and said, "Thanks. Where's yours, Mike?"

"One simpleton on the team is enough." Finley extended both arms with open palms. "Be my guest."

Hanson stepped forward, shining his flashlight on the drawings held open by one of the other agents.

"According to the diagram, this alcove ends right at this spot. It shows a solid three-foot thick concrete wall lining the whole section."

Steve mumbled, "I think they hired the same builder I'm using in Sonoma."

"This place was built in 1910."

"Jack Rothstein could be older than he looks, which explains why it's taking him so long to finish our simple remodeling project." Steve neglected to consider all the change orders issued by him and Edie.

Steve tried getting into position to swing the heavy axe in the cramped passage. Everyone, including Amber, gave him a wide berth. About to take the first swing, he paused and stared at the wooden planks across the back wall. He took a step closer and angled the axe head onto the floor for leverage. Next, he raised his foot and kicked the heel against the middle of the wooden planks. He didn't kick too hard, but the entire panel fell inward. With a gentle whoosh, it slapped onto the floor and sent a cloud of dust swirling into the supposed non-existent space beyond the terminus of the basement alcove.

This time Mike Finley said, "Sonofabitch."

CHAPTER 24

EDIE PAULING AND CATORI TORRENCE sat on a bench inside the enclosure for the Loof Carousel at Riverfront Park in Spokane. Rosa cried, pointing to the brightly painted gyrating ponies as they rose and fell on shiny stainless steel poles during their endless journey. Edie had held Rosa in front of her on the molded saddles for three consecutive trips. Her butt ached and her stomach felt queasy, but Rosa was ready for more.

Several hours ago, Paco had dropped Steve off at Fairchild Air Force Base before driving back to police headquarters in Plummer. Catori, recovered from her vivid experience on the balcony outside of Room 1909 at the Spokane Falls Lodge, had decided to stay with Edie. So far neither spoke of Catori's vision, but with a watchful eye, Edie kept guard on Catori's emotional rollercoaster ride, allowing Catori to finish sorting through the details. She knew enough to let the process play out in Catori's head.

Edie idly rocked Rosa's stroller to the rhythm of the musical chimes accompanying the carousel while Catori tickled Rosa's chin. Together they diverted the baby's attention from the dancing horses, and Rosa busied herself with a small stuffed white German Shepherd squeaky toy.

Without looking up, Catori said, "Do you think it's possible to visit Beth?"

Edie smiled to herself and picked up her phone. After a brief conversation, she thanked the other party and ended the call. "DHS is about to move Beth to the Ninety-Second Medical Group facility at Fairchild Air Force Base. It's an outpatient clinic, but it'll be easier to keep her under lock and key on the base. It took a little arm twisting for her doctors to agree to the transfer, but they finally concurred that she was stable enough to make the move. They were encouraged by the latest MRI and will start easing her out of the coma by tomorrow."

Catori nodded and smiled. "Great."

"We've got time to kill before they complete the move and she's settled in, so let's go grab a bite to eat in the mall before we head over."

* * * * * *

Hours later, Edie and Catori finished the process of gaining access to the air force base via the Route 2 gate in Airway Heights, the small community west of Spokane, and adjacent to the base. They followed directions to the clinic located near the western border of the vast complex and found a parking space near the main entrance.

Edie was relieved to see their credentials verified at the front desk, and once again by the two guards stationed outside Beth's room. Those added layers of security gave her more confidence Beth would be safe.

Edie and Catori walked into Beth's room and closed the door behind them. They stood at the foot of the bed and watched the incessant hissing of the respirator in sync with the rise and fall of Beth's chest.

Edie's thoughts shifted to Sampson. So far neither the local officials nor the feds had uncovered any useful information regarding her brother's whereabouts. She put her anxieties aside and concentrated on the image of Beth Dawson.

What secrets remained hidden in her shrouded brain? Her mind flashed to the broken fragments sealed in the evidence bag along with the medallion that had saved Beth's life. Edie hoped the memories locked away in Beth's mind would be whole once she regained consciousness.

Catori grasped Edie's hand and led her to the side of the bed. She placed her other hand softly against Beth's forehead and asked Edie to stroke Beth's arm.

Edie's fingers tingled from the initial contact. She had expected to feel a clammy, cold sensation. The smooth, dry texture surprised her. Following Catori's directions, Edie shut her eyes and her body seemed to dissolve around her. She felt weightless and then shocked when a combination of Beth's and Catori's energies swam into her head.

Nestled in her stroller and unaware of the change in her mother, Rosa slept soundly at the foot of the bed, gurgling sounds accenting her gentle breaths.

The next image emerging in Edie's consciousness was Rosa, fully awake in Catori's arms. Edie, lightheaded, lifted herself up to a sitting position. She looked around and found they were no longer in Beth's room but huddled in the corner of a large lounge area.

Edie blinked her eyes, still trying to reorient her head. She stared down at her hands, not knowing what to expect. She felt a slight numbness, otherwise they looked okay.

"Here, Edie," Catori said, handing her a cup of water. "Drink this."

Edie nodded and did what she was told. As Catori eased the empty cup away from Edie's lips and placed it on a side table, Edie's back stiffened and she grasped the sides of her head with both hands. She then covered her eyes, rubbing them with her fingertips. When she removed her hands from her face, she looked sharply at Catori.

Catori shrugged and a small smile creased her face. She placed Rosa back in the stroller and kneeled in front of Edie. She grabbed hold of Edie's hands, exerting a slight pressure. For an instant, Edie's body tightened, but then relaxed.

"Sorry, Edie. If I told you, you would've tensed up; blocking me out. I needed you to be open and willing to accept something new."

"You mean like when I say to Steve that he's full of crap and doesn't have a clue?"

"No, like when you get a bug up your ass and ignore what everybody else is telling you."

"You've been living in California too long. You need to spend time in New Jersey." Edie started to say more when....

"Oh!" Edie's hand went to her chest. Her eyes danced around the room. She moved Rosa's stroller closer and almost picked her up and bolted out of the room.

"It's okay, Edie. There's nothing to worry about. Possibly a few minor aftereffects." She paused. "At least that's what I think."

"What do you mean—you think?"

"First time I tried it. Lomasi pulled me in to her visions several times. It was kinda weird, but not so bad."

"Well, coming from somebody who has frequent-flyer mileage with her body cemented to the ground, I'm not sure how to take those words of encouragement." Edie swallowed and shook her head. "But for now, why don't we swap notes... or share our diaries... or do whatever the hell we need to do. I can feel and see things, but nothing's clear. What I do sense though is—none of it is very good."

"We'll do this together, Edie. I could've tried the old-fashioned way. A little girl talk. But we may not have much time. Before we went to see Beth, I had the impression you were a big part of the story. By bringing you with me—into this vision—I hoped to save a little time. Let's try to piece this together."

CHAPTER 25

STEVE CASELLA STOOD IN A sub-basement of the National Museum of Natural History with Mike Finley and three agents from the first lady's security detail watching the dust settle after he kicked in the wooden barrier hiding a narrow tunnel. Amber knew where to go and took off through the opening, leaping over the splintered boards scattered next to the newly discovered access panel. Her fading barks swallowed up by the darkness.

The men pushed forward, crouching down to avoid hitting their heads on the low ceiling and protruding utilities. They followed the moving beams from their flashlights, negotiating their way through the cramped passage. Amber had long since disappeared around the first bend. The tunnel sloped downward, and they moved as quickly as they could over the damp, slippery floor.

The musty odors got stronger. Amber's barking sounded closer as they reached a part of the tunnel that sloped upwards. They caught up with her and watched the dog jumping up at a circular metal hatch in the ceiling. A pushcart sat against a side wall of the tunnel. Although they struggled, their combined efforts failed to move the stubborn hatch.

Hanson found a relatively dry spot to roll out the architectural drawings. After reviewing his bearings and doing a few rough calculations, he speculated they were standing somewhere underneath the National Museum of

American History, across the street from where they had started.

Finley scanned the area while Steve and two other agents continued to push against the hatch.

"Doesn't look like that thing is gonna budge," Finley said. "Let's backtrack. I'll get an investigative team down here and see if they can come up with anything." He reached into a pocket and pulled out a small object. "Fred. Attach this tracking device to the hatch. We can pinpoint exactly where this thing comes out from up top."

They returned to the Museum of Natural History and the scattered piles of foam blocks under the demolished trap door leading to the stage in the Baird Auditorium. Steve watched the other agents climb up the ladder as Finley shouted additional orders into his handheld. He looked down at Amber. "A promise is a promise, girl."

Amber whined and rolled over on her back.

* * * * * *

Once back outside, Steve gave Amber a much-needed break. He took her for a quick walk around the deserted National Mall and then headed over to join in on the concentrated activities near the service entrance to the National Museum of American History. After Steve caught up with the others, Finley led him to a little-used storage area in the museum's basement.

They had used a forklift to slide aside a heavy galvanized steel trash container set on top of the exit hatch to the tunnel that led under the roadway and into the sub-basement below the Baird Auditorium. The hatch was now open, and Steve glanced at the flashing LED on the locator device they'd earlier attached to the bottom.

Steve held his hand out, and Finley retrieved the first lady's panties from his briefcase and handed him the package. He reached back in and pulled out the second one.

A nearby agent who'd watched the scene, leaned in closer to Finley. "Wow. You've got good organizational skills, Mike. I guess the labels prevent mixing them up. You wouldn't wanna return them to the wrong owner."

He tried to peek into Finley's briefcase, but Finley brushed him back with daggered eyes.

Steve shook his head and re-scented Amber. He gave her the command to search. Amber looked at Steve briefly and chuffed. Steve smiled at his canine companion and said, "So if you're so smart and can figure out what to do, why are you still hanging around with us dumb humans?"

As Amber padded off and got to work, Finley turned to Steve. "I've always considered myself shrewd for not getting married. Now I'm positive I won't be bringing home a dog anytime soon."

"You should see it when Edie and Amber join forces."

Amber made quick work of searching the immediate area. From the open hatch, she circled out and charged through a doorway into the main warehouse section. She alerted on the floor at the far end by the loading dock. And then she scooted closer to the closed overhead door. Her claws screeched sharply, and she barked at the heavy barrier.

FBI investigators combed over the entire site, starting from the storage area behind the main stage at the Baird Auditorium, through the catacomb of steel framework beneath the auditorium, and the circuitous tunnel leading to the warehouse and loading dock in the National Museum of American History. They uncovered no useful information to help locate the first lady and the president's daughter.

In the meantime, Finley leaned on the supervisor of the museum's shipping and receiving department and turned up something they could at least sink their teeth into.

"Listen to this, Steve," Finley said, pausing to catch his breath. "Earlier today, four trucks picked up stored artifacts from this warehouse." He waved a handful of shipping manifests in his hand. "The items were mini submarines kept in the museum after the World War II and Cold War exhibits closed. They're being shipped to other museums around the country as part of a rotating exhibit exchange. We got the four destinations where the subs are first headed."

Finley jabbed a finger at the top sheet. "According to this, the last truck departed almost at the same time the service locked down the entire area." He shook his head. "Damn! Probably squeaked through right before the barriers got thrown up."

"It all fits, Mike." Steve looked down at Amber. "If Amber's nose is on target, the first lady's scent ended on the loading dock." Amber tilted her head and ran back to the overhead door, scratching the floor. "Good girl, Amber. Nobody's questioning you."

Finley nodded at Steve. He couldn't keep still and paced around while glancing at his phone—willing it to ring. "I'm not taking any chances. We've issued BOLOs for all four of the trucks and advised local law enforcement at the scheduled destination sites to look for the trucks too."

"You really think if the first lady is sitting in one of those trucks—they're going to make their scheduled delivery?"

Finley stared at Steve. He started to respond but the phone chimed in his hand. He punched the screen so hard he cracked a fingernail and tore the screen protector. "Yeah? Talk to me." His face scrunched up. "Sonofabitch! Okay. We're on our way."

CHAPTER 26

IN LESS THAN THIRTY MINUTES after leaving the Museum of American History, the SUV with Mike Finley driving, lights and sirens blaring, exited Interstate 270 and headed in the direction of the Lakewood Country Club, outside Rockville, MD.

Steve and Amber looked right at home watching Finley scream past the clogged traffic on the Capital Beltway and thread his way around slow-moving vehicles for the rest of the trip. Finley filled Steve in on the information from the phone call and what the investigators had found at the scene.

Right before reaching the country club, Finley braked and swung the SUV onto a narrow residential street. A hundred yards later he braked harder, and they spun through the entrance of a gated community.

They had no trouble spotting the flashing lights and at least ten police and emergency vehicles parked at the far side of a drainage pond skirting the tree-lined border behind the first row of houses.

Without slowing, he cut his wheel left and the SUV jumped the curb. They bounced down the incline toward the water. A uniformed officer waved for him to stop. When Finley got closer, he stuck his shield out the window and brushed past inches from the startled cop. He continued by a grove of trees to a narrow basin cut between the main road and the upscale housing development.

The SUV skidded to a stop in the marshy soil.

Finley and Steve jumped out.

Steve paused to fasten a lead on Amber, and they hustled down to the crime scene. They saw a large box truck wedged in a dense grove of white ash. The rear door had been rolled up and paramedics stood nearby, leaning up against the side of an emergency response vehicle.

There was no urgency for them to get to work.

Several gurneys sat unattended and empty next to the truck.

As Steve and Finley approached, they noticed that except for the activity at the front of the truck's interior, the huge cargo space was empty. If there had been a submarine on board—it was long gone before the first responders arrived on scene.

Steve looked at the drainage pond. Finley shook his head. "It's shallow and they already cleared it. Nothing there. Human or machine."

Edging their way to the rear of the truck, they peered inside and watched the investigators finishing up. Blood spatters covered a good portion of the front and side walls. Dried pools of blood formed an irregular pattern around the three bodies.

Finley, his face rigid, looked at Steve.

He pounded a fist in his open hand.

The body of Badiyah Jamail lay on top of the other two inert figures. Her severed head hung from a hook on the truck's front wall. The other two bodies had been identified as the men who worked for the shipping company.

There was no sign of either the first lady or Brianna.

Steve put Amber through the paces, but she came up blank, other than a tentative alert near the rear door of the truck. The damp earth on the path surrounding the drainage ditch showed clear signs of a second truck of similar size. The differences in tire tracks indicated the weight of the second vehicle was significantly increased on its exit path. A thorough canvassing of the area came up empty. The entrance gate was neither manned nor locked, and none of the residents in the adjacent houses saw anything.

This had all occurred in broad daylight, and the investigation had reached another dead-end.

Chapter 27

FRUSTRATED FROM HAVING SEARCHED THROUGH every nook and cranny of his underwater prison for at least the tenth time since waking up, Sampson Pauling placed the only item of interest he found on the tiny table in the galley area of his miserly confines.

After reading and rereading the single sheet of torn paper for a good part of the last hour, he cursed and ambled over to the lower bunk. He sat back on the cramped cot and stared at the metal springs on the upper bunk.

"If that's supposed to be a clue to what the hell is going on, they should've kidnapped somebody with more than half a brain to make any sense out of it." He lowered his body onto the cot, feeling like the last of one-too-many fish in a sardine can. "You catch that, you bastards?" Sampson spoke to unseen ears as his eyes darted about, still looking for a hidden mike or camera.

He muttered and took in a deep breath, slowly exhaling and closing his eyes. A second later his eyelids fluttered, and he imagined a noose closing around his throat. His hands flew to his neck and swiped at empty air. Then he realized the pressure came from inside his chest, blocking his ability to scream out. He gasped for his next breath.

The last thing Sampson recalled was a sensation of movement as his torso rocked sideways on the mattress.

Everything went black, and he sensed his body tumbling into the abyss.

* * * * * *

He heard a voice.

Or voices.

Hollow sounding and muddled. Coming from far away.

His head still encased in darkness.

Sampson strained to make out the words. Something wet and cold covered his face. Maybe those sonsofbitches had come back.

Well, it's about time.

"You bastards are gonna pay for this." Pushing himself up, Sampson yanked off the wet washcloth from his face, opened his eyes, and once again smacked his head on the upper bunk.

Blurry images danced in front of him. The faces of two people came into focus. Sampson rubbed his bruised head and tried to stand up. A wave of nausea overcame him, and he sat back on the cot, both feet anchored to the floor. He blinked several times and grabbed at the upper bunk for support.

"He doesn't sound very happy to see us, Mom," Brianna Griffin said. "But you're right. It is Sampson Pauling. Good thing you stopped me from whacking him with the skillet." She turned and placed the hefty fry pan back on the three-burner cooktop.

Sampson lowered his arms but didn't try to move. He stared at First Lady Alison Griffin, and her daughter, Brianna.

"Are you okay, Sampson?" the first lady asked. "Those men told us we'd have company, but we weren't sure if there was someone inside who would hurt us."

Brianna was staring at Sampson's torn shirt and the bandage. She then pointed at his arm. "In case you're interested, I think I saw the rest of your shirt caught on a sharp piece of metal on the outside of this thing."

Sampson smiled, thinking his opponent may have been bigger than he thought.

"What are you doing in this place?" Brianna asked. "You sure look different than the last time I saw you. All tucked into a tuxedo at your sister's wedding." She pulled a pair of jeans down from the upper bunk. "You might wanna slip these on. A little wrinkled, but I don't see any rips."

Sampson's eyes darted to his legs and the boxer shorts he had on. He accepted the jeans from Brianna. With considerable effort, he twisted his bulky frame into the trousers while the first lady and Brianna busied themselves looking around the rest of the enclosure.

This time when Sampson tried, he stood up without losing his balance.

"I could ask you ladies the same question. And by the way, do you happen to have any ideas about exactly where we are?"

"Sure," Brianna said. "We're in a steel cylinder floating underneath a large body of water."

"Brianna, I think Sampson is aware of those facts." The first lady turned to Sampson. "But I'm afraid we don't know anything more specific. How long have you been locked up?"

Sampson scrunched his brow. "I'm guessing maybe two days, but there're no clocks and it's difficult to tell day from night through that little porthole. The glow from the lighting keeps everything gray. Once in a while a fish swims by. But anything beyond several feet is invisible."

He rubbed his stinging eyes. "I think they pumped a sedative gas into the air system before you guys showed up. I remember feeling the whole chamber shift, and then I must've passed out."

The first lady nodded. "When they took our blindfolds off, we were standing on a floating platform. There were high walls around the perimeter—with several small openings." She gazed around the cramped quarters. "This vessel had just risen to the surface. Sheets of water were still flowing off its outer shell. They opened a hatch at the end. One of the guys—"

"You mean Islamic terrorists, Mom," Brianna interrupted.

"Brianna, we don't know for sure—"

"Of course we do. I told you that sleaze ball Badiyah was nothing but trouble. She was in on the whole thing. You don't see her inside here with us. Do you?" She put both hands on her hips and shook her head. "When we get out of this cage, I'm gonna find her and—" Brianna pounded her fists together and stomped on the floor.

The first lady nodded at Brianna with a tight smile. "Anyway, Sampson, one of our kidnappers jumped inside and opened the inner hatch and pushed us through. Before we knew what happened, both hatches shut and we began sinking below the surface."

"Before they tossed you inside, did you see anything?"

"Well, I think we're in a lake. I got a brief glance at mountains surrounding us, and the water seemed calm. No waves or anything." She turned toward Brianna.

"I thought I spotted houses on the mountainsides when they dragged me across the deck," Brianna added. "Maybe several docks along the shoreline, but it's difficult to be sure. I managed a quick look before one of the *Islamic terrorists...*"

She paused and tilted her head at her mom. "Grabbed my arm and shoved me through the hatch." She folded her arms and gave her mother a look. "And you know what the guy also did?" The first lady raised her eyebrows. "The slimy creep pinched my ass. Guess he couldn't wait for one of his seventy-two virgins."

The first lady walked over and embraced Brianna. Brianna kissed her mother's cheek and slipped into the seat at the galley table. Sampson watched as she reached for the torn paper he had discovered. She gave it a casual glance.

He looked pointedly at the first lady. "If you don't mind my asking, how in the hell did anybody get close enough to you guys in the first place? Aren't you surrounded by secret service agents wherever you go?"

"Not so hard when it's an inside job," Brianna mumbled. "Nobody ever listens to me."

The first lady ignored Brianna's comment. "One minute I was speaking at an auditorium filled with children at the National Museum of Natural History, and then a fire alarm started blaring. The kids were running in all directions—screaming and crying. Next, we were led to the back of the stage. It all happened so fast."

"Pushed by the Muslim bitch, you mean," Brianna said.

Sampson stared at Brianna but saw the image of his sister Edie when she was a teenager. He blinked his eyes and turned to the first lady. "Where the hell were the agents from your security detail? Aren't they by your side like glue?"

"Now that you mention it...." The first lady hesitated. "I didn't see—"

"Mom?" Brianna interrupted again. "So, you didn't tell them to back off away from the stage so the children wouldn't be frightened?"

The first lady looked puzzled and shook her head.

"I knew it. Badiyah Jamail was in on it from the start. That little prick." Brianna placed a hand over her lips. "Oops. Sorry, Mom. I meant to call her a bitch." Sampson saw a smile peeking out from behind Brianna's hand.

"Then," the first lady continued, "the floor literally dropped from underneath us. We were tied up and gagged, and then these guys shoved us inside big sacks... probably gave us tranquilizers. I remember waking up several times after they dumped us out. In fact," she spun her head around the chamber, "the lighting was dim, but I think we were in a place similar to this... whatever this is." To Brianna, she said, "You remember any of that, honey?"

Brianna looked back up from the paper on the table and frowned. "Yeah, but it was a lot smaller. And it looked old—an antique maybe. I think I saw seats at one end. And like a steering wheel and a lot of gauges. Also two big glass panels. But I couldn't see anything on the other side. It was all black. Only a dim light inside whatever we were in. At first, I thought we were in an airplane." She looked around. "But I think you're right, Mom. It did look sorta like this."

"A small submarine?" Sampson asked.

The first lady and Brianna looked at each other. "Yeah, I guess," the first lady said. "But the strange thing is we were moving, but the ride was bouncy and jarring. Not like being underwater."

"Right, mom. I'd bet we were traveling on land. I think I could make out road noises and vibrations; and I swear every once in a while I heard horns beeping."

The first lady nodded. "We never got a look at the outside though. As soon as we stopped, they opened the hatch and put the blindfolds on. Everything else happened so fast. We only got a brief look around when they took off the blindfolds and pushed us in here with you."

"So, what do you think is going on, Sampson?" Brianna asked. "You seem to have been working on figuring things out." She pointed to the paper on the table.

"What're you talking about? I don't have a clue." He looked over Brianna's shoulder. "I found that paper stuck under the refrigerator. I have no idea what it means."

"All those numbers and symbols look like map coordinates or GPS codes. I thought you wrote all that down."

Sampson shook his head, and for the first time since banging his thick skull when he had awoken on day one, a smile spread across his face.

He patted Brianna on the shoulder. "I'm sensing we got way more than half a brain seated at this table."

CHAPTER 28

THE NARROW SAIL AND DIVING planes cleared the surface as the sleek hull bobbed against the bumpered moorings inside the floating platform. Corrugated steel panels near the platform's outer perimeter shielded most of the scene from prying eyes. Two men climbed out of the vessel and walked across the platform, stepping down into the waiting launch. Aside from the submarine's two-man crew, they were the only passengers on board today's journey underneath the northern border.

The lines were dropped and the boat drifted back from the platform. Twin engines revved and the sleek craft picked up speed and headed to the southern end of Lake Pend Oreille. By the time the powerboat approached the main facility, the overhead door had rolled up, allowing the sleek craft to disappear inside.

Up until about a year ago this underwater research facility was the property of the U.S. military. It now belonged to a private corporation owned by one of the aliases of Mr. Clean. Once the two men entered the plush office space on the third level of the main building, Bartholomew strode to the bar cabinet and prepared himself a gin and tonic. His companion, Aamir Rahaman, did not consume alcoholic beverages. Bartholomew tossed him a bottled water from the refrigerator.

Rahaman took a swig and made several phone calls. The phone conversations were not in English, which always annoyed Bartholomew, but he chose to ignore this affront, satisfied he wouldn't be dealing with the man much longer. This phase of the campaign was coming to an end.

"As we expected," Rahaman said to Bartholomew as he walked up beside him, "my men completed the entire operation without any problems."

Bartholomew glanced at Rahaman. "One would assume so, given your guests are safe and sound." He waved a free hand toward the large window facing the waters of Scenic Bay. "Somewhere out there, beneath the surface. And the old mini sub from the museum is well on its way to its final destination at the bottom of Puget Sound."

Rahaman stared at Bartholomew. The two had agreed a long time ago on a mutual dislike for one another. Bartholomew was well aware Rahaman had an inherent loathing of him. He'd overheard him arguing with his grandfather on several occasions regarding his impulsive and, what Rahaman called, foolish actions.

"I am still displeased with your last-minute change in plans. I do not like things that complicate our jobs. Especially what is going on with this Pauling character you have placed in the same pod."

"Aamir," Bartholomew said with a subtle sneer transforming his face, "the only reason it was even necessary to make contact with him and his girlfriend in the first place was the inadequate safeguards in your databases. Our systems had never once been compromised until we integrated your servers with their antiquated software into ours."

"You cannot be certain of this."

"Oh, but I am, Aamir." Bartholomew patted Rahaman on the back. This always drew an instant edginess from Rahaman at the perceived insult.

Bartholomew ignored his companion's discomfort. "Have you completed the next arrangements? Remember, the timing is critical."

Aamir Rahaman didn't respond. He narrowed his eyes and stared at Bartholomew.

CHAPTER 29

THE FAA HAD JUST LIFTED the ban on commercial air traffic. After a frustrating day of dead-ends and a tense conversation with President Tyler Griffin, Steve Casella settled back for the first leg of the US Airways flight from Washington, D.C., to Spokane. He'd be changing planes in Phoenix.

Amber lay curled up in the narrow space in front of him. Before the landing gear had fully retracted, she was sound asleep, her gentle snores drowned out by the cabin noise. Steve knew he should get some needed sleep as well, but his head was spinning with too many questions and no answers.

After finishing up at the bloody scene inside the abandoned truck in Maryland, Agent Mike Finley and Steve had returned to the White House for a meeting with the president. The day had started out bad enough with the horrendous attack in Jerusalem but had spiraled completely out of control with the news of the attempted airliner hijacking on American soil and the daring kidnapping of the first lady and the president's daughter.

Steve declined a cocktail from the flight attendant and asked for a coffee, although the added stimulant was probably not necessary. As the jet reached cruising altitude and followed the sun's westward decline, Steve took a sip from his cup and opened up a notebook. He stared down at the jumbled writing he'd scribbled while investigating the first lady's disappearance. The anticipated trip to Teterboro Airport in New Jersey to investigate the foiled hijacking of the Alitalia airliner had been postponed.

What stuck most in his mind was the haunted expression on the face of the president. Steve could almost feel the crushing weight on Griffin's shoulders. He wondered how much more pressure the man could endure.

As of now, there were no leads as to the fate of the first lady or Brianna. The FBI was digging into the background of Badiyah Jamail. No one could be sure if she was an unwitting victim of the kidnapping or was complicit in the act. If she were party to the undertaking, her beheading may have been orchestrated as a serious message from the perpetrators.

To the president's credit, Steve admitted, he listened intently to the briefing on the work Edie had documented regarding the complex links and funding strategies channeling to terrorist organizations around the globe. Steve had also recapped the recent events in Spokane.

It was beginning to look like not only the two hijackings were linked, but Beth's assault and Sampson's disappearance might be tied to the kidnapping of the first family.

The timing of these events could not be considered a coincidence. With the tensions escalating in the Middle East, the president needed accurate information to make a decision that could change the face of the world for generations to come.

* * * * * *

Exhaustion at last overtook Steve. Following a plane change in Phoenix, he dozed off after slipping into his seat for the final leg of the journey. When the flight landed in Spokane, he grabbed a taxi to drive him back to his house in Coeur d'Alene. It was past three A.M. when he collapsed into bed next to Edie. She stirred, but Steve kissed her on the forehead and told her to get back to sleep.

He managed a few hours of fitful slumber, spiked by fleeting dreams of his father and their failed relationship. He woke up with a start, seeing the image of his father's face when he told Steve his mother had just died. After that day, things had been strained between them. The arguing ended when the authorities found his father dead in a federal holding cell.

Pulling off the sweat-soaked sheets, Steve wiped the moisture from his face and padded into the shower. The scalding water worked into his rigid muscles. Invigorated, he dried himself off, wondering what this next day had in store.

CHAPTER 30

THE PRESIDENT SAT ALONE IN the Oval Office as the morning sun cast its first shadows across his desk. He had never suffered the gravity of this job more so than the last few days. The silence from the South Lawn was deafening. No more barking dog to wreak havoc in the Rose Garden.

After a restless sleep, he'd faced his two older boys with the grim news of their mother and sister. He himself couldn't get a grip on the reality of the kidnapping.

Griffin's mind drifted back to the days leading up to the events on Ellis Island when he was still the vice president. Those bastards had gone after his family too. At least when the sniper on top of the Statue of Liberty took a shot at him, it all began to make sense.

Why the hell didn't these latest bastards leave his family alone and come right at him? He preferred the direct approach. He shook his head, feeling guilty his decisions again put the lives of family and friends at risk.

Griffin had listened to Mike Finley's account describing the latest dead-end in the investigation. Finley and Casella had been the last people to leave the Oval Office late yesterday. Casella had summarized the progress and status of the Amber Alert project. Lots of interesting links and innuendos, but nothing concrete; only the typical conspiracy theories that surfaced from time-to-time. Right now he had to deal with the immediate problem.

From Casella's summary, the president understood the events occurring in the Pacific Northwest were most likely related to the global issues he faced. It looked like Edie had touched a nerve, and this young girl, Beth Dawson, might've got caught up in the backlash. But so far nothing was clear.

The crisis in the Middle East had reached the boiling point, and tough decisions needed to be made. The clock was ticking down on the Israeli prime minister's warning to retaliate. If Israel continued making aggressive overtures against Iran, the president was confident the Iranians would launch a counter-offensive to prevent Israel from making the first move.

The United Nations security council had been meeting all day to address the crisis. They were demanding President Griffin appear at the U.N. headquarters in New York to dissuade the Israelis from committing any immediate acts of violence and to assure the world the United States would intervene on behalf of the U.N. and quell the potential escalation of hostilities between Israel and Iran.

In addition, the president's advisors reported that the U.N. was preparing long-range global proposals to address the worldwide tensions and the growing tsunami of conflicts battering the increasing numbers of besieged states. The Israeli Iranian situation could be the tipping point for the world to demand an end to unilateral action. The time had come for the U.N. to step up its authority and power.

President Griffin had a different answer in mind.

He had been elected to this office on the promise to restore the power and influence of the United States. The world had floundered while the United States took a back seat to international events. The former president, Alice Andersen, had seen it coming, but her failing health prevented her from staying on the job long enough to complete the necessary policy changes.

Without leadership, the weaker nations kowtowed to insurgencies and terrorist organizations. The failing states throughout the Middle East were prime meat for the Islamic militants building caliphates throughout the region. Under the guise of freedom and tolerance, western nations had been covertly undermined by organizations tentacled to the most dangerous elements of these radical jihadists. And now the borders of sovereign nations were being overrun as people fled the horror of their homelands.

Terrorist groups such as ISIS vowed to take the fight to every western state: to recruit jihadists from within and to clandestinely march warriors into the midst of the non-believers. An uncontrolled internet provided fertile ground for an almost instantaneous radicalization process to grow an endless supply of converts.

The president envisioned a missing link—a hidden connection driving the Islamic revolution to even greater heights. He believed the annihilation of the Jewish state represented only the first step. The endgame was the eradication of two thousand years of Christian civilization.

Yesterday, after Finley left the president's office, Griffin placed a call to his secretary of defense and ordered an immediate increase in military presence throughout the Middle East. All aircraft carriers and battleships were to move into strategic positions. Key armed forces bases overseas were placed on the highest level of alert.

After considerable debate and consultation with his cabinet, the president ordered the United States military's readiness level to DEFCON 2, matching the highest level since the Cuban Missile Crisis and the first Gulf War.

At the moment, three Trident submarines armed with nuclear missiles cruised the Persian Gulf. This information had been intentionally leaked and served as a calling card to the Iranian leaders. The remaining fleet of Tridents maintained positions in classified sectors around the globe. Any one of them was capable of launching up to twenty-four Trident D5 ballistic missiles. Each D5 missile carried up to eight one hundred kiloton nuclear warheads with a potential range of over 6000 nautical miles, depending on the number of warheads and the designated upgraded specifications for the individual missile.

There was a sharp knock on the door.

The president jumped in his chair. "Jesus Christ," he muttered. In a stronger voice, he said, "Come in."

Mike Finley burst through the door and ran to the president's desk. He placed a single sheet of paper in front of the president.

President Griffin,

We have the first lady and your daughter in our possession. For now, they are unharmed. If you do as directed, they will be returned to you. If you fail to follow our instructions, they will die. The United Nations has requested the United States to intervene in the imminent conflict between Israel and Iran. You must appear before the General Assembly of the United Nations and denounce any aggressive actions being threatened by the state of Israel. You must convince Israel to stand down and allow the United Nations to investigate the incident in Jerusalem. You will state that the United States strongly condemns any unilateral actions by Israel against Iran or any other nation. And that the United States will support all United Nations resolutions regarding this conflict and any future United Nations policies for strengthening international laws.

If you fail to carry out these specific demands, you will never see the first lady or your daughter again.

The president grabbed the edge of the desk with both hands. His fingers dug into the aged wood. Dark eyes stared up at Finley. "Where the hell did this—"

Finley touched the president's shoulder and swallowed. "The first lady's secretary found it in her inbox. It was in a sealed manila envelope. It's been checked out for any signs of toxins as well as fingerprints. All clean."

"And what? This happens to show up in the White House? How do you explain that?"

"Well, sir, it appears Badiyah Jamail had it delivered to the first lady's secretary before—"

The cold stare from Griffin stopped Finley before his words interrupted. "Mike." The president stood up and stared out the window. He glanced toward the telltale sounds of an approaching helicopter angling down to the South Lawn. Without turning, he repeated, "Mike. I trust you're doing whatever it takes to... to find Alison and Brianna. If you need anything—just do it."

Griffin spun around and faced Finley. For a second, his eyes flashed down to the note Finley placed on the desk. "You understand, if we deny support to Israel, it's the same as launching a nuclear attack on Iran. Make no mistake about it. The Middle East will blow up, and we'll be headed straight into World War III."

Finley stood straight and gave a small nod.

"Who are these maniacs, and what the hell are they trying to do?"

The president didn't expect an answer, and his words hung in the air.

"Mr. President, the chopper landing on the South Lawn is taking me to the airport. It's a longshot, but I'm going to personally check out every destination point where those museum shipments were supposedly headed. Right now—we've got no other leads to go on."

CHAPTER 31

REFRESHED, BUT WITH ONLY A few hours sleep after returning to Coeur d'Alene, Steve walked into the kitchen. He saw Edie and Catori sitting at the kitchen table. Amber was licking up the remains of Rosa's breakfast on the floor, while the baby smeared yellow and green slim over her scalp. He grabbed a mug from the cabinet and sat down across from Edie, pouring the steaming coffee from a carafe on the table.

"Anything on Sampson?" he asked.

Edie shook her head and Steve filled them in on the highlights of what transpired in D.C. He cut his summary short when he sensed strange vibes coming from Edie and Catori. "Is there something you guys care to share?"

Edie shrugged. "Nothing much. Yesterday I got a small glimpse into Catori's world."

Steve looked at Catori. Catori smiled and touched Edie's hand. Steve noticed Edie's hand twitch, but she allowed Catori's hand to stay put.

"We went to see Beth after they transferred her to Fairchild Air Force Base," Edie said. "She's still in an induced coma. The doctors think they'll have her conscious again soon, but Catori insisted on jump-starting things a bit."

Catori added, "I brought Edie in with me—into one of my visions. I needed her perspective on what Beth stumbled into since she last talked to her."

Steve homed in on the words: *brought Edie in with me.* He looked at Catori and then back to Edie. "And?"

Edie rubbed her eyes and shook her head. "Catori and I have been trying to piece together something concrete." She let out a long sigh. "The whole experience was kind of like a dream. When I woke up, my head spun with all these strange images. I could almost see what we were looking for—what Beth was trying to tell me—but then everything got jumbled. Now it's all a blur." She looked at Catori, her eyebrows raised.

"Well, it's possible whatever Beth found could've been recorded on that broken memory chip. The one found with her medallion." Catori shrugged. "Even with Edie's assistance, I got mostly images from what happened back in California last year. The Kessler Foundation, the Nordic Brotherhood, and also a few hints about the Muslim Brotherhood."

She ran her fingers through her hair. "That might be important, but I'm not sure how it all fits in, since probably most of it came from Edie and me—not Beth. It's like a giant spider web entangling everything I'm seeing."

Closing her eyes, she continued. "I sensed several names from Beth, but no solid connections. I think that's why Beth needed Edie to take a look at what she found. I'm hoping that chip might hold the key."

When Catori opened her eyes, Steve shook his head.

"What?" Catori's voice sounded resigned.

Steve's lips tightened. "Got word back on the damaged memory chip." His head continued shaking. "It was smashed up pretty bad. No way to retrieve anything useful from it."

Catori nodded and pressed her eyes shut again. After a short pause her eyes blinked open and she turned to Edie. "I'm sure Beth will be awake in a day or two. Then you two can put your heads together. What I'm struggling with now are these strange images of Sampson. And neither you nor Beth can help with that." She got up and walked toward the sink and then turned, leaning against a cabinet.

"I'm sorry, Edie." Her voice cracked. "It's gotta be all in here someplace." She clasped her hands on top of her head. "I... I can't put it together."

She slipped down the side of the cabinet and sat on the floor, legs splayed out in front.

Edie ran to Catori's side and gave her a hug.

Catori arched her head back and whispered, "Please... don't let me be too late."

Edie's phone rang.

"Edie? This is Connie Wilton."

"Hi, Connie. How are you and Joe?"

Steve and Edie met Joe and Connie Wilton several years ago. They were instrumental in helping Steve find answers about his father's involvement in a political scandal. And if it weren't for the Wiltons' help, Steve and Edie may never have survived long enough to put all the pieces together and prevent the conspirators from completing their mission.

Connie Wilton, a slight woman in her late sixties, had a full mane of long red hair that framed a smiling face and accented the twinkle in keen green eyes. Her husband, Joe, a retired attorney from Seattle, was solidly built and sported a crown of white hair on a six foot-two frame. These days he looked more comfortable in T-shirts and blue jeans—usually sweat-drenched and soiled as a result of his non-stop efforts at keeping busy.

"We're fine, dear. We just returned home to Coeur d'Alene late last night. Joe needed to grab more tools from his shop. We've been working up at our cabin for the last two weeks. There's no TV, phone, or even cell service in our part of the lake. So, the first thing I did when we got home, after grabbing my squirrel gun and shooting a few varmints, was to turn on the TV. Then I saw the reports out of Spokane. Oh... my... God. It's terrible about what happened to that poor girl. Falling out of the gondola. It's a miracle she survived."

There had been no mention of the attack, or the fact Beth Dawson had also been shot. Those details were being kept from the media.

"Then I saw your brother's picture splashed all over the TV, and the police asking if anyone had seen this man. I had to call you."

Edie stood up a little straighter. "What do you mean, Connie?"

"Well, at first, Joe told me I was making a mistake; and I needed a new pair of glasses. But I told him my eyesight was just fine."

Edie made out Joe's voice in the background, telling Connie to get to the point.

"Our cabin's located near the southern tip of Lake Pend Oreille. The other day I was sitting outside the cabin on our deck looking at the scenery with my binoculars."

Connie told Joe to hush up. She wasn't spying on anybody.

"This large SUV pulled up to the pier at the Naval research facility in Bayview. We can see it all from our deck."

Connie continued arguing with Joe. "What difference does it make who owns it now?" To Edie, Connie said. "Anyway, three men got out of the SUV and helped another... large man... from the rear seat. He must've been drunk or sick because they needed to pull him out and onto his feet. Then they all but carried him to the end of the pier and onto that big floating platform the Navy—I mean this private corporation—uses to do whatever they do out on the lake."

Edie walked to the sink. She didn't have a clue as to what Connie was getting at. But she knew her well enough to understand that this wasn't a social call.

"The man being ushered along looked familiar. The last time I saw him was at your wedding. At first, I would've sworn it was your brother, Sampson. I called Joe over, but by the time he peered through my binoculars, the men had disappeared behind the walls on the platform. Joe convinced me I had to be wrong. What would Sampson be doing at Lake Pend Oreille? I put the whole incident out of my mind. Until this morning when I learned Sampson and that girl were in Spokane together. And now everybody is looking for him. So, regardless of what Joe says about my eyesight, I'm guessing... it's possible... I might've seen Sampson... or someone who looks a lot like him... getting out of that SUV."

In the background Edie heard Joe mumbling, "Jesus, Connie, I sure wish you were the only eyewitness to a crime one of my clients was accused of. With that kind of confidence, I'd have him walking out a free man."

"Oh hush, Joe. You're the one who made me doubt my own eyes in the first place," Connie said.

"That's why my clients paid me the big bucks."

Edie ignored the bantering and struggled to focus. "Sampson? Drunk at a Naval research facility?"

"Where are you now, Edie? Is Steve with you?"

"Steve and I are in Coeur d'Alene, at his fa—at our house."

"You do have Rosa with you too, don't you?"

"Of course."

"Listen, dear," Connie said, "Joe and I are heading back to the cabin as soon as he finishes loading his tools in the Jeep. Why don't you follow us up there? Give me a call when you're ready, and we'll meet you at the bottom of the hill." The Wiltons' house sat on ten acres about three miles from where Steve and Edie were staying.

Connie continued, "Better you see for yourself what I'm talking about; then it will all make sense."

Edie agreed and was about to end the call when Connie added, "And by the way, Jimmy Martin is up at the cabin right now. He's helping Joe with the heavier work. Gives Jimmy a chance to fish and SCUBA dive. We've found it keeps his mind from worrying about government conspiracies."

"Like the Naval research facility?" Edie asked.

Connie laughed. "No. Like Joe keeps reminding me, the Navy sold the whole facility to a private corporation, so Jimmy doesn't need to worry about any more conspiracies in our neck of the woods."

CHAPTER 32

STEVE FOLLOWED JOE WILTON'S JEEP Grand Cherokee along the interstate into the city of Coeur d'Alene and then north on US 95. After turning east on Hwy 54, they passed through Farragut State Park and the small town of Bayview, nestled on Lake Pend Oreille's southern shores.

He caught a glimpse of the main gate to the former Navy Acoustic Research Detachment before heading up the narrow, winding lane along the western slopes of Scenic Bay. Ten minutes later, the two SUVs pulled in front of a tiny cabin perched on the hillside overlooking the lake. Jimmy Martin's red, rusted old Ford Ranger was parked along the right edge of the driveway. A set of wooden stairs behind the cabin led down to a dock and boathouse.

Steve stepped from the Escalade and gazed at the peaceful vista stretching across the tapered curves of the bay. Sharp peaks spiking above the stealthy depths clasped the glassy facade like gnarly hands cupped to embrace the pellucid liquid, molding its banks into beautiful, contrasting features defining a jagged mountainous path to the north.

The picture reflected in Steve's eyes did little to suggest the violent birth of this vast inland empire. Eons ago, an incredible tumbling water wall of incalculable volume raged through the once docile territory.

Crafted by a melting glacier's final hold on a monstrous body of water, this savage onslaught of destruction had been unleashed when a giant frozen plug gave way to the forces of nature. With it came the power to carve deep gorges in its inevitable attempt to seek a path to the Pacific Ocean, burying ancient riddles far beneath the now placid surface of Lake Pend Oreille.

Connie Wilton rushed to the rented Escalade and fawned over Rosa. Seeing Catori step out of the SUV, Connie smiled and gave her a big hug. "Oh, it's been ages since I last saw you. And you keep getting more beautiful."

Joe Wilton interrupted the reunion. "Come on, folks, let's go inside." He put an arm around Edie's shoulder. "I'm sure you're anxious to see if we can be of any help in finding your brother."

Lingering pockets of fresh paint engulfed them as they walked into the family room of the lakefront cabin. The furniture had been moved away from the walls and formed a tight circle in the center of the room, resembling a modern-day version of a wagon train preparing for an attack. A paint-encrusted aluminum ladder heaped with folded canvass tarps sat in the far corner.

Connie Wilton headed to the kitchen. A moment later she popped her head out and said, "Joe, the power's out again."

Joe didn't look surprised. His steps never hesitated, and he kept on talking. "We're redoing the lower level. Jimmy's been helping me plumb-out a new bathroom." He led them through the French doors to a wide patio deck overlooking Scenic Bay. Joe leaned over the railing and called down to the man fishing off the end of the dock. "Hey, Jimmy. Come on up and say hello to your old friends. And, can you start up the generator?"

By the time Jimmy Martin schlepped his way up the long, weathered staircase and joined them on the deck, Joe was ensconced in educating them on the history of the Navy's Acoustic Research Detachment in Bayview. He paused long enough for Jimmy to greet his guests.

Jimmy Martin stuffed a stained blue cap into his back pocket, revealing medium-length sandy blond hair plastered to his scalp. Average build, he was now in his late thirties, going on fifteen. His demeanor—the opposite of Joe Wilton—always nervous and jumpy. His close-set blue eyes in perpetual motion, darting about his surroundings, on a constant lookout for a concealed motive.

For a second, his sharp eyes landed on Edie. She gave him a slight wave and a wink. He always acted like a lost puppy dog around her. She had brought him back from the brink of a total meltdown that would have ended up with him either dead or in prison for the rest of his life.

After a warm greeting, Jimmy grabbed a beer and leaned up against the deck's railing, facing his friends; but now and then checking his perimeter. Something Amber could relate to.

Once everyone settled in again, Joe Wilton looked back to Edie.

Steve and Edie had been firing questions at Joe, trying to understand how any of this connected with her missing brother. "I thought you were joking when you said the Navy ran a testing facility right here in the middle of the Pacific Northwest. Can't be anymore landlocked than Idaho. Figured it to be another outlet for big government waste." Edie glanced at Jimmy, who nodded a silent approval. "But after you explained the lake's unique characteristics regarding soundwaves and its isolation from other interfering elements, I guess it makes sense." This time Jimmy's face remained neutral. Edie checked that Rosa was still sleeping in the stroller and pulled the lacy white blanket back up to her neck.

Steve, still studying the distant research facility at the tip of the bay, straightened up. He placed Connie's binoculars back on the patio table and turned his attention to Joe. Steve hadn't mentioned anything about the kidnapping of the first lady in D.C. The president had been adamant about keeping the circle tight. Until now, he wasn't even sure how it related to Sampson's disappearance.

When Joe mentioned the Navy had done submarine research at this facility, the hairs on the back of his neck stiffened. "Joe? Is there a Naval museum located in the area?"

Joe's brows crinkled. After a slight hesitation, he nodded. "Yeah, there's one in Farragut State Park. We drove right by it on the highway. Farragut was a training base during WWII. Over a quarter million recruits passed through the camp. The museum is located near the visitor center. Why?"

Steve's heart rate picked up as he tried to recall the delivery addresses on the shipping papers Mike Finley had waved in his face yesterday. He didn't remember Idaho being on the list of museum destinations—but he didn't like coincidences.

Edie looked at Steve, folding her arms. "What are you getting at, Steve?"

Steve took a breath and decided to make an exception to the president's orders. He explained the details of how they thought the kidnappers got the first lady and the president's daughter out of D.C.

Connie looked up in amazement. "How in the world could they keep a lid on something like that?"

Jimmy Martin placed both hands on his hips. "When you're the government, it's what you do."

Joe was shaking his head. "This museum is inside the old brig for the training camp. The cells are used to display artifacts—mostly photos, letters, personal items— no room for anything big. Outside in the courtyard they got an old fire engine and a Ford flatbed." He glanced at Jimmy Martin. "The old truck's probably in better shape than Jimmy's Ranger."

Jimmy dropped his arms, opened his mouth, but then shrugged. He reached for his beer and took another pull.

Steve considered the comment he made to Finley about the unlikelihood of the kidnappers delivering the first lady to one of their scheduled museum stops. On the other hand, when they switched trucks, why go to the trouble of transferring the submarine to another vehicle? Maybe it was safer than yanking the first lady and her daughter out in the open where prying eyes could identify them. The evidence at the scene suggested that the second truck had backed up close to the first, making it easy to quickly transfer the heavy cargo.

Right now, none of this made sense. He didn't know what to think. The sight of a damn submarine in a gated community in Maryland certainly would've raised a few eyebrows. He didn't think the drainage pond could've been a likely place to hide even a mini-sub. Besides, they found nothing there.

Steve looked at Joe. "Sorry for the interruption. Why don't you continue telling us about those underwater pods?"

Catori, silent throughout the conversation, kissed Rosa on the forehead and walked to the edge of the deck. She placed both hands on the railing and stared into the depths of the crystalline waters. Lake Pend Oreille, one of the deepest in North America, reflected the intensity of the vibrant blue skies: like a chameleon, hiding another world beneath.

"As I was saying," Joe responded. He hesitated and Steve followed his eyes to Catori's image. "The Navy's program tested different submarine prototype designs."

Steve was listening to Joe, but he kept a watchful eye on Catori. Her long flowing hair rustled in the gentle breeze coming off the lake.

"They needed to isolate the various components to understand how to identify specific sound signatures," Joe said. "Each pod contained individual elements of the entire submarine. To name a few, there were pods for propulsion systems, weapons launching devices, power generating equipment, ventilation systems, and simulations of the crew's living quarters."

"And what'd they do with these pods?" Steve asked. His legs were pushed aside as Amber jumped up and padded over to Catori. She sat back on her haunches. While looking down at the water lapping against the pebbled shore, Catori scratched the dog's ear.

"They submerged the pods in different parts of the lake." Joe pointed to the distant facility. "Check out that large floating platform at the edge of the pier. Even without the binoculars you can see how big it is."

Steve and Edie nodded in unison, and Joe continued. "They towed it around and used it to lower the pods under the water. From what I understand, the data got transmitted back to a laboratory in the research center. They analyzed the acoustical signals generated from the pods."

Steve asked another question. "So, they didn't test complete working subs?"

"They did that too. At least I think so. Not full-scale sizes for the larger subs, but I heard they perfected mini sub designs right here."

"And after they sold the facility? What does this new company do?" Edie asked.

Jimmy Martin coughed. He walked over and placed the empty beer bottle on the table. He looked out over the bay and then stared at the research facility.

"I'll tell you something." Jimmy reached into his back pocket and grabbed his cap, pulling it snug to his head. The brim shielded a portion of his eyes as they scanned the bay again. "When the government ran this operation, I wanted to see what they were up to. And also have me a little fun." Jimmy looked at Joe Wilton. "Joe lets me keep my little fishing craft in his boathouse. It's got one hell of an engine; not to mention, it's damn loud."

Joe stood up and asked if anybody needed a refill. Jimmy was just getting started. Joe returned with a cooler, and set it down on the deck.

Before continuing, Jimmy's hand flew into the cooler and twisted another bottle open. "On occasion, I'd take my boat for a spin and head down to the end of the bay, toward Bayview. From the surface, you can't see where the pods are when they're beyond a certain depth. The

Navy never hassled me too much about going out there. Besides, the area isn't restricted or anything. And I know my rights."

He paused, eyes darting toward Edie and then diverting to his shoes. "Push them when I think the government's not being truthful." A brief smile twitched across his face. "They did get a little antsy when I put on my SCUBA gear. That's how I knew I was getting too close to one of their experiments. They'd send a patrol boat over to see if I needed any help, and then politely ask me to do my diving in another area. For my own safety, they said."

Jimmy paused again, checking his audience. "Now here's the interesting part. Ever since the government sold the facility, things have changed. I've only tried this once. This new company has a different attitude. They told me to get the hell away, and they didn't use very polite words to get their point across. They also said it was for my own safety, and I guess they meant it, because I saw the telltale bulge of shoulder holsters under their windbreakers. And all their patrol boats were well-armed."

Steve looked back and forth between Jimmy Martin and Joe Wilton. He settled on asking Joe another question. "You did say this company still does contract work for the government?"

Joe nodded.

"Are they still doing acoustic research?"

Joe shrugged. "No way to tell for sure. But they're still towing the floating platform around the bay. They seem to be raising and lowering pods—or something—in and out of the water. Their crews tend to be larger too."

Connie broke in. "That's where I think I saw Sampson. Being led onto the floating platform."

Steve thought of something else. "Since we got here, I haven't seen any activity out on the water. The platform appears to be deserted. In fact, you've got a powerful pair of binoculars, and I haven't seen any movements at all—anywhere in the whole research complex. Is that normal?"

"Well," Joe said, "they don't follow any set schedules, so—"

Connie interrupted. "You're right, Joe, but this week there's been a lot more going on. And now that I think about it—remember when we were driving through Farragut State Park this morning? I saw a steady stream of trucks heading in the opposite direction. And I remember when we passed the research facility, the parking lot looked empty."

For the first time since they started the conversation about the research facility, Catori spoke up. "Why don't we take a little boat ride?" She turned to Edie. "You still got your brother's suitcase in the back of the Escalade?"

She kneeled down in front of Amber and massaged the dog's ears.

Chapter 33

Before heading down the stairs to Jimmy Martin's speedboat, Edie grabbed a few articles of Sampson's clothing from the suitcase stashed in the back of the Escalade. Steve pulled Amber aside and focused her on Sampson's scent.

Connie Wilton insisted on taking care of Rosa and stayed behind at the cabin. The rest of them climbed into the open craft. Jimmy stood at the helm, under a small, camouflaged canopy. Joe and Edie settled into seats at the stern, and Steve and Catori kneeled on the bow seat with Amber crouched on the narrow bow platform.

Jimmy kept the powerful outboard near idling, the thirsty engine coughing and stuttering in protest. Using both his GPS navigation unit and following distinct landmarks as guidelines, he maneuvered in a tight grid pattern, systematically covering the waters of Scenic Bay. Each leg brought them closer to the research facility at the western shore near the tip of the bay.

"If I hadn't seen this done before," Catori said to Steve, "I'd never thought it possible."

Without taking his eyes off Amber, Steve said, "It is amazing. So far, I've only worked with Amber using controlled testing situations, but I've seen what other detection dogs have picked up under actual search conditions."

He hesitated, a dark thought passing through him. He had tried to convince Edie to wait at the cabin. The usual underwater tracking scenario involved searching for bodies snagged below the surface. He didn't want Edie to witness such a possibility.

Steve noted a distinct shift in Amber's posture. Her ears slanted back and she crept forward; nose extended over the bow. Steve raised a hand for Jimmy. He twirled a finger around for Jimmy to circle back to the area where Amber's behavior first changed. Edie worked her way to the bow and Steve grabbed onto her shoulder. Amber's reaction heightened. She barked and pawed the bow.

Jimmy cut the engine, but it was impossible to drop an anchor: the water's depth in this area of the lake approached a thousand feet.

Catori asked, "How deep can a dog detect the scent?"

"I'm not sure, since the scents normally diffuse to the surface. But with shifting currents, we may not even be close to…." Steve let his words drift off and held Edie tighter. He avoided mentioning anything relating to cadaver searches.

Jimmy peered over the starboard side. Seeing nothing, he shrugged and opened up the storage bunker bolted to the transom. Joe helped him pull out the SCUBA gear and strap the tank to his back. Jimmy rolled off the swim platform and disappeared below the surface.

Amber leapt from the bow, chasing after the ebb and flow of bubbles that indicated Jimmy's position. Steve finally convinced Amber to swim over to the stern, and he and Joe grasped the dog. Once back onboard, she stood on the swim platform and continued to bark at the water's surface.

For what seemed like hours, Edie sat at the bow, both hands covering her face. Joe pointed to the water at the port side as an indistinct shadow evolved into Jimmy

Martin. Bursting through the surface, Jimmy tore off his face mask and mouthpiece. "I spotted a steel cylinder. And it's freakin' big. Like an oil tanker. Probably one of those pods you talked about, Joe. It's tethered about twenty feet below the surface. Can't see what's inside, but I felt the hull vibrating. Could be power for a ventilation system."

Jimmy swam around to the stern, and they helped him back on board. Edie asked, "Did you try banging on the pod?"

This time Jimmy looked her straight in the eye and nodded. "I did. But even if I got a response, I don't think I would've heard anything. Sorry."

Edie bit her lip. "When you were down there, Jimmy, we followed where you went by watching the bubbles. If there's a working ventilation system—to keep a person alive—why don't we see any bubbles coming to the surface?"

Joe Wilton answered. "It doesn't mean anything, Edie. It'd be a closed system with a carbon dioxide scrubber to recirculate the air inside. You wouldn't see any visible bubbles."

"Where's the closest place to pick up cell service, or at least find a landline?" Steve asked Joe.

"In town." Joe pointed to a cluster of buildings near the former Naval research facility.

Steve looked around, his eyes settling on the old research site. He pointed. "Let's go knock on their damn door and ask to use the phone." He checked his jacket to make certain an extra clip was in place.

Jimmy started up the engine and pushed on the throttle. He pointed a thumb over his shoulder. "If you guys need any reinforcements, I got more than SCUBA gear in my bunker."

Steve glanced inside. "Jesus H. Christ, Jimmy! What the hell kinda fish you after?"

"The same ones you're looking for, Steve."

The bow of the lightweight craft sailed high out of the water and then settled into a solid planing position as Jimmy aimed the speedboat toward the research facility. Water sprayed over the bow, and the gap narrowed quickly.

Steve's eyes turned back to the spot where the pod lay submerged, wondering what they'd find inside.

Chapter 34

ALL ARRANGEMENTS HAD BEEN FINALIZED. President Tyler Griffin would be traveling to New York City to address the General Assembly of the United Nations. He had spent most of the day dealing with cabinet members, advisors, and leaders of the congressional intelligence committees in an endless procession marching through the Oval Office.

For the more sensitive exchanges, he met with key individuals in the Situation Room. The majority of his efforts focused on reports from the intelligence agencies. He had demanded his military advisors present him with worst-case scenario plans regarding the use of force, including pre-emptive military strikes against Iran and other nations responsible for sponsoring terrorist groups.

The president signed a number of executive orders to turn up the heat on domestic Islamic organizations with possible ties to terrorist activities. National Guard troops would soon deploy to both the southern and northern borders in an effort to maintain a semblance of control. The attorney general had been purposely kept away from the particulars of the president's actions.

Stuck in an unending loop, President Griffin's mind kept replaying images of the events leading up to the latest crisis in Israel. Nation-states throughout the Middle East were falling like rows of dominoes. Fleeing refugees escaped their homelands as terrorist groups overran failing governments. An exodus of biblical proportions threatened the European borders. Ultimately, this effect would ripple and jeopardize the entire world.

Many refugees had found their way to both the North and South American continents. They joined the large numbers of souls fleeing the oppressive governments closer to American soil.

Vetting this vast number of converging humanity was an impossible task for the any of the designated federal agencies in charge, and the U.S. Border Patrol had already been overwhelmed. With the heightened threats of terrorist activity, drastic measures needed to be taken.

The United Nations called for a moratorium on all national priorities; proposing a unified international council to implement a worldwide declaration of law. Banking and commerce systems were on the verge of collapse, and key international leaders urged a different monetary system be instituted for the purpose of seizing private assets throughout the world.

The few remaining democratic nations looked to the United States for leadership and guidance. Others had given up and pleaded for the United Nations to step in and unite a collapsing world.

The president had been tight-lipped on what he planned to say at the U.N. A number of standard-bearers in both political parties rallied together to force the president to advocate alignment with the U.N. proposals and to convince Israel to abide by those same criteria.

Since being sworn in to the office of the presidency, Tyler Griffin had been fighting this insidious infiltration of what he recognized as anti-American sentiments. These threats to the basic tenets of the constitution and the American way of life could soon become more powerful than any overt terrorist actions.

The hairs on the back of his neck bristled as he recalled the sinister threads Steve Casella and Mike Finley had described, pointing to another organization behind the vast Islamic network. That would have to wait. He needed to take action on the current conflict but couldn't shake the calculated possibility of all these events being orchestrated by the same unknown group. He didn't like the thought of being pulled like a puppet on a string.

Before leaving for his speech at the United Nations, the president returned to the Oval Office to consider his actions. He had spent the previous thirty minutes in the private residence of the White House talking to his children. The last words he said to them still echoed in his ears. He told them to remember one thing: he loved them all more than anything else. He then asked them to pray together for their mother and sister.

To himself, Tyler Griffin asked Alison to forgive him if he got this wrong.

The president contemplated the consequences of how he handled the current situation. The world may not get another chance. He knew damn well Alison and Brianna would not.

Could he go through with this?

Did he really have any choice?

CHAPTER 35

JIMMY NAVIGATED THE SPEEDING BOAT to the edge of the research facility's wharf and cut the engine. Two long piers spanned by a closed multi-tiered structure extended out into the bay. Part of the structure linked to a larger building on a massive concrete pad. On the outside edges of the piers, wide concrete slabs angled below the water's surface. Pairs of rusted rail tracks were bolted to the ramps. Several steel-webbed cranes rose high above the structure.

They bumped hard against the dock and Steve jumped out to secure the bow and stern lines. At this point they didn't go for stealth, since anyone in the vicinity of the entire lower half of Scenic Bay had already been assaulted by the deafening sounds of Jimmy's engine.

The dock planks were in reasonable shape. They were old and dry with only traces of the usual road-tar smells surviving the baking rays of the sun. From all appearances, the former Navy Acoustic Research Detachment looked deserted.

The entire complex was eerily still.

"This place is a lot smaller than I expected," Steve said to Joe. "Mostly open land and parking spaces."

Joe nodded. "The temporary structures got torn down when the Navy sold the place. The new outfit probably made a lot of money on the scrap sheet metal. Only thing left is the original red- and yellow-brick research building and this warehouse complex on the pier. As you can see, they could easily launch and service good-sized vessels using this set-up. The basic infrastructure looks solid, but I don't see much machinery or heavy equipment remaining. Almost looks like an abandoned ferry terminal."

"Hard to imagine anything useful still comes out of this facility. And right now, with no welcoming committee, I'd say it's probably deserted." Steve shrugged and jogged across to the floating platform moored near Jimmy's boat. The platform rode about two feet higher than the dock's surface. He pulled himself up and took a quick look around. The platform was close to forty feet long and twenty feet wide. A narrow band of decking surrounded the perimeter. Corrugated steel panels with several yellowed, square plastic windows walled off the inside of the platform.

Steve peeked inside and saw a large opening in the floor deck running almost the entire length of the platform. A crane, considerably smaller than the ones built adjacent to the warehouse structure, was mounted on board, the upper framework rose high above the outer walls. This one appeared relatively new compared to the others. He looked at the base of the crane and the control panel. A large generator was housed behind the mounting frame for the crane.

Steve stepped back to the perimeter decking on the platform and called over to Jimmy. "Can your little boat tow this thing?"

Jimmy gave him a look. "Shit, yeah."

Edie and Catori worked with Jimmy to swing the boat into position while Steve asked Joe to help check things out on the platform. He took a closer look at the crane and turned to Joe. "You wouldn't know how to operate those hoist controls, would you?"

"Not a chance, but I know someone who can." He pointed across the empty complex to a small rustic building outside of the facility's fence. "Go grab those bolt cutters out of Jimmy's bunker and I can introduce you to Winston. He's the owner of the Bottom of the Bay. That tavern I'm pointing at."

Steve said, "I *could* use a drink, but—"

"Winston used to work at this facility when the Navy ran the show. He retired about ten years ago and bought the Bottom of the Bay. Back in the day, Winston operated these damn things."

"In that case, let's go talk to Winston. And maybe he'll let us use his phone to call in the cavalry. I don't like the feel of this place. The feds need to do some prying."

Steve grabbed the cutters and explained the plan to the others. He directed Amber to stay put. Then Steve and Joe sprinted across the crumbling asphalt parking lot. By the time Joe caught up, Steve had the fence cut back enough to slip through.

The first thing Steve noticed when they walked through the door to the Bottom of the Bay was that the place was quiet—and dark. From the tired look of the faded stained walls and yellowed natural pine ceiling, any additional lighting would have detracted from the atmosphere. The only person in the bar sat in a booth near the window. He held a large tumbler of scotch in his hand. A copy of the Coeur d'Alene Press lay spread out on the table.

Joe introduced Steve to Winston and pressed him into assisting with lifting the pod out of the water. At first, Winston appeared apprehensive at meddling in activities at the former Naval facility. Steve flashed his fed credentials and told him it was a matter of national security. That tweaked Winston's interest enough to set his tumbler back on the table. But only after draining the remaining amber liquid.

Winston looked up and let out a long alcohol-tainted breath, making Steve's eyes water and reminding him of the last wildfire strike team he'd been on cutting line in the Angeles National Forest.

When Steve asked to use the phone, he learned the reason Winston had been sitting alone in the dark. Earlier today, phone and electric services had gone down. Steve looked at Joe.

Joe responded, "Usually the power outages are confined to the more remote areas out near our cabin. This is a little troubling."

Around that same time, Winston added, cell service had also been cut. He told them there was no estimate for when any of the utilities would be restored. He couldn't be sure but believed the closest working phone was at the main visitors center in Farragut State Park. About a ten-minute drive. Winston offered the use of his car if Steve wanted to head over and make a call. Being more concerned with what they might find in the pod, Steve asked Joe to make the trip while he took Winston back to the floating platform.

By the time they returned to the dock, Jimmy was almost ready to move out. Winston looked over the controls on the floating platform's crane and nodded. "This set-up is state-of-the-art. A lot different than when I ran this beauty a decade ago. But I do believe I can make this baby purr." He stroked the main operations panel as one would caress a lover.

They used the GPS unit on Jimmy's boat to guide them back to the coordinates he'd entered when they first located the submerged pod. Steve took over the helm as they approached the site to allow Jimmy to don his SCUBA gear. Winston fired up the generator and fed out the crane's cable. Jimmy dove under and coupled it to the lift brackets on the pod.

Jimmy followed Winston's directions on how to release the mooring cables at the bottom. Winston manipulated the controls and began the process of bringing the heavy pod to the surface.

Steve saw Catori's face turn a vivid red as she listened to the sensual words Winston used to cajole the controls into performing to his satisfaction. Steve imagined if Jimmy had a pen and paper he would've taken notes, recording the erotic, lyrical intonations for posterity.

Steve also kept a close watch on Edie. She seemed oddly removed from the entire scene, her arms folded tight against her chest. Amber stayed close to her side, arching her sleek frame against Edie's knees.

As soon as the pod broke through the surface, Amber barked and charged along its side. She skidded to a stop, and her nose pushed against the tattered remnants of a piece of fabric snagged onto what looked like a cable-latching clamp protruding out near the hatch.

When Steve took a closer look, he spotted dark splotches on the material, possibly blood. He chanced a quick glance at Edie but remained silent.

Once they secured the pod to the floating platform, Winston explained the procedure to open the hatches. As

Steve plunged through the outer hatch and disengaged the inner locking mechanisms, Edie came to life. Before he could stop her, she followed him inside.

Edie's gasp echoed through the metallic chamber.

The pod was empty.

Steve called Amber and she searched the confines. Catori waited outside, her hands wiping randomly at the streams of dripping water from the curved hull. Amber located two items stuck in the springs of the lower bunk.

The first, a silver necklace with a silver cross.

On the back, the inscription read:

To Brianna Griffin, with love, Nana.

The other item Amber found was a single torn piece of paper.

CHAPTER 36

THE PALE BLUE FORD TAURUS traveling east on US Route 40 slowed and turned into a gas station five miles north of Baltimore. Keeping his head down, the tall, lanky man twisted tired legs out of the car and shuffled inside to pay the attendant before pumping the gas.

Close to his seventieth birthday, the once imposing six-foot-two figure now portrayed the wan appearance of a much older man. He kept his head lowered, more out of habit than to avoid any security cameras. After all this time he didn't think the feds or anyone else would still be looking for him. Everyone considered his disappearance a mystery, but his death a foregone conclusion.

During the long recovery from his so-called death, he'd had a few subtle changes made to his once carefully sculpted facial features. Age and the near-death experience did the rest. He still didn't like to leave an electronic trail, hence the avoidance of the more convenient pay-at-the-pump credit card transaction.

The man finished filling the tank and checked his watch. Steering clear of the interstate for most of the trip had eaten away more time than expected. According to his calculations—there was nothing wrong with his mental acuity—if he drove the final leg of the trip on the interstate, he'd make it on time for his scheduled visit.

The notion of walking into a federal prison on his own accord precipitated a slew of nightmares, but he had to admit it got the adrenaline coursing through the ancient vessels once again. At least his decrepit appearance was good for something. Even if the authorities had still been looking for him, they'd never recognize the sad old man standing right in front of them.

Everything he could put in place ahead of time had been taken care of. His connections were not what they used to be, but he retained enough clout to grease the appropriate palms. As it turned out, getting on this prisoner's approved visitation list hadn't been too difficult. He'd never gone to law school, but he could act like a presumptuous asshole with no problem at all. This job description fit well with his previous occupation.

The man nodded with satisfaction and eased himself back in the driver's seat. He picked up the entrance ramp to I 95 near Aberdeen and headed north. He calculated that in less than two hours he'd be pulling into the visitor lot for the Federal Correctional Institution at Fairton, located in south central New Jersey.

The remaining portion of his trip allowed him plenty of time to think.

* * * * * *

The man had followed all aspects of the final failed incident, including the lengthy investigations, the arrests, and the subsequent plea bargaining of one of the feds key witnesses. It didn't surprise him when the fat little pig had sung like a canary to try and save his own ass. This got him into the medium security facility at Fairton, instead of the feds locking him into a more fitting maximum-security prison and throwing away the key.

The slimy two-bit hood had named a lot of important people involved in the scheme. The old man smiled: if the authorities had thought he was still alive, he was certain his fate would be a lot worse than that of the two-timing bastard in Fairton.

He recalled the events of that last night after the whole plan went to hell. He should've smelled a rat. During those long months of recovery, he concluded that the self-absorbing prick of a senator who had summoned him to the meeting was too stupid to be in on the plot designed to make him permanently disappear. He'd been just another pawn in the game. In reality, they'd all been used. This revelation came to him during his many months of convalescence.

Senator Henry Whitcome was the only face that came into view. Al Rozano was dead. Officially, a suicide; not that he ever believed that story. And Arthur Constantine supposedly killed in a boating accident. The body never found.

If things went okay with his current vendetta, he'd then hunt down the retired senator and strangle the asshole himself. Even if the old fool wasn't responsible. Just for old times sake.

Then he laughed out loud. Wishful thinking. He barely had enough strength left in his hands to hold his dick to take a leak. Some days he wished his mind didn't still function so well. It pissed him off to remember the old days when his pathetic dick actually worked.

He glanced at his reflection in the rearview mirror, surprised to see a small smile on his face. It used to be chemically fixed into a slight smirk that accompanied his perpetual stare. All bracketed by a curtain of leathery tan.

His face turned dark as he recalled what happened that night.

It had looked like an accident up ahead at the curve. A fender-bender, but the road nevertheless still blocked. A figure appeared in his headlights, waving his arms and running toward him. When he opened his window, a musky scent penetrated his senses. He must've been close to the river. Before he had the chance to speak, two other men materialized out of the darkness, yanked open his car door, and dragged him to one of the vehicles obstructing the road.

The first man, tall with buzz-cut hair, stood in the glow of the headlights and shouted orders. A light mist rolling off the Potomac gave him the look of a ghostlike apparition. One of the men called to the first man by name: Bartholomew.

Bartholomew, the apparent leader, didn't look all that old, but his face reflected a brashness and an expectation that no one would dare question his commands.

Months later, he learned his car had been left abandoned near that spot. Front axles embedded in the muddy shoreline. No signs of any struggle. The media ran with the story for days. The mysterious disappearance of such a controversial figure made for great press.

The follow-up pieces and speculations kept him entertained while he recovered from the botched attempt on his life. Bartholomew may have been a hard-assed assassin but doing things his way turned out to be a rookie's mistake.

He often wondered if Bartholomew had learned anything from his carelessness that night. He found it hard to believe the asshole could be a leader in any big operation. Either way, he'd still prefer never to see the bastard again.

They'd thrown him in the trunk, and he heard Bartholomew tell the men to stage the scene. He'd take care of the rest. The car door slammed shut and the man was flung around the trunk as the car sped away. He calculated they'd driven at least an hour, making a lot of turns, traveling over increasingly bumpy and rutted roads before stopping. When the trunk popped open, Bartholomew, his face shrouded behind the intense beam of a flashlight, spoke his first words to the man.

"Get your ass out of the trunk. You damn goombahs screwed-up big time. I'm here on behalf of my grandpa to clean things up. Take out the trash, so to speak." Bartholomew laughed. The man could only imagine the grotesque sneer hidden behind the light.

Bartholomew shoved him away from the car, his feet slipping on loose rocks and gravel. Expensive Italian dress shoes didn't provide much traction. As he stumbled through the underbrush, he watched the rays of the powerful flashlight disappearing into a shadowy void. He sensed the closeness of a dangerous precipice. His foot reached forward, kicking air. He stopped and Bartholomew kept talking.

"Shit happens, old man, when you rely on brainless goons who don't have a fucking clue. That's why we need to step in and cut a few strings. We're nowhere near done with our venture, but we've got no more use for problems like you."

The man turned back toward Bartholomew. Still blinded by the flashlight, he didn't see the gun in his hand. From a distance of approximately twenty feet, Bartholomew fired off two quick shots. The man staggered one step back and his limp body did a freefall for at least ten feet before impacting with thick branches reaching out from unseen shrubs.

From above, Bartholomew smiled as he listened to the cracking and crunching sounds of the man's body cascading down the steep embankment. When he scanned the area with his flashlight, he saw nothing but a path of broken boughs and darkness creeping at the limits of the beam.

Bartholomew shook his head. He looked at his small-caliber pistol. The instructions called for two close-range shots to the head. He glanced over the ridge again and saw nothing. Placing the weapon back in his pocket, he shrugged. "They're never gonna find that asshole anyway." He turned and walked back to his car. This was one of the first times he'd strayed from his orders. A path he'd turn to again on future missions.

The man always carried cash. Tonight, the denominations on the bills weren't important, just the number of bills stuffed in the thick leather wallet in his inside coat pocket. The man prided himself on being well-dressed and never considered removing the jacket of his charcoal gray pinstriped suit while being tossed about in the trunk.

The impact of the first shot, although greatly suppressed by passing through his cash-laden wallet, still lodged in a fleshy portion of his chest. When he came to, he could breathe okay—lungs not collapsed—so there had been no penetration into the chest cavity. It did hurt like hell when he took a deep breath. The second bullet, more superficial, had probably fractured at least one rib.

His body lay nestled in a dense tangle of leafy bushes. He carefully wiggled his arms and legs, sending sharp impulses of pain, so he couldn't rule out any other broken bones. He squirmed around to reach a hand into his pocket. His cell phone had a small crack in the corner of the screen but otherwise appeared functional. Except there was no cell signal.

In addition to the bullet wounds, the harrowing fall caused multiple injuries, and the man struggled for hours to make his way back up to the road. By the time he neared the top, the first grayish specs of dawn teased darkness from the long and ill-fated night. With a final grunt, he swung his body onto the flat surface, only yards from where Bartholomew had last stood.

This time when he checked his phone, he was rewarded by the sight of a single flashing bar. The call went through to a special emergency service, and he connected with the doctor. Not his favorite plastic surgeon, but one retained by the union for those times when it might be inconvenient or detrimental to call 911.

The physician turned out not to be the type of doctor a man of his stature would ordinarily seek out for one's preventative healthcare or treatment for any acute medical emergencies. Although his injuries did not appear life-threatening at the time, poor initial care of his wounds precipitated a nasty systemic infection. Bouts of fevers born from the stubborn contagions kept the man bedbound for an extended timeframe. Missed fractures failing to heal properly resulted in the current inability to navigate his body to the extent he desired. His age, also a factor, accelerated his downward spiral of less than adequate mobility.

The physician hadn't been well-versed in the art of plastic surgery, however the man had little opportunity for any second opinions. The alterations changed his appearance enough to lessen the possibility of him being recognized, but at the same time resulted in a look that tended to frighten young children.

The man repaid the doctor's services by grabbing a scalpel and slicing his throat. He also took care of any other incidental witnesses to his continuing existence.

* * * * * *

The man arrived in Fairton and pulled into the Federal Correctional Institution visitor lot right on schedule to meet with his unsuspecting new client. He wore a charcoal gray business suit and carried an elegant chocolate brown briefcase. The suit was the same make and style as the ones he wore back in the day; although the size and final cut were a far cry from the original. Inside the briefcase were all the credentials necessary for him to gain access to the prison and engage in a private legal consultation as the recently appointed representative for Anthony Funetti.

The man's credentials identified him as James H. Edelstein, attorney-at-law. He had seen the name imprinted on an antique brass nameplate on an exclusive office building near the White House.

CHAPTER 37

STEVE AND EDIE STOOD STARING at the pod now secured to the floating platform bobbing in the waters of Lake Pend Oreille. Amber's nosework in finding the blood-stained piece of fabric caught onto an exterior cable linkage, and her positive alerts once they opened the hatches convinced Steve that Edie's brother had definitely spent time inside the submerged vessel. The silver necklace and cross belonging to the president's daughter proved he had company.

They quickly concluded that the chain of events from the Pacific Northwest to the nation's capital were linked and part of a much larger plan. The timing of the airline hijackings, as well, appeared too coincidental. They needed to inform the president and steer the investigation in this direction.

Steve examined the empty pod and found nothing useful to help locate Sampson or the missing first family. Another dead-end. He climbed outside the pod and stretched his arms, joining the others on the platform's outer deck.

Catori held the torn paper found in the pod. She and Winston huddled together in an animated conversation, while Jimmy spread a nautical chart of Lake Pend Oreille on the deck.

Edie looked up as Steve stepped toward the group. "The paper that Amber found inside. Winston says it contains the coordinates for the research facility and a navigation route heading toward the northern end of the lake."

Winston knelt down and ran a finger along Jimmy's nautical chart, tracing the proscribed route from the coordinates written on the paper. After several moments he paused and scratched his head. "Let me see that again."

Catori handed him the paper, and he flattened it out over Jimmy's chart. Winston mumbled and shook his head. Catori watched where he planted his finger on the chart. She asked, "What's wrong?"

"Well, up until we reach this position." He pointed at a location about a half mile south of the city of Sandpoint, near the northern edge of the lake. "The coordinates follow a precise path along the deepest parts of the lake. But according to this, the bottom rises sharply and the lake remains shallow through this whole area." He moved his finger over the top section on the chart. "See?"

He looked again at the torn paper and then back to the chart. "These coordinates indicate a different heading, only the route continues at the same depth. And these last coordinates—at the torn edge of the sheet—show a route east of Sandpoint, about a mile beyond the northern shores of the lake. The heading is due north." Winston blew out a long breath. "So these positions have got to be all wrong. I sure wish we had the rest of the paper. Guess I'm too damn old to see straight anymore." He looked around at the others.

"Can one of you young men or ladies help me to my feet?"

Steve and Jimmy grabbed Winston under his shoulders and eased him up.

* * * * * *

Propped over the chart, Catori remained frozen on her knees, arms spread out on the deck. She slowly pushed herself away and stared up at Edie. She leaned back against the corrugated steel wall of the platform.

Catori hadn't told Edie or Steve the entire story when they discussed their shared experience in Beth Dawson's hospital room. And except for an abbreviated description she'd related to Edie about the dead Russian, she had kept the illusions and sensations from the nineteenth-floor balcony in the Spokane Falls Lodge to herself.

Plastered against the wall on the floating platform, Catori's body shook from conflicting images of the dead Russian, ancestral burial grounds, and the appearance of Coyott, who mocked her attempts to pick through the shattered dreams.

Catori's eyes rolled up as her eyelids slammed shut.

The sound of rushing water filled her ears, and she visualized salmon jumping and fighting on their programmed journey. Then the waters became still, and hundreds of eagles swooped down, diving deep beneath the surface of a placid lake.

An icy liquid embraced her—she gulped for air and shut her mouth to stop from swallowing the water as her whole body plunged into darkness. As if pulled far beneath the surface, her arms and legs contorted with the frigid currents taking her deeper and deeper. The vortex spun her until she believed her lungs would explode. A dim light grew brighter, and she burst through the surface, gasping for air.

Catori had earlier threaded additional bits and pieces together about the dead Russian, Dimitri Gruzinsky, by a more modern means of communications: the Google search engine.

And now with today's vision, everything fell into place.

Catori's eyes opened wide, her head shook with violent coughs, and her breathing slowed.

She swallowed the perceived sweet vestiges of the serene waters.

The color returned to her face.

"Edie?" Her voice calm, but insistent. "I don't think we need the missing piece of that torn paper. Let's head back to Joe's cabin."

Steve looked at Edie. They both recognized Catori's demeanor.

"I'll cut us loose, Jimmy," Steve said. They climbed into Jimmy's boat and abandoned the empty pod.

They hoped Joe had gotten through to D.C.

CHAPTER 38

PRESIDENT GRIFFIN STARED ACROSS THE coffee table at Charles Rutherford Smithfield, the American ambassador to the United Nations. The walls of the Oval Office felt more like a prison cell as the president awaited news from Mike Finley about the fate of his wife and daughter.

Within hours, he would be facing the leaders assembled at the United Nations and still struggled with how he would address the current conflict in the Middle East. He wrestled with his conscience and the dilemma the kidnappers brought to the table.

As the president and leader of the free world, he needed to set aside his personal concerns for the safety of his wife and daughter and do the right thing to prevent the current crisis from escalating once again. The Iranians scoffed at any Israeli threats and had vowed to take this opportunity to wipe the Jews from the face of the earth.

At this point no one was certain if the Iranians had finally assembled a viable nuclear weapon. The delivery system didn't present much of an obstacle. Hell, they could easily find a dozen assholes to throw the damn bomb into the heart of Israel.

Griffin suspected the Russians had been working behind the scenes to sabotage any negotiations and facilitate the Iranians in bypassing the sanctions and embargos. Besides, he wouldn't put it past the Russian president to have already provided the Iranians with a fully functional nuclear device.

Since their defeat during the Cold War, the Russians looked for any opportunity to fill the void on the global stage whenever the United States failed to show strong leadership. Even with a military in shambles, they continually tested the waters, looking for any signs of weakness coming out of Washington.

The American ambassador continued to bluster, and the president lost his patience. "So, *Chuck*, why don't you get to the point?"

Griffin chose his words carefully, with the knowledge Charles Rutherford Smithfield would bristle at the bastardization of his name. No one in the polite circle of his associates would ever call him anything other than Charles. Griffin prided himself on the fact that people like Smithfield considered him uncivilized and vulgar.

By the expression on Smithfield's face, Griffin could almost read the man's thoughts: *What else could you expect from a man whose roots in this country are so shallow. And for God's sake, his family journeyed to this country along with hordes of barbarians stuffed into the bowels of a ship—dumped off in the New York harbor. How the hell could someone like him be elected to the office of the president?*

When the Ambassador spoke out loud, the president nearly missed what he was saying, but he had no trouble detecting the scorn in his tone. "Mr. President, the secretary general asked me to speak with you before you address the General Assembly this evening. He has expressed concern for how you intend to handle the situation."

Griffin leaned forward, his anger punctuated by the sharpness in his eyes.

Smithfield hesitated, but then charged forward. "We are wrestling with a humanitarian crisis. The Middle East is on the verge of collapse. And the European nations are bracing for an onslaught of refugees beyond comprehension. If Israel chooses to escalate this little incident, it could set off a powder keg."

The president spit out the next words. "*Little incident?*" His eyes sliced right through the ambassador. "This *little incident* as you call it—" The president pounded a fist on the coffee table hard enough to splatter coffee from the delicate cups. "This little incident has destroyed one of the holiest sites in the world, and at the moment we have no idea how many bodies are still buried beneath the rubble. Have you even bothered to look at the pictures of the carnage and devastation—*Chuck?*"

"The secretary general, on behalf of the security council needs your assurance that you will do everything in your power to make sure Israel does not retaliate. They insist the Israelis take their grievances to the U.N. and cease making threats against the sovereign nation of Iran for the acts of a few radical terrorists. They asked me to speak with you—"

"And I thank you for taking the time to enlighten me, Chuck." The president rose, signaling for Smithfield to do the same. He placed a hand on the ambassador's shoulder and guided him toward the door. "On your way back to New York, you may want to consider exactly who you're working for, but don't waste too much time. And by the way—*Chuck*. I read your latest recommendation on how to improve our relations with the Cuban government. I'll take it under advisement. Great idea. Not only to turn over our Guantanamo Bay facilities to Cuba, but to give them a trillion dollars in reparations. Yeah, they do need a better prison to lock up all those pesky dissidents."

As the president shoved the ambassador out the door, he resisted the urge to stick a boot in his ass to reinforce his point. "Next document I want to see coming from you... would be your letter of resignation. By tonight, if it doesn't conflict with your plans."

The president closed the door behind Smithfield and glanced at his watch. It was getting late and still no word from Finley. He tried to erase those thoughts from his head and walked to his desk. He dropped down into the leather chair.

With his arms folded, he considered the message delivered to him by his own ambassador to the U.N.

Was it beyond the realm of possibility to believe the secretary general had used Smithfield to threaten the president of the United States?

CHAPTER 39

JIMMY MARTIN KEPT THE THROTTLE wide open as long as possible. The speeding craft left a sizeable wake as it entered the cove: he'd let Joe Wilton make apologies to the neighbors—again. At the last second, Jimmy cut back on the throttle and slammed the protesting gears into reverse. Steve had been poised to secure the bowline, but Jimmy's actions almost sent him over the bow and headlong across the end of the dock. The boat faltered and then slipped expertly into the slip next to Joe's boathouse.

They all rushed up the stairs leading to the cabin. Winston trailed, cursing softly when he stared up at the steep flight. Over his shoulder, Steve said, "I'm sorry about this. We'll get you back to the bar as soon as we can. This was the quickest route back to land and my SUV."

Winston waved him off and placed both hands onto the galvanized steel railings. "Don't mind me, young man. I'm old enough to piss and moan—and get away with it."

When they reached the top, Joe Wilton stood waiting on the lower patio. His eyes searched Edie's face. "You find Sampson?"

"The pod was empty." Edie patted Amber's head. "But we're pretty sure he was there. And he wasn't alone."

Joe scrunched his brows. "The phone at the state park worked okay. But the best I could do was to leave a message for Agent Finley." He shook his head.

"Apparently he's in the middle of something important. I got the damn national security story you guys like to recite. Told them who you were and what you were working on. The bureaucrat took the message. Said he'd have Agent Finley call you when he got the chance." Joe paused. "When I got back to the research facility, I saw Jimmy rocketing toward the cabin, so I drove Winston's car here."

Edie explained what they'd found in the pod and a brief account of Catori's revelations.

"Hell," Joe said. "That bureaucratic asshole in D.C. is going to be sorry he brushed me off."

Jimmy Martin said, "Fer chrissakes, Joe. We're talking about the federal government. They'll probably give him a raise and a big promotion."

"We need to hit the road, Joe," Steve said as they all headed inside. Standing in the family room, Steve shook Winston's hand. "Thank you for all your help. When we get back, I want to meet you in the Bottom of the Bay and buy a couple of rounds for the house."

"Glad to be of help, son."

"Edie," Connie said. "Joe and I are more than happy to take care of Rosa. If you say no, Joe and I are going to follow you guys. If you remember, I'm not such a bad shot, and I'm itching to bag me something besides those damn varmints." She kissed Edie's cheek. "Now, you go find your brother."

Edie nodded and wiped a tear from her eye. She ran out to the Escalade and brought back the rest of Rosa's belongings and gave her baby a big hug. By the time she got back to the SUV, Steve had the engine started; Catori and Amber were sitting in the back seat.

Jimmy Martin leaned into Steve's window. "You sure you don't want me to join you guys?"

"Thanks, Jimmy. You've been a great help, but where we're heading, things could get a little complicated."

Steve glanced in the rearview mirror at Catori. He slammed the SUV into reverse and backed out of the driveway.

CHAPTER 40

STEVE BACKTRACKED ALONG THE NARROW road through Bayview and out to the highway cutting across Farragut State Park. Edie continually checked her cell phone for service. When they reached US 95, Steve headed north. He didn't have to ask Catori if she was sure of their destination.

Edie's face brightened. "Steve—I've got a cell sig—" Before she finished, Steve's cell phone buzzed. He hit the Bluetooth button on the steering wheel and Mike Finley's voice filled the SUV. Amber barked and placed her front paws on the middle console.

"What the hell is going on, Steve? I've been trying to get a hold of you ever since the office contacted me. What's this about bringing a team out to investigate a Naval research facility in the middle of Idaho? Does this have anything to do with Edie's brother?"

"Listen, Mike," Steve said. "It's more than a request to investigate. This is not only about Sampson: you need to get out here now. It's the first lady—we found—"

Finley interrupted. "Alison and Brianna? Hang on a second." Steve heard Finley shouting orders to someone. To Steve, he said, "Go ahead."

Steve swallowed. "They were here. And so was Sampson. But they're gone now. Like in Maryland. It looked like another dead-end, but we've got a possible lead on where they were taken." He glanced at Catori, and in a more forceful voice said, "Mike. We've got solid information that the first lady has been taken to Canada.

We're heading there now. Just left Bayview, a small town on the southern end of Lake Pend Oreille. We're about an hour and a half away from the closest border crossing. And then another thirty minutes from where they're keeping the hostages. Where the hell are you?"

"I was about to check out the last site from the shipping manifest we found in the museum warehouse in D.C. The other three turned out to be dead-ends; like everything else. The last one's in Tacoma, down the road from Seattle. It's a longshot, but we had no other leads. We were on final approach to Sea-Tac Airport. And now we're about to join up with you guys. Hold on." Steve listened to more muffled conversation. "Okay, Steve. You anywhere near Sandpoint, Idaho?"

Catori answered. "We're about thirty minutes away."

"Good. Drive to the airport—and stay put."

CHAPTER 41

TWENTY MINUTES AFTER ENDING THE call with Mike Finley, Steve drove the rented Escalade over the narrow viaduct onto the northern shores of Lake Pend Oreille. A short time later he stopped in front of an obscure general aviation building near the north end of Sandpoint Airport. Steve spotted the letters *CBP* imprinted on the white fuselage of a Bell UH-1 helicopter parked on the side of a small hanger.

He scanned the western skies and observed a Gulfstream making a steep bank for its approach to runway one. The sleek craft carrying Agent Mike Finley dropped in hard, skimming over treetops and lines of parked school buses. White puffs accented the wheels grabbing onto the tarmac.

Edie and Catori stood close to Steve, shielding their eyes from the harsh rays reflecting off the gleaming aircraft as it taxied toward the waiting U.S. Customs and Border Protection helicopter.

Finley hurried down the Gulfstream's extended stairway. Amber sprang forward to greet him. He tussled the dog's neck and double-timed his strides toward the anxious group.

Steve took two steps toward him and spoke first. "Hey, Mike. Good to see you." He twisted his head at the Huey. "I'm guessing the chopper's our transportation. Glad we waited for you."

Finley raised his arms, both palms held out. "Whoa, Steve. I've got the wheels in motion, but we need an agreement in place with our neighbors to the north. Neither DHS nor the U.S. Border Patrol can just swoop into Canada and orchestrate a raid. This isn't like we're protecting the border or chasing drug runners."

Edie stepped next to Steve. "Mike. Are you going to tell the president his people are sitting on their asses because of some bureaucratic process while his wife and daughter are held captive by terrorists?"

"You know damn well Griffin's screaming bloody murder about this whole thing, but we can't start an international incident until we're positive they're being held on the other side of the border." In a calmer voice, he added, "Give me something to work with." Finley's eyes flashed between Steve and Edie.

Catori was still standing to the side with arms wrapped around her chest. "Look at me, Mike." She placed her hands on her hips. "I'm what you've got to work with." She walked up to Finley: so close her neck craned as she looked into his eyes. "The information we've got can only tell you where the first lady, Brianna, and Sampson have been. If you insist on waiting for solid, physical evidence of where those bastards took them, you're going to find them dead."

She reached out, touching his arm and then pressed both hands across her heart. "I can lead you to them. It took a while for it to fall into place." She glanced at Edie before continuing. "I missed the signs at first, but now everything makes sense."

Catori shrugged, a weak smile passed quickly.

Steve jumped in. "Besides, Mike. You've got nothing else. Otherwise, you wouldn't be wasting taxpayer dollars flying all over the country grasping at straws."

"Mike," Catori said. "I can see the location as clear as I see your face." Her eyes stared without blinking. "I'll get you close." She pointed to Amber. "And I'm willing to bet, she'll bring home the jackpot."

Finley let out a long breath. He nodded. "I guess I can live with that. But—" He raised a single finger in the air. "There's the minor issue of putting together a task force with the Canadian authorities and assembling a strike team. That could still slow things down."

"I don't think that's a problem, Mike," Edie said. Since reconnecting to the internet, she'd been busy working on her tablet. "We get on your chopper. Then make a quick stop at the Kingsgate Border Crossing and ask one of the Canadian Mounties to assist us on a joint operation. That's all the approval we need."

"What the hell are you talking about?" Finley asked.

Edie turned her tablet around and shoved it near Finley's face. "See this? It gives us the ability to act immediately. For once, the legislators did something useful." She tapped the front of the tablet and handed it to him. "Read it, Mike."

Finley read through the text, nodding slowly and then looked up shaking his head. "I don't think so, Edie. This agreement is for a very specific purpose."

"I realize that."

"We can only be granted jurisdiction over the border if we're part of a joint vessel patrol on shared waterways. Look at the title of the agreement: *Integrated Cross-Border Maritime Law Enforcement Operations.*"

"I realize that," Edie repeated.

"There's not a body of water within miles of this border crossing—let alone spanning international boundaries. The basis of this legislation is to improve border security in the Great Lakes region." Finley waved a finger. "And don't give me that same line again."

Steve said, "You need to understand how we think they transported the hostages across the border."

"I'm listening," Finley said.

Steve directed Finley to the hood of the Escalade and opened up a nautical chart of Lake Pend Oreille, along with maps of the Idaho panhandle and British Columbia. "We've come to the conclusion Lake Pend Oreille is directly linked to a lake in Creston Valley." He shuffled around the papers, pointing out the locations. He unfolded the torn paper found in the submerged pod. "These coordinates correspond to an underwater route leading in a northerly direction from Lake Pend Oreille. The last coordinates and depth readings are cut off right in this area." He indicated the position on the map.

"And where's the evidence suggesting this route continues, not only across the border, but up to this particular lake?"

Catori tapped Finley on the shoulder. "Again, that would be me."

Finley rubbed his hands over tired eyes and sighed. "Damn. And how in the hell am I going to convince the Canadians about all this?"

Edie said, "If we got probable cause to think they transported the victims across the border via a common body of water, that's enough to justify the immediate launch of a joint strike team. I'm sure you can get an unsuspecting Canadian working at the border to take a little ride. You only need the presence of one law enforcement official from the Canadian side to validate our jurisdiction. With your renowned powers of persuasion, that person doesn't need to be made aware of the precise mission until we're far enough into Canadian territory."

Finley walked away from the Escalade.

He took a dozen steps and turned back. "Okay, let's board the chopper before I come to my senses." He slapped the side of his head. "Jesus Christ. I can't believe I'm about to kidnap a Royal Canadian Mountie. I won't even get the chance to turn in my retirement papers. Maybe I'll at least get to keep his hat."

CHAPTER 42

THE BLADES ON THE HUEY rotated, gaining momentum. The engine's vibrations escalated, and the lumbering aircraft jolted and rose.

Before the ground grew smaller, the helicopter shifted attitude and shot forward, barely clearing the closest hanger and flirting with a number of power lines. The heavy bird hugged the treetops, sliding over intervening peaks and gorges like a rollercoaster. During the short flight, Steve, Edie, and Catori remained silent while Finley rapid-fired a number of calls.

In a clearing near the Kingsgate Border Crossing, the Huey touched down long enough for several armed U.S. Border Patrol agents and a single Royal Canadian Mounted Police officer to climb on board. As the chopper flew across the Canadian border, a second Huey holding additional U.S. agents shadowed its flight.

This second helicopter soon broke off on a northerly path toward the narrow lake to perform a high-altitude flyover and check out the large stone mansion perched on the eastern shores. If conditions permitted, they'd insert personnel for a more precise surveillance of the target.

The helicopter carrying Finley and his passengers set down in a remote valley on the far side of the western ridges bordering the lake. Plans would be finalized once the second helicopter completed the initial reconnaissance flight.

The sole Canadian, Corporal Roy Tremblay, had made several attempts after boarding the helicopter to verify the authenticity of the joint mission, along with who and where the target was located. Finley had replied by telling Tremblay to deposit all communication devices in a locked container to prevent any accidental transmissions from jeopardizing the integrity of the operation.

After landing, Tremblay lost his patience and demanded answers.

The young Canadian officer had been on the job for less than three years. He stood two inches shorter than Finley but exuded an almost equal amount of fire in his blood. His training had taught him to restrain from using it until he understood the entire situation. Standing on Canadian turf with this small band of American cowboys—and cowgirls—he would need every ounce of that training to maintain his composure.

The Mountie removed his hat and held it with both hands over his belt buckle. His thick, light brown hair and neatly trimmed sideburns framed a handsome face. He remained silent, eyes glaring into Finley.

Finley glanced down at the hat and then nodded to Tremblay. With a subtle gleam in his eyes, he turned to Edie and Catori.

"Ms. Pauling and Ms. Torrence. You have my permission to brief the corporal as to the nature and the scope of this mission while we wait for the second helicopter to report in."

He ignored the shocked looks on their faces and continued. "Remember, this is a highly sensitive operation, authorized by the president of the United States. Do not say anything to compromise what we are about to do."

He walked far enough away to avoid the inevitable protests from the Canadian representative.

Corporal Tremblay bristled at Edie's attempt to justify the utilization of the maritime agreement for the basis of the joint operation, insisting he didn't see anything in this so-called mission coming close to being cooperative.

Catori had been studying Tremblay's reaction to Edie's pleads. In a quiet, but firm voice she asked him to sit on a nearby rocky outcropping. After waiting for him to settle down, she then wove her incredible tale from the beginning.

While telling the story, Catori never once took her eyes off Tremblay.

Edie drifted away and found Finley.

"What do you think they'd charge us with if we cuff him to one of those trees?"

Finley didn't answer.

"Seriously, Mike, if we're this close to finding them, we can't let anything get in the way."

She bit her tongue and continued, "Mike, I caught only a glimpse of what Catori saw in her visions—we don't have much time. I can feel it. We can't wait for back-up or a legitimate authorization." She paused and glanced at Catori, seeing the intensity on her face. "I trust her. She's saved the day more than once."

Finley's lips tightened. "You think I don't remember? That's the only reason I'm standing here listening to you guys." He waited a second and then added, "The president gets it too. He told me to act on my instincts."

When they both looked back at Catori and Tremblay, they noted a change in the corporal's demeanor. He was nodding his head vigorously and making strong gestures with his hands.

"On the surface, I'm a pragmatist," Tremblay was saying as Edie returned.

"But," he continued, "this vision you described about an underground river linking these two bodies of water? To me, it's not an absurd tale."

The droning rumbles of a distant helicopter grew louder. They looked up and saw the chopper returning from its surveillance operation.

"We don't have much time," Tremblay said. "So I'll make this brief."

His voice became animated as he spoke. "When I was a boy, I helped my father in our tavern. It's been in the family since the early nineteen hundreds. Back then it was also an inn, owned by my great grandfather. The stories he told have been passed on to my grandfather, my father, and then to me."

Edie sat down next to Catori, her eyes glued on Tremblay.

"Shortly before my great grandfather died, there had been a young Russian immigrant staying at the inn until he found a more permanent residence. One day the Russian brought my great grandfather a gift: a fish he picked up on the shores of his private lake. An eagle had supposedly dropped it." Tremblay paused, seeing the expression on Edie's face as she turned to Catori.

Catori's face remained impassive. In a low voice, she said, "The lake next to the large stone house I've seen in my vision."

It wasn't a question.

Tremblay swallowed before continuing.

"The locals didn't consider this fish indigenous to the waters in Creston Valley. The native tribes who once lived in the region believed it to be sacred, coming from the gods. According to the legend, eagles brought the fish as a sign of a new destiny for the tribe. The ancestral ghosts fled these valleys and disseminated to the south. The fish represented a vast underwater route symbolizing the journey of the dead. The living members of the tribes, who roamed the surface and followed the visions of their ancestors, encountered another creature."

He stopped as if grasping for a name.

"Coyott," Catori whispered, "the ghost of the ancient god of light."

Tremblay nodded, his eyes bulging. "Yes, they believed this creature to be deceptive. Sometimes it helped; sometimes it would lead them on disastrous journeys."

Amber padded up to Tremblay and rested her snout on his lap. Tremblay looked at the white German Shepherd, and then at Edie.

Edie shrugged. "Someone once said Amber bears a resemblance to this mythical creature, and at times, she can also be a trickster."

"At first, the Russian laughed at my great grandfather," Tremblay said, keeping an eye on Amber. "Looking for answers he couldn't find, the Russian became consumed with watching the great eagles hunting in the waters of his lake. Although my great grandfather considered it true, I'm not convinced the legend is factual. But from this and other tales he told, I do believe in the existence of vast underwater networks beneath us."

Catori placed a hand on Tremblay's shoulder. "Your great grandfather's story may be flawed, but it is, in essence, the legendary basis of my tribe's beliefs. Part of which I only learned recently."

Tremblay watched the helicopter land and the blades spinning down. "I don't know if those three Americans are being held captive on that property or how they got to Canada. But if there's a chance they're in the Creston area, I'd like to be a part of this. You Americans don't have sole ownership to probable cause."

CHAPTER 43

ONE AGENT EXITED THE HELICOPTER and jogged over to Mike Finley and Steve. "What's the situation look like?" Finley asked. He glanced at the helicopter. "And where are the rest of your guys?"

Agent Mitchell gave Finley a slight nod. "We've observed a minimum of three people at the site. All located inside the space adjacent to the floor-to-ceiling windows along the rear upper deck. Could be additional personnel, but it's been difficult to get any clear imaging from inside the house. The outer walls are solid rock and absorb most heat signatures. So far, there's been no further images picked up through the other windows. And we can't confirm anybody's being held captive inside."

Mitchell paused, listening to an incoming communication. "There's a small airfield. It's vacant. Also a dock and boathouse. Nobody inside. The structure's large enough to house a substantial cruiser. The lake is not very big, so I'm not sure it makes sense for something that size."

He hesitated. "Back to the number of bodies. You'd think if they had the first lady, they'd have a hell of a lot more guards. The other thing is there's no indication of any high-tech security systems. If this is supposed to be a sophisticated group capable of snatching the first lady two blocks from the White House, they're being damn sloppy."

Finley nodded but remained silent. Edie, Catori, and Tremblay joined the group.

"What else you got, Mitchell?" Finley asked.

"We inserted Cocheran and Swazy about a mile from the house. They'll set up surveillance: inform us if anybody comes or goes. Swazy's one of our best snipers. He's going to move in as close as possible. He didn't see any good spots. No high ground. The house is in an ideal position. And it's like a fortress. No way we can get close without being spotted. Maybe that's all the security they think they need. Swazy's going to work his way over to a dense grove of cottonwoods about a hundred yards north of the house. I got Cocheran covering the only road leading to the place."

"Good work, Mitchell." Finley turned and walked away, reaching for his secure satellite phone.

Steve was grilling Mitchell for more details when Finley returned. "Give us a minute," Finley said to Mitchell and Tremblay. After they'd distanced themselves from the others, Finley handed the phone to Edie, pulling Steve and Catori aside.

They watched Edie running fingers through her hair and kicking the dirt but didn't catch any words. Steve turned to Finley. "Talk to me, Mike. We're running out of time."

"The president's made the decision," Finley said, glancing at Edie. Finished with the call, she took a deep breath and headed back. "Since Edie's brother is also being held hostage, he wanted to explain things to her personally."

Finley took the phone from Edie and stuck it in his pocket. Edie grabbed Steve's hand, her eyes never wavering from Finley's face. He returned her stare but remained silent. She gave him a slight nod and looked up at Steve. "Things are happening in Washington. The whole world is about to ignite. In thirty minutes, the president heads to New York to address the United Nations. The terrorists have given him the script. Israel gets thrown under the bus, and he's supposed to let it all play out. They want the United States to defer all authority to the United Nations." She reached out and touched Catori's arm. "If there's any possibility Alison, Brianna, and Sampson are in that house, he wants us to move now. I told him we had no doubts."

Edie paused, squeezing Steve's hand harder, and addressed Finley. "Mike, Tyler says it's your show. Lay it out."

Finley signaled for Mitchell and Tremblay to rejoin them. "The president is fully informed of the situation we're facing. When I updated him on what you found in Bayview and how we wound up in Canada, he came to the conclusion that he's either been deliberately misled by the terrorists or something's changed. Either way, time has run out. We go in now." He looked at Mitchell. "Any updates from your guys?"

Mitchell shook his head. "Everything's quiet. They still can't confirm the exact number of bogeys or if there are any prisoners."

"And you see no way to go in without them spotting us?"

Mitchell confirmed his assessment.

Finley pursed his lips and spoke. "Okay. This is what we're going to do."

CHAPTER 44

BARTHOLOMEW HAD GROWN TIRED OF the man's complaints and accusations. Not for the first time, he wondered how his grandfather put up with the arrogant bastard. He remembered when he met Aamir Rahaman. It had been right here at his grandfather's estate overlooking the pristine lake in Creston Valley: over a year ago. Bartholomew had pretended not to listen to Rahaman's condescending remarks or his air of superiority.

When he had pulled the trigger of his favorite sniper rifle and felled that magnificent creature, one of the last remaining bald eagles in the region, he imagined turning the rifle on Rahaman and placing a bullet through the imbecile's forehead. He sensed that time could now be soon.

For an instant, a cold wave of fear washed over him. When he looked out on the lake, he got an ominous sensation, not the usual calm and reassuring reaction to the familiar sights. But like on other occasions, he chose not to be distracted by anything contradicting his current agenda.

"You are a fool, Bartholomew," Aamir Rahaman spit out. "We are on the verge of bringing the United States government to its knees, and the Israelis will be forced to act on their own. The beginning of the end for all infidels." A look of disdain spread across his face. "How dare you move our prisoners at the last moment before victory."

"Perhaps Grandpa saw a fatal flaw in your plan, Aamir." Bartholomew didn't try to hide the sneer.

The third man in the room, remained seated in the corner watching the large TV screen, concentrating on the latest news bulletins out of D.C. and New York. Bartholomew glanced over to the sound of a reporter's voice describing the scene on the White House South Lawn as the president prepared to fly to New York. Once he spoke to the United Nations, the chain of events would be finalized; the inevitability of World War III a reality. He smiled to himself.

Bartholomew's response to Rahaman had not been truthful. Grandpa, or Mr. Clean, as he was known to Aamir Rahaman, did not initiate this latest change. He had no idea the prisoners had been removed from their underwater hideaway near Bayview.

Once again Bartholomew had acted alone. In recent months he had observed subtle changes in his grandfather. Time had taken its toll. For years Bartholomew watched as his grandfather's physical health declined and the strong image withered into a shell of the once powerful man.

This Bartholomew accepted. It was the more recent apparent unraveling of the old man's mental acuity that had disturbed him. The bouts of confusion and sudden lapses had become more frequent. At least that was Bartholomew's perception. So, he had acted.

"This is insane," Rahaman continued. "I was about to join your grandfather with the others. We had everything in Bayview secured. The meeting to discuss the final phase has been scheduled. I spoke to him right before you showed up. He said nothing of any changes."

"There was no time for any explanation, Aamir. Trust me, this is for the best."

"But I must call my men. We need to strengthen our position. This place is vulnerable, and we cannot defend ourselves. The prisoners must be guarded."

"We are safe at this location. No one has any idea who owns this estate. Even you don't know the real identity of my grandfather." Bartholomew smiled. "And the prisoners will never be found in this house. The previous owner failed to follow through on his dreams, but with the modifications we've made, the accommodations are quite suited for our needs."

The man who had been glued to the TV screen tilted his head and looked out the large window facing the lake.

Rahaman glanced at his watch. "Where is my transportation? I insist on being taken to your grandfather. By this time, everyone else has arrived at the location." His eyes followed the other man's movements toward the window. He looked skyward. "Is that a plane? This must be my ride. With the right connections I can still make it to the meeting in time."

Bartholomew looked at Rahaman but didn't speak. He too had heard the distant drone. But he also knew no transportation had been arranged for Rahaman. At least not off this property. He had more immediate plans for this detestable character.

As the thumping sounds grew louder, he recognized the distinctive signature of a helicopter. He turned to the other man. "Go check it out, Rick."

Rick grabbed the binoculars from a large storage bunker near the patio door and stepped out onto the deck. Bartholomew and Rahaman walked over to the glass doors but remained inside.

Rick pulled the binoculars to his eyes and focused on the slow-moving helicopter approaching from the south. It hung at a fairly low altitude, making broad arcs along the lake. They could feel the expansive windows facing the lake begin to vibrate from the growing low-pitch buffeting from the incoming chopper. Rick swung the binoculars around but there were no other aircraft. The skies were clear.

"What have we got, Rick?" Bartholomew asked.

"It's a Huey. Ahhh… looks like a U.S. Border Patrol emblem on the side."

Rahaman grabbed Bartholomew's arm. "You have proven me correct and have destroyed all we have accomplished. You led them right to your door!"

"Relax, Aamir. I've seen this before. Sometimes the U.S. Border Patrol runs maneuvers with the Canadians. Usually a Canadian chopper accompanies them, but… it doesn't look to be a threat. And there's no way anyone could've discovered the prisoners had been moved to this location. We've been running these subs back and forth for over a year now. You know for a fact how many of your men we've smuggled in and out of the United States." He aimed a good part of those sentiments at calming down his own reservations.

The helicopter shifted course and slowed. This heading brought it closer to the house. And it gradually lost altitude.

Rahaman, ignoring Bartholomew's words, screamed louder, his eyes darting from the chopper to the bunker by the door. "It is going to land. Is this a part of their exercise? We cannot let it happen."

Bartholomew's face tightened. He swallowed hard before continuing. "I believe my grandfather mentioned that on occasion border patrol helicopters have set down here before. He has tried to maintain good relations with the local authorities. This should not be a problem. We need to remain calm. Show them we have nothing to hide."

The sweat now began to flow freely down his neck, dampening his shirt.

Eyes glazing, Rahaman turned away from Bartholomew; he reached into the bunker, pulling out an assault rifle and stumbled out to the deck.

Bartholomew charged after him.

Rick dropped the binoculars from his face and stared at Bartholomew and Rahaman. In a rage, arms shaking, Aamir Rahaman raised the weapon toward the helicopter.

As the first round blasted from Rahaman's rifle, his body stiffened, and the weapon flew from his hands, crashing to the deck. The entire front of Rahaman's face exploded, and he collapsed.

In the next instant, Bartholomew and Rick mirrored Rahaman's last actions. The approaching helicopter dropped in fast before flaring and hitting the ground hard on the expansive lawn on the north side of the stone house.

Bartholomew and Rick lay sprawled on the deck next to Rahaman's body. They never saw the second helicopter materialize over a ridge on the western shores of the narrow body of water.

Rivulets of blood cascaded between the deck boards and splashed into the lake waters, mingling together as the waves driven by the percussions from the helicopter lapped against the shore beneath the cantilevered deck.

CHAPTER 45

WHILE THE LATE AFTERNOON SUN cast long shadows off the gleaming white fuselages of the two U.S. Border Patrol Bell UH-1 helicopters in the remote valley a few miles north of the U.S.-Canadian border, the silhouette of Marine One on the South Lawn of the White House melted into darkness as daytime hues gave way to the graying night skies.

Mike Finley faced the small group and outlined his plan for approaching the lakefront estate in Creston Valley. His voice confident, belying the tension etched in his eyes.

Steve stepped forward and started to protest, but Finley held up a hand. "We can't go blazing in with two choppers: too damn threatening. We want them to see us and make up their minds we're on a routine patrol: not an assault team raiding the property."

"I'm not questioning that, Mike. But Amber and I should be on the first chopper."

Before Finley responded, Tremblay added, "There's no way in hell you're gonna keep me from going with you. You forget? This is a joint international mission. And I'm the sole representative of the Canadian government."

Finley sighed and nodded. Edie's mouth opened, and Finley spun the rest of the way around to face her before any words spilled from her lips. His finger shook in her face. "Don't even think it, Edie. You and Catori are staying back in the second chopper." His eyes blazed into her. "And don't give me any of your feminist—sexist crap. You're civilians."

Finley lowered his voice, softening his next words. "I know it's your brother in there." His hand lightly touched her shoulder. "This is our best shot, and we don't have much time. You talked to the president. I'm not entertaining any more discussion on the matter. At most, you'll be sixty seconds behind us." He didn't point out that if things turned deadly, the pilot of the second helicopter had orders to immediately get them back across the border.

The blades on both Hueys began slow revolutions. Steve gave Edie a kiss and caught up with the other agents boarding the first helicopter. By the time he clipped Amber's harness into the restraint link, the blades had reached maximum RPMs and the heavy chopper lifted.

Edie and Catori waited only a moment before running over to the second helicopter. The first Huey made a gentle sweeping arc further to the west before circling back to approach its target from the southern edge of the valley. They were going to come in slow and loud, making themselves visible and as non-threatening as possible. Following Finley's orders, the pilot flew in a leisurely pattern, performing easy, gradual turns; weaving a random course, but steadily closing the distance to their destination.

Mitchell received intel from his two men on the ground. Cocheran's reports remained unchanged: no activity on the road. Swazy, hidden in the grove of cottonwoods, had managed to climb one of the huge trees. From this vantage point he had an excellent view of the rear deck and the main floor. His last transmission had been more confident about the number of people observed at the house.

Swazy spotted a man standing on the deck who had just pointed binoculars at the approaching helicopter. For the moment, no signs of any threatening activity came from the house.

Finley gave the pilot the order, and the Huey made another measured turn. It headed toward a large clearing adjacent to the north side of the house. In a protracted maneuver, the pilot flared the aircraft and prepared to set it down.

Finley waved and smiled at the man holding the binoculars. The man appeared calm, not particularly nervous about the approaching helicopter.

An instant later, additional activity stirred on the deck as another man scrambled through the patio door. He held a rifle in his arms. On board the helicopter, agents now had a clear view of the deck and the rear portion of the house. The pilot made a slight adjustment before making his final descent.

A third man burst through the door.

The first man dropped the binoculars from his face and stared at the frantic actions of the other two men on the deck. They saw the third man waving his arms at the man with the rifle, and his mouth opening wide. The movements of the second man on the deck turned even more agitated; his stride unbalanced and jerky. He started to raise the assault rifle.

Finley nodded to Mitchell, and Mitchell relayed the order.

Perched in the cottonwood approximately a hundred yards north of the stone house, Swazy let out a slow breath and squeezed the trigger. He repeated the exercise two more times. All three men on the deck dropped from the precisely placed shots.

Even before the struts of the first Huey crushed the thick blades of grass, the second helicopter shot over the hills on the western side of the lake, skimming the treetops and screaming toward the house. Thunderous echoes resounded up and down the valley. It set down close to the first helicopter.

Mitchell's two men maintained surveillance on the perimeter while the other agents swept through and cleared the house. They obtained more accurate thermal imaging pertaining to the inside of the dwelling—the house appeared empty. Swazy had been correct in his last assessment. And those three bodies were accounted for—dead on the deck.

Next, the agents quickly cleared the boathouse. They found a small submarine hidden inside—empty.

There were no signs of the first lady, Brianna, or Sampson.

* * * * * *

Catori stepped from the second helicopter and walked around the exterior of the stone house. She glanced at the lake, the nearby grove of cottonwoods, and the distant mountain peaks, but the house itself drew her in.

A sudden chill slapped at her consciousness; but it didn't come from the waning rays of sunlight. It emanated from another time.

A low, mournful chant filled her head. And hurt her heart.

Her gaze coalesced on the foundation stones. She reached out to touch a nearby cornerstone, expecting to feel the radiating warmth from the day's sunlight. Instead, she jolted back from the icy pricks stinging her hand.

More layers from her visions peeled back.

She once again witnessed the Russian, Dimitri Gruzinsky, as he fell from the hotel's balcony in Spokane in 1974.

His ties to this house remained great, but Catori bore a stronger bond to long forgotten ancestors who had lived, toiled, and died in this valley.

And were then driven from their homes.

Remnants from their graves formed the foundation of the Russian's house—and thereby his dreams.

And in the end—his death.

So obsessed with this house, Dimitri Gruzinsky expected to rest for eternity within the walls, held up by the countless gravestones torn from the ancient Ktunaxa's resting place.

When Catori next looked up, she found herself standing on the deck.

After noticing the others inside, she stepped around the three bodies, avoiding the bloodied decking planks, and walked through the door.

"We've checked the entire house, Catori," Finley said. "No signs of the hostages."

She could hear the frustration in his voice.

Edie stopped looking out the window. She turned back to the others. "Those guys on the deck must've been hiding something. Otherwise, why did they try to stop you?"

Catori stared at Finley. "Finding them has something to do with the Russian's obsession to be buried at this spot."

Finley let out a sigh. "If that's true, they could be anywhere. There are hundreds of acres to search."

Edie shook her head. "No—it's the house." She looked at Catori. "After you described bits and pieces from what you'd seen on that hotel balcony, I researched Dimitri Gruzinsky. He had chosen to be buried inside this house. When he found out it couldn't happen—because of the Canadian laws—he became despondent. He disappeared—until they discovered his body in Spokane."

Catori nodded and smiled thinly. "I believe I also came across that same information."

Up until now, the incessant barking of the dog restrained in the helicopter had been ignored.

Steve shrugged. "I'm going to get Amber."

CHAPTER 46

ANTHONY FUNETTI PACED ABOUT HIS cell in the Fairton Federal Correctional Institution, annoying his cellmate to no end.

"For chrissakes, Tony. Give it a rest." He glanced up from his magazine, ready to toss a shoe at Funetti. "You think because they assigned you a different mouthpiece, you're gonna get outta this joint anytime soon? Use your head. You were involved with an assassination attempt on the vice president of the United States. And now the guy, Tyler Griffin, is sitting in the White House. You screwed with the life of his sister and her husband—including her husband's family. Not to mention a few other less fortunate bodies getting in the way. I doubt Tyler Griffin is the kinda guy to live and let live. A new plea-bargaining deal's never gonna get you out. Relax and enjoy the place."

"Go fuck yourself. It's about time I got a real lawyer working for me. The loser they assigned me for the trial had been fresh outta law school, probably just got her first period. I think I coulda nailed her, if I wanted to put a bag over her head."

The cellmate waved the magazine in Funetti's face. "Pshhh, like she'd wanna fat pig like you touching her."

Funetti grabbed the magazine and crumpled it up. He took another look at the business card the guard had delivered to him yesterday. He pointed at the name. "James H. Edelstein. Finally, I got me a Jew lawyer. He'll make something happen. So be nice, and I'll refer your case to him too."

The cellmate shook his head. For a moment, a brief look of pity swept across his face. "Tony, I overheard what you was saying in the mess hall. I know about your brain tumor. That you don't got much time left. Just wanted to say... sorry."

Funetti swallowed and gave a quick nod but remained silent.

"You're still a fuckin' jerk though," his cellmate said and smiled.

Funetti had fought the odds. His partner, Marty Calebrese, had told him he'd die of a heart attack or his career choice. Fate had other ideas for the one-time union goon.

Calebrese had been the healthy one of the pair, but it didn't matter in the end. On that day when he took aim at the vice president from high atop the Statue of Liberty, Marty Calebrese had died from two shots coming from someone else's sniper rifle.

Tony Funetti had suffered only minor dog bite wounds from a crazed white German Shepherd. He had watched in horror as the dog licked dabs of Calebrese's brain spatter off that damn firefighter's head. Him and his bitch of a girlfriend—the journalist. He should've finished them off and piled their bodies next to the dead park rangers instead of bringing them up to the torch.

Looking back, who the fuck cared what Marty Calebrese had ordered him to do. Though he should've listened when Marty told him to shoot the dog. Wouldn't be sitting in this goddamn prison cell if he had killed the dog in the first place.

Funetti absently rubbed the scar on his arm as his head snapped back to the present. "That's more like it, asshole," he responded. "You were starting to talk like a little pussy there for a minute."

A guard banging on the bars interrupted their discussion.

Anthony Funetti, sometimes referred to as Tony Two-Step, was led down the long corridor, through several doors, and into one of the privacy chambers in the visiting room. The door slammed shut behind Funetti, and he walked over to the table.

The new attorney had his head lowered, sifting through a sheath of papers.

Without looking up, the man said, "Sit down, Tony."

Something about the man's voice sent a chill down the nape of Funetti's neck. He hesitated, but then slid out the metal chair. It made a sickening screech across the floor. Funetti sat down, leaning back in the chair and folding his arms across his chest.

Still not facing Funetti, the man continued, "I don't want to see you react in any way to make those guards standing behind the window suspicious." He placed his pen on the table. "If you do, I'll fucking strangle you. Then you won't need to worry about any cancer finishing you off."

Funetti let his eyes glance at the man's hands which looked weak and disfigured, but the tone of the man's words stopped him from disagreeing with the threat.

What the hell kind of lawyer is this?

He didn't even look like a Jew.

Funetti gave a slight nod and added in a tired voice, "I understand."

The man slowly raised his head and Funetti reluctantly met his eyes. His entire body felt as if it had been struck with icy crystals. He searched the man's face, sensing a familiarity, and also an imminent danger.

Finally, he shrugged and stretched out his arms, palms up. "So what gives?"

The man's lips turned into a smile that stopped before reaching the folds of skin under his eyes. "You remember Al Rozano, don't you?"

"Yeah, so?" Funetti's eyes became lost behind the slits.

"Well, Big Al worked for me. And that means—so did you." The man's smile transposed, showing rows of yellowed teeth. He leaned closer to Funetti. "You fucking squealed like a pig to save your sorry ass."

Funetti finally saw through the layers.

Instinctively, he pressed back away from the table.

"Holy crap. Philip Lucchesi? Head of the Consolidated Brotherhood of Tradesmen?" His mouth formed a perfect circle. He looked over his shoulder to see if the guards were paying any attention.

In a lower voice he said, "But you're fucking dead."

"You must be thinking about Jimmy Hoffa. But let me get to the point. First, if you weren't almost dead by now, I'd a put you in the grave myself for your chicken shit canary act. I'm willing to let bygones be bygones. And right now, you happen to be in the ideal position to take care of something."

Lucchesi's face closed in on Funetti. "Based on what happened on the Statue of Liberty's torch platform, you might find satisfaction from this as well. So this is what you're gonna do."

* * * * * *

"So how's your new Jew lawyer, Tony?"

The cell door closed behind Anthony Funetti. He'd sat in the privacy room with Philip Lucchesi until visiting hours ended. Having recovered from the initial shock of seeing the former national president of the CBT alive, and the realization Philip Lucchesi was not going to kill him on the spot, Funetti considered what Lucchesi had ordered him to do.

During the walk back to his cell, he concluded that he had nothing left to lose, nor did he have a choice in the matter anyway. It wouldn't be much of a stretch to understand a man like Lucchesi could probably have him eliminated in a heartbeat. For a moment, he toyed with the possibility of singing to the feds one last time, but he'd probably be dead before signing on the dotted line.

There would be a fair amount of pleasure doing this anyway. What better way to go out? He had always reckoned, if he got the chance, he'd put a gun to his own head before the damn cancer got the last laugh.

Funetti regarded his cellmate. "He ain't no Jew. And he ain't no lawyer. He's a walking corpse, much the same as me."

He looked out the cell door to make sure the guards weren't hanging around. "I need your help on a job."

CHAPTER 47

AMBER DIDN'T NEED TO BE re-scented.

She didn't need any commands or any encouragement. Least of all, she didn't need any leash to restrict her efforts.

The second Steve unbuckled Amber from the restraint, she bolted out of the Huey, spanning almost ten feet of open air before her claws grasped hold of the slippery turf. She leapt up the deck stairs. Steve stood watching as Amber disappeared inside the house.

Her barking never let up.

By the time Steve entered the house, Amber's barking sounded lower in volume but, if possible, more frantic. Steve grabbed hold of Edie's hand and they tried to catch up with her. The others followed.

During the earlier search, all rooms had been checked, cleared, and the doors closed.

They found Amber scratching a batten oak door at the far end of an old-fashioned pantry. When Steve pulled open the heavy door, Amber scrambled down the rustic wood staircase to a basement. He flipped on the switch next to the doorway, and the room flooded with a harsh bright light as Amber's tail-end skittered around the corner.

At the bottom of the steps, Steve and Edie picked up Amber's barks coming from the other side of an arched opening flanked by massive oak support columns. As

Edie flicked on the next light switch, Mike Finley and the others caught up with them.

They all peered at Amber clawing and lunging at another hefty oak door. A tarnished brass bar held the door shut.

Finley called to Steve. "These rooms have been cleared. This one," he said, pointing to the door holding Amber's attention, "is a dead-end."

Steve looked over his shoulder. "This whole investigation has been one dead-end after the other. It's time for a change."

He lifted the brass bar to the screeching sound of a rusted hinge. As he pulled on the door, the same horrid sound echoed again.

Amber didn't charge through the open doorway. Instead, crouching low, she padded across the threshold.

Finley had been right. Only one means of entry or exit. And they had just walked through it. The room measured about twenty feet square and had no windows. The outer walls were comprised of solid stone with firm joints, no decomposition or moisture evident. Thick, smooth plaster covered formidable interior walls. The exposed edges of the concrete floor revealed no cracks. An aged, oval sisal rug covered part of the floor's surface. Faded, but otherwise in good condition.

Amber circled the perimeter once. With her head in the air and mouth open, she channeled scent, concentrating the molecules deep in her nasal chambers. In mid-stride her body arched toward the center of the room and her snout swooped to the floor. She resumed barking, and the tenor escalated, becoming shrill and more determined.

Near the center of the room, her front paws dug into the rug. At the same time, her jaws worked at a feverish pace; sharp canines shredding the tough, natural fibers, obliterating the woven patterns.

As Amber continued her frenzied efforts, the others jumped forward and rolled, pulled back, shoved the rug aside.

At first the tight edges hidden in the concrete expansion joints went unnoticed. Amber's claws grated hard against the merciless floor. Several cracked, drawing blood. Steve and Edie knelt on either side of Amber, hands and faces flat against the cement.

"I'll be a—" Finley said. "We missed this."

"If this is an opening," Steve said, "I don't feel any air flow. It must be completely sealed." He looked at Amber, whose snout now appeared glued to the floor. "Well, at least mostly."

Edie concentrated on a scarred spot where a piece of Amber's nail stuck. She grabbed the utility knife clipped to her belt and scraped away more of the softer, and what looked like, recently mixed cement. Underneath the surface she found a recessed metal pocket embedded in one corner. Steve joined in, jabbing in another corner with the pointed edge of the pliers from his multi-tool.

Agents responding to Finley's commands gathered up tools from the chopper and, in a matter of seconds, they hooked hammer claws into two of the metal pockets and yanked the small, square section of concrete upwards and let it fall back away from the opening.

Peering inside, they discovered a ladder bolted to a lower wall.

And three familiar people staring back up.

If this was Dimitri Gruzinsky's crypt, he planned to spend eternity in style.

The subterranean space wasn't large, but was well-lit, containing ample food supplies and drinking water. It was also equipped with a modern ventilation system and basic plumbing fixtures. Apparently the new owners did some remodeling, as well as repurposing of the space.

Regardless, the first lady, Brianna, and Sampson wasted little time in climbing out of the modified crypt.

Sampson, last out, stared at the tears streaming down Edie's face. He took a deep breath and exhaled the words. "Beth? Is Beth okay?"

CHAPTER 48

FROM THE CONCRETE PRISON, THEY brought the hostages to the spacious chamber on the main level that overlooked the lake—and the three bodies on the deck.

Finley procured a secure satellite link to Marine One. The president's flight was now descending toward the Downtown Manhattan Heliport on Pier 6 for his upcoming address to the United Nations.

"Mr. President?" Finley said. "I've got two lovely ladies standing beside me who'd like to speak to you." He handed the phone to the first lady and walked to the far side of the room, looking out the west-facing glass. His head stayed discreetly turned from the first family.

Mike Finley had always admired the president and his relationship with the first lady. He now absorbed the intimate warmth coursing through the room. The relief the president experienced in knowing his family was finally safe traveled across the ether, filling Finley's own spirit with a tangible emotion, not a normal part of his usual daily consciousness.

In a rare moment of weakness, a hollow tremor shimmered through his body. A wave of envy for Tyler Griffin hit him in the gut. Not for the powerful position and stature afforded to the president of the United States—he wanted no part of that aspect of the man— but for the love Griffin shared with his beautiful family. This made Finley contemplate where he himself had gone wrong.

Staring out the window, Finley watched the sun dropping toward the western hills.

Had the sun already set on any opportunity he might have to fill such a void? Could he change things in his life?

He wasn't even sure if that was something he wanted.

Brianna's voice broke his reverie. In a matter of seconds, she filled the room with infectious laughter, gripping tears, and a quick bout of erupting anger. Finley was relieved to feel his own face relax and a small smile return.

This young girl had the makings of one fine future leader of the free world, or one hell of a ballbuster of a wife. Not that one excluded the other.

He breathed a sigh of relief and thought it was now up to her father to make sure the world remained in one piece long enough for her to get those chances.

* * * * * *

Earlier today, they learned Beth Dawson had been revived from her medically induced coma. Still groggy, she didn't remember any details of her assault. Many of her earlier memories remained clouded as well, but the doctors were confident her memory would return over time.

Although Beth's voice sounded gravelly and weak, it was still music to Edie's ears when she handed the phone over to Sampson. She couldn't bear to see the big fat tears flowing freely down her brother's face as he spoke to Beth.

Standing in the open doorway and facing the deck, she busied herself by watching Steve as he examined the three bodies cut down by the sniper.

Steve motioned to Finley, and Edie stepped aside to allow him to pass through the patio door. She noticed a peculiar haunting look on Finley's normally stoic visage.

Wearing vinyl gloves, Steve kneeled by the body of the man with the heavy beard and sifted through his pockets. Catori stood, arms folded, looking over his shoulder. When Finley approached the scene, Edie listened to Steve describe the various identifications held by the man. He cited one address given as San Francisco: the street and number matched the recently destroyed mosque.

From the way Amber had reacted to whatever hidden scents originated from the dead terrorist, she probably concurred with the fact he had at least visited those premises; somehow involved with the deadly chemical brews discovered there several nights ago. Steve recognized one of the man's aliases as Aamir Rahaman, the supposed attorney for the ICCA.

Sampson came up from behind Edie. "Thanks, sis. For a while I wasn't so sure I'd be seeing you again. But I should've guessed you guys were on the case." He put an arm around her shoulder and bent down to kiss the top of her head. His eyes shifted to the scene on the deck. Catori looked up and gave him a wave and a big smile.

Sampson nodded. "I'm guessing that young lady had something to do with the posse showing up at our doorstep."

"That's an understatement," Edie said.

"I tried thanking those two federal agents who're now holding a powwow over that bearded devil, but Steve and Mike told me to get a grip and stop with the mushy stuff."

"Powwow? So you're tired of making sexist remarks? Trying out nativist comments now?"

"What can I say?" He jammed a thumb over his shoulder. "After being confined with the two first females, I've exhausted my repertoire of thoughtful sensitive remarks pertaining to the opposite sex."

He slowly shook his head and pressed his lips together. "Edie, those damn Muslims got this all wrong. The way they treat their women. And it's a good thing for us. Because if they allowed them a smidgen of the freedom you gals get here—they'd no doubt whoop our asses."

"I guess for now I'll let the 'you gals' comment ride. I'm pleased your enlightened mental faculties are slowly returning."

"Damn," Sampson smiled. "This whole adventure has given me time to think about one thing in particular. It's convinced me to stay away from all natural bodies of water."

"Is that all you've learned?"

"Nope. Steve's been trying to talk me into buying his old RV. I'll be damned if I ever want to be inside anything resembling that underwater travel trailer again."

"Not even if it were only you and Beth cozied up inside?"

He smiled. "Well, that might be helpful in replacing those bad memories she's having trouble remembering. But only if I can first erase the image floating in my brain about you and Steve running from Nana's house and climbing into his RV. I don't want to think about what my little sister and that honky were doing inside that thing."

Edie playfully punched him in the arm. She noticed Steve had pulled off his gloves and stepped back from the bodies on the deck. She strolled over to him. They melted into each other's arms and held the embrace.

The first star of the night faintly glowed, punctuating the end of a long and trying day. At this moment, the looming world crisis lay light-years from her thoughts.

CHAPTER 49

AFTER MARINE ONE LANDED IN Manhattan, the president hardened his resolve during the short drive to the United Nations building. Finley's report from where they recovered the first lady and Brianna had him re-energized and steadfast.

He needed more answers to the larger questions, but it was time to act with conviction, put an end to the escalating violence in the Middle East, and prevent the world from tumbling into another global conflict.

Sitting at a negotiating table, compromising on ideals, and agreeing to an unending list of concessions had failed the previous administrations. The world was now a more dangerous place as history repeated itself. Each generation, believing they knew better than the prior one, fell into the same traps.

The president glanced out the window as his limo approached the United Nations Plaza. He saw throngs of people chanting and holding signs. It was utter chaos. Opposing sides whose differences could not be swayed. The president let out a breath as the limo swung away from the crowds and came to a stop near the guarded entranceway. The same irreconcilable differences existed on the floor of the assembly chamber as they did around the world.

A phalanx of secret service agents ushered him inside. President Tyler Griffin planned on demonstrating to the world that the United States of America would once again flex its muscles and take a leadership role in world events.

He was elected by the American people to lead this nation and wasn't about to hand over the White House keys to the United Nations.

The president advised his entourage that they'd be heading directly to the General Assembly chamber. There would be no briefing with the U.N. security council prior to his speech. He was at least fifteen minutes late and didn't want to keep the world waiting any longer.

His own advisors and staff appeared nervous. The president had no notes, and there would be no teleprompter. He hadn't leaked a word of what he was going to say to even his press secretary, who had been barraged by the media all day.

As President Tyler Griffin walked up to the podium, he gazed at the world leaders filling every table in the cavernous chamber and the gallery overflowing with spectators.

For a brief instant, Tyler Griffin visualized his grade-school class trip to the United Nations. He remembered the week of detention he'd received for walking up to one of the tables, removing his shoe, and pounding it on the top, shouting unrecognizable words in an attempt to mimic the infamous Russian leader, Nikita Khrushchev.

This time Griffin settled for a sharp rapping of knuckles on the podium. He began by looking over his shoulder and acknowledging the officials seated behind the striated green marbled dais.

After thanking the leaders of the U.N. for the opportunity to address the world leaders, Tyler Griffin drew a line in the sand.

"I ask you all to take a moment of silence to pray for the latest casualties in this unending siege on humanity."

A hush fell over the packed assembly room. He scanned the crowd, making eye contact with the Israeli and Iranian ambassadors.

He uttered no words for almost half a minute. "There are those among us who have hailed this latest atrocity as the moment to stand together and unite the world as one. And the only way to absolve our differences is to become a single entity. To look to the general council of the United Nations for guidance."

President Griffin paused and spread out his hands. "They would have the world believe that the root cause of conflict is based on national sovereignty. And dissolving nation-states would bring harmony—eliminate strife. We are told individual laws of a nation force us to take sides against each other."

Griffin reached into his coat pocket and pulled out a well-worn pocket edition of the Constitution of the United States of America. He held it out to the assembled crowd.

"I am the president of these United States. I have been elected by the people of my nation to protect and defend this particular constitution. And I have sworn on the Holy Bible to do so." He placed the book back in his pocket.

"No charter, no proclamation, no resolution brought forth by the governing bodies of this so-called world institution will ever change my job description. The U.N. was formed to provide a platform for nations to air grievances and provide a means to stabilize events and prevent wars. It appears this may no longer be the case. The time has come to remind the leaders of the United Nations of their responsibilities to their own countries."

The president pounded a fist, not a shoe, on the lectern. "Let me make this clear. There *are* differences in the great nations of this world. And there is *no* moral equivalency with those savages who promulgate and instill a state of fear. I am here to remind you—the United States of America will never tolerate or appease any terrorist groups, or any nation who sponsors those groups."

He looked directly at the Iranian ambassador as he said those words and continued. "The United States considers the recent attempt to hijack an international airliner and use it as a weapon of mass destruction on American soil to be a direct threat to our country. And most likely an act of war."

He now turned briefly to the Israeli ambassador. "The Israelis have even more reason to believe the same, following the latest devastation in Jerusalem. We will stand beside Israel and their right to protect themselves, as we plan to do for the United States as well."

When the president paused again, the Iranian ambassador stood and stomped out of the assembly. He was followed by at least ten more ambassadors from key Islamic states. "I am fully prepared to use my executive powers to stop any further aggressions and to act against any nation that continues to support terrorist activities."

His next words were like darts aimed at the back of the Iranian ambassador. "We will first start with Iran. We have in our hands sufficient evidence to implicate them in the two most recent attacks and, of course, their ongoing sponsorship of terrorist organizations."

The Iranian ambassador had reached the door when he spun around in disbelief and listened to the president's next words.

"When I return to Washington, Mr. Ambassador, I will inform my secretary of state that all negotiations regarding sanctions against your country, and the fruitless discussions to allow the U.N. to inspect your nuclear facilities will immediately cease. Your president will receive official word to this nature. Under the direct supervision of the United States military, your nuclear program will be dismantled. You will allow us immediate access to all nuclear facilities. Including military sites. By the time I return to Washington, our armed forces will be in position to enforce these demands. So, if your president and supreme leader choose to ignore this, I am prepared to initiate immediate military action."

President Griffin glanced at the Israeli ambassador. "Mr. Ambassador, Israel should continue to act in its own best interests, and rest assured, the United States will be there to support our allies."

CHAPTER 50

THE PRESIDENT OF THE UNITED States literally and figuratively held his finger on the nuclear button. Not since the Cold War confrontations more than half a century ago did the world wake up to the threat of nuclear annihilation.

Early the next morning, the Situation Room thrummed with heated activity. The frenzied arguments and screams of protest and fear were the same in that secure facility as what was being repeated over all media outlets, government chambers, barrooms, and every kitchen table throughout the world.

President Griffin prepared for the constitutional challenges and congressional hearings, but none of that would change the current dilemma. In less than twenty-four hours, the world could be engaged in the next world war. Griffin had vowed to confront the devil head-on and the line could not be moved. To do so would only serve to strengthen the enemy and cripple the ability of the United States to maintain its role as the sole remaining superpower.

This time, Griffin was not about to let history repeat itself. He would not sit back and appease the enemy until they grew too strong to defeat.

While the president's cabinet and key members of the congressional intelligence committees argued and threatened one another, Griffin stayed out of the melee, reading his daily briefs and sipping his coffee. He kept an ear on the heated discussions but liked to allow the arguments to run their course without any presidential input to cloud the thinking. He sometimes got his best advice by listening to the experts duke things out.

Griffin wasn't certain how this would end in the short term, but he still needed to anticipate the potential long-range consequences and what was at stake. He visualized the black and white pieces spread before him on a giant chessboard. But the grays got in the way. He feared unseen strings leading him like a puppet, moving pawns on a worldwide stage.

The president's eyes shut tight, and his hands rubbed tired lids.

When did this country lose control of its destiny?

The founding fathers had strived to ensure that the freedom and strength of future generations could not be subverted by a few corrupt individuals.

But what of an insidious scheme slowly eating away like an undiagnosed cancer?

Not a slippery slope, but an orchestrated program to strip away the fundamental beliefs and independence once guaranteed and preserved by a single document.

All the signs had been there, growing and digging into the moral and legal fiber of the nation.

Had the founding of this nation been a hoax? A cruel joke to set the stage for this very day? How many government leaders had been in on it or coerced to play a role?

Did they even know?

Was it too late?

Tyler Griffin had gotten his start in politics by taking the bait from a single comment made many years ago by his wife. He saw a group of local politicians in his hometown forcing one greedy project after another onto uninformed voters. Alison had told him to stop complaining and do something about it.

The stakes were now higher, the organizations he fought much larger and more dangerous, but he wasn't about to stop now.

He opened his eyes and looked over his shoulder. He riveted his gaze on the powerful image on the presidential seal. The bold, piercing eye of the bald eagle stared back at him.

Griffin was positive that the eagle blinked first.

When the door to the Situation Room's main conference center opened, no one except the president paid any attention. The terrified duty officer hesitated by the door before entering. The president motioned for the man to come in.

Like on death row, the duty officer marched over to the head of the long table where the president was sitting. With his hand shaking, he placed a single sheet of paper in front of the president and croaked out a weak message. Griffin nodded and the man rushed out the door.

The president's voice boomed over the loud discussions taking place. "Everyone please take their seats and hold off on your conversations—I understand the supreme leader of Iran will be transferred to our secure line. I believe he has a message for me."

EPILOGUE

CHAPTER 51

PRESIDENT TYLER GRIFFIN STOOD IN the sunroom of his colonial estate in Stillwater, New Jersey. His family remained busy around the isolated property, away from the media onslaught surrounding the harrowing events of the last several days. Following his historic speech at the United Nations and the showdown with the Iranian leaders, the president had taken a brief respite to   privately at the safe return of the first lady and Brianna.

An address to the nation was scheduled for later this evening, and the camera crews were due at the front gate within the hour. The president insisted on delivering his message in the sunroom, next to the woodstove and neatly stacked pile of firewood. He'd spent part of the morning splitting about a half cord of oak from several trees he'd felled on his property last fall.

This evening the president would present his case to the American people. He needed to instill confidence to the citizens of this nation, as well as the world. America would act as a superpower and prevent further escalations of nuclear threats by negotiating from a position of strength.

Before Tyler Griffin faced the nation, he needed to face his own family. He called them into the house and asked them to sit at the kitchen table, a fitting symbol of the importance of his family. When they had all taken their seats, the president—husband—father—looked each one of them in the eye.

He then settled his gaze on Alison and Brianna.

"There's something I need to say." He reached into his pocket and unfolded a copy of the terrorist's letter delivered to the White House by Badiyah Jamail. After a slight hesitation, he read the threatening words out loud. When finished, he closed his eyes, reliving the moment Finley had handed him the paper in the Oval Office.

"As it turned out...." He paused and a grim smile flickered for a moment across a drawn face. He then looked directly at Alison and Brianna. "You were rescued in time. But before that I had to make a decision. To do what the kidnappers demanded or take the chance they would kill you."

He picked up the sheet of paper, his hand shaking. "From the moment I read this note, to the moment Mike Finley called with the news you were safe, I wrestled with what to do." He ripped the paper up and dropped the shredded document on the table. He stared down at the pieces, willing them to disappear. "The fact that in the end I didn't have to make that decision doesn't change things."

Tyler Griffin pushed his chair back, stood up, and placed both hands on the table.

His voice faltered. "May God forgive me for contemplating such a choice. I'm still wrestling with what I would've done."

Several tears dripped down his face, and his family ran to his side. Alison cupped his chin and kissed him lightly. She pulled Brianna next to her and nodded.

Brianna, at first unnerved by the sight of her father's raw emotions, started slowly, "Dad, after Mom and I figured out why we were probably taken, and you'd be dealing with a major crisis…." She stopped and looked at her mother. "Mom told me she was confident you'd do the right thing, and if you didn't, she'd—"

"Make your life a living hell." The first lady finished Brianna's sentence. "We didn't fight this hard to get to the White House to let it all fall apart when things got tough."

A smile spread across Brianna's face. "You knew exactly what you needed to do." She tilted her head and waved a finger. "Of course, if you guys would've listened to me in the first place, Badiyah would've been long gone before any of this happened." She stepped forward and leapt into her father's arms.

* * * * * *

For now, a major crisis had been averted. The president's forceful response to the imminent threat from Iran had caused those leaders to reconsider America's role in world affairs. Inspectors from the U.S. military descended on Iran almost before the ink dried on the disarmament agreement. U.N. inspectors were allowed to observe, but they played no role in managing the process. American forces remained on high alert, ready to deploy to any potential threats at a moment's notice.

Tyler Griffin's message had been heard. The lesson had been learned. But a considerable amount of work still needed to be done. Taming this overt act of terrorism was a good place to start, but the insidious cancer infecting the world had spread, metastasizing around the entire globe. The Muslim Brotherhood represented a dangerous part of this movement, but other roots still lay hidden.

It was time for the Amber Alert project to take a major leap forward. Mike Finley had been given the green light to put unlimited resources on the covert project, however the nature and scope of the tactics and solutions would still remain guarded—until the infiltrated parties could be exposed.

In fact, the findings could be too damaging to the governments of many nations, including the United States. National trusts and international trade and commerce could be more crippled than fear from a worldwide military conflict.

CHAPTER 52

THE DOCTORS RELEASED BETH DAWSON from the clinic at Fairchild Air Force Base. Thus far, she remembered only small fragments of the events leading to her encounter on the gondola. She hadn't identified her assailant, but the Skyride attendant who'd worked that night made a positive identification of Bartholomew.

Sampson and Beth flew back to the East Coast. The doctors told them that getting her into a familiar environment might trigger her memories to return. She sensed she had important information for Edie but had no clue as to any of the details.

When shown a picture of the medallion that had saved her life, she stared at the indentation to the eagle's head made by the bullet but shrugged at the shattered computer chip.

With regards to this piece of the puzzle, her mind was no better than the broken memory card scattered at the bottom of the evidence bag.

Steve and Edie returned to their home in Sonoma. They gave the construction crew two weeks off. Most of the demo work had been completed and the place was beginning to shape up.

After a quiet dinner on the deck, Steve and Edie, along with millions of Americans, listened to President Griffin's address to the nation and his vows to keep the homeland safe and assure the world the United States would remain in a position of leadership.

Edie was finishing up bathing Rosa when Steve walked into the remodeled bathroom, slipping a little on the wet tile floor. She glanced up with an expectant smile, but it froze at the look on his face.

He handed her the phone, grabbed the towel, and wrestled with the task of drying off the baby. Edie sat on the edge of the tub and listened to the words of the former president, Alice Andersen.

Edie's mind transformed through a kaleidoscope of emotions. Tears streamed freely down her cheeks and one hand rested on top of her head, fingers twisting tight curls into her straight, black hair. Her lips trembled, twitching with an occasional brief, tiny smile. Edie thanked President Andersen and placed the phone on the vanity.

Rosa stopped squirming and stared at her mother, pulling away from Steve's arms. Edie kneeled down and pulled her baby close. Steve placed an arm around Edie and whispered, "I'm sorry, babe. How did it happen? Alice didn't say."

Before speaking, a parade of images danced through Edie's head. Most of them good—real good. This gave her strength. "Let's get this big girl to bed."

Later, Edie and Steve sat together on the leather sofa in the great room. Steve drew Edie close. Edie nursed the apricot sour Steve had prepared in honor of Nana. It had been Nana's favorite drink. But only on special occasions. Otherwise, she stuck with hot tea.

"Nana was visiting Alice on her farm in Virginia," Edie said. "Ever since Nana was a little girl, she wanted to ride a horse. She rode a pony once and always mentioned it while we watched those old western movies on TV."

Edie paused; a distant smile came and went.

"Funny thing is—she grew up on a farm, but they never owned a single horse. For her fifth birthday her parents took her to this place in Saddle Brook, New Jersey. The ponies would go around and around in wide circles inside a small corral. But Nana swore she was a cowgirl in the foothills of western Montana."

Edie stopped and listened, thinking she heard Rosa fussing, but then shrugged and continued.

"Alice said Nana kept begging her to at least go for a short ride. Late this afternoon, Alice's Parkinson's disease appeared to be behaving itself, so she agreed to take Nana on a peaceful ride across one of the pastures. She saddled up two of her most gentle horses, and off they went. On the way back, Nana's horse encountered a snake. The horse bolted for a fraction of a second, but Nana lost her balance and fell. She hit her head on a rock and never regained consciousness."

Wiping a tear and taking a deep breath, Edie said, "Nana's greatest fear was being laid up for months and dying in a hospital bed, helpless, with people standing around crying and carrying on. Said she'd do everything in her power to not let that happen."

Edie let a small smile spread slowly across her face. Steve hugged her tightly and kissed her forehead. After several minutes of sharing stories about Nana, he got up and made arrangements to fly back East and say goodbye to the person who most influenced Edie after her mother died at the hands of a drunk driver.

While Edie listened to Steve making the calls, a sudden chill coursed through her body at the abrupt image of Rosa riding the painted horses on the carousel at Riverside Park in Spokane.

She shook it off but wondered if a bit of Catori's influence hadn't been planted in her brain. Or even more disturbing—in Rosa's.

CHAPTER 53

VINCENT CASELLA, OR UNCLE VINNIE, had been a model prisoner. He'd adapted remarkably well during his tenure in the Federal Correctional Institution at Fairton. By boxing up the tough guy mentality on day one, he rode out his sentence in relative comfort, knowing on the outside, his family had transformed the businesses and the family's image.

He could live with that. There was no changing his own past. He had a nasty reputation for getting things done his way. Knocked a few heads around. Made more than a few enemies.

Uncle Vinnie's rehabilitation had nothing to do with the criminal justice system, except for his incarceration giving him ample time to assess his career choices and business practices. While locked away on unrelated charges to his typical methods of solving problems, he watched his businesses become legitimized and thrive.

His extended family had dragged the enterprises away from extortion, intimidation, and bribery. A close relative, Dominick Casella, had managed to transition all aspects of the diversified endeavors into profitable businesses. And he never threatened or killed anybody during the entire process. Uncle Vinnie knew this for a fact, since although Dominick was intelligent and hardworking, he didn't harbor any of the Casella criminal genes.

Somehow Uncle Vinnie possessed the last remnants of this colorful, though undesirable genetic family trait. But he was willing to accept that times had changed.

He knew that when he got out of prison, he would never practice law again, but that had been always just a means to an end. Although he'd never go so far as to think of himself as a law-abiding, respectful citizen, he'd give the family a chance to do so.

Through the prison grapevine, Uncle Vinnie learned that Anthony Funetti had also wound up at Fairton. The two had a history together, although they parted ways a number of years ago. In the early days, Uncle Vinnie and the local unions had a lucrative business arrangement. Anthony Funetti, a young wannabe wise guy working for the CBT union, had been bailed out on several occasions by Casella's law firm. Over the years, Uncle Vinnie and the union also parted company, as the result of unresolved conflicts of interest.

As it turned out, Uncle Vinnie played a role in identifying Anthony Funetti as one of the key union goons involved in a scheme to strong-arm Vice President Tyler Griffin's family business into unionizing. A plan that turned ugly, resulting in several deaths and a plot to assassinate the vice president to stop him from becoming a presidential candidate.

During the escalating union threats against Griffin Mills and Home Center, the company owned by the vice president's family, Tyler Griffin asked Steve Casella to do an independent investigation into incidents of suspected arson at several of the company's sites.

At the time, Steve knew nothing of his own family ties in New Jersey. Edie's persistent digging changed everything. All of a sudden, Steve was introduced to a brand-new family with a somewhat tainted background.

Steve and Dominick, during a surprise visitation to the Federal Correctional Institution, described the escalating violent incidents occurring at the Griffin Mills and Home Center. Uncle Vinnie recognized the typical union tactics at work and pointed the investigation toward Anthony Funetti and his partner, Marty Calebrese.

The paths of Anthony Funetti and Uncle Vinnie never crossed at Fairton. Uncle Vinnie continued to keep a low profile, counting the days till his parole hearing. He was ready to put his past behind him and let his family continue to run the businesses. There was no way Dominick could ever be coaxed over to the shady side of New Jersey politics and business. He'd come to admire Dominick's gentle, yet steadfast persona and grew fond of him, even though he'd never stop ribbing the poor boy.

Uncle Vinnie, one of the most streetwise products of his generation and chosen vocation, never saw it coming.

The day, sunny and warm, the recreation yard crowded. Activity around the basketball hoops bustled with pent-up energy. Uncle Vinnie strolled the yard, keeping to himself, except for casual conversations with several inmates and guards. Uncle Vinnie got along well with most of the correctional officers, and his exuberant personality encouraged bantering with even the seasoned personnel. He was detouring around one of the hoops, trying to avoid getting in the way of the younger inmates.

Admiring the clear blue sky, he didn't see the group of players bouncing the ball toward him. An instant later, the converging mass of sweaty bodies appeared to swallow him up. The swift moves of the players and their loud chanting masked and drowned out whatever happened in their midst.

As the crowd dispersed, Uncle Vinnie lay motionless on the ground. The games were usually rough, and inmates often took their knocks. It took several moments for anyone to notice the lack of movement, the unnatural position of the body, and the pool of blood seeping out from underneath Vinnie Casella.

Six months ago, the Fairton Federal Correctional Institution had upgraded their ambulatory treatment clinic. After gutting an unused administrative structure, they constructed a small, but fully functional hospital ward with a modern emergency center capable of handling most major trauma incidents.

This saved Vinnie Casella's life.

In a matter of seconds, the staff physicians got to work. If they had taken the time to transport him to one of the nearby hospitals, the blood loss would have been critical. Uncle Vinnie had been brutally stabbed in the upper abdomen, the shiv twisted up, penetrating his diaphragm and puncturing a lung. He also suffered a head injury from the impact with the concrete surface in the yard.

Quick surgical work had stopped the bleeding and stabilized his vital signs. He was on a respirator and suffered from a concussion. Prison doctors made the decision not to transport him to a major trauma center. After several initial medical crises and resuscitations, the doctors believed they had the situation under control and Vinnie Casella would make a slow, but complete recovery.

When the emergency procedures had been completed, they placed Vinnie in one of the hospital beds in the ward. In the bed next to him, Anthony Funetti rested during one of his chemotherapy treatments.

* * * * * *

The next morning Anthony Funetti returned to his cell. The chemotherapy treatment in the correctional facility's hospital ward left him drained, but he was still pissed. "What the fuck did you not understand?"

His cellmate put down the magazine. "What's your problem, Tony?"

"My problem? You almost got Casella killed. Your guys were only supposed to rough him up enough to land him in the hospital ward for a week or so. Not the morgue."

"This ain't a fine science. Not like you can interview the schmucks before you hire them. Besides, I thought you had a hard-on for the guy. Every time anybody mentioned his name, your face got all red and you screamed like a banshee. What would it hurt if the guy died? Is it so important for you to do it yourself?"

Funetti pointed a finger and nodded. "Oh, I'm gonna finish off the motherfucker when the time comes. You can bet your ass. But for now, I need him alive."

The cellmate put his hands over his ears. "Hey. I don't wanna hear nothin' about what you're up to. Me and the boys did the job. The less I know the better."

"Right," Funetti said with a smile. "Everything's arranged. I'll be going out like a man. Not giving the cancer a chance to rot out my brain."

CHAPTER 54

NANA'S FAREWELL PARTY TURNED INTO a great opportunity for the Paulings to celebrate her life. Through the tears, the three siblings, Edie, the youngest, Sampson the oldest, and Thomas the middle child, swapped stories of the woman who had touched their lives. Edie's stories were different than those of her two older brothers.

When their mother had died, both brothers had already been out of the house. Only fifteen, her mother's death had hit Edie the hardest. For the most part, Edie and her mother had been on their own. Her father, a Navy SEAL, spent a good deal of her childhood in other countries fighting terrorists. Nana had stepped up to the plate after the death of Edie's mother and guided the devastated young girl into adulthood.

It was only later in life, while Edie attended college, that she and her dad began to bond. That had been cut short when he died attempting to stop a suicide bomber from gaining entrance to the American embassy in Pakistan. Edie, traveling with her father, felt the rumbling of the bomb blast from their hotel room and knew she'd be returning home alone.

Once again, Nana was there to help.

Catori attended Nana's funeral and provided comfort to Edie and her family. From their first encounter with this inscrutable young woman, Steve and Edie never ceased to be amazed as they watched the strength and power emanating from this tiny angel.

Several days after Nana was put to rest, the family gathered in Thomas and Kristie Pauling's home on the outskirts of Morristown. Thomas had met and fell in love with Kristie Griffin, the president's sister, when working on the then Senator Tyler Griffin's reelection campaign.

Moments ago, Sampson and Beth had made a quiet announcement of their engagement. Sampson shed rare tears as he related the story of them visiting Nana with the news prior to her leaving for President Alice Andersen's farm in Virginia.

The men headed out to the poolside patio to drink to Sampson's engagement. Exhausted from all the excitement, Rosa crashed in her highchair, and Edie quickly transferred her to one of the guest bedrooms.

Returning, Edie noticed a peculiar, yet familiar look on Catori's face. Kristie and Beth shepherded Catori to the sofa but were at a loss of what to do next. Edie moved closer and gazed into Catori's eyes.

Catori glanced at Edie and then she reached her arms toward Beth. Probably thinking Catori wanted a little help to stand back up, Beth extended her own arms. Catori grasped Beth's hands and rose. Her eyes closed and she allowed Beth's arms to drop at her side.

Beth started to speak, but Catori's eyes fluttered back open, and she placed a hand against Beth's chest. Beth tensed, and then her body relaxed. Catori slowly removed her hand. She rested both hands on Beth's shoulder.

"You have a back-up."

Beth's face scrunched up.

Then her mouth opened.

She looked at Edie.

Beth's hands shook as they moved toward her chest. Fingers fumbled with the top two buttons on her blouse. She grasped the silver chain and pulled out the medallion. Her eyes focused on the front side of the silver object. She stared at the wheel of life symbol on the front of the medallion.

Beth nodded her head and she smiled at Catori.

With a sudden air of confidence, she flipped over the medallion and pushed her thumbnail into a narrow groove near the bottom. There was a tiny click, and she caught the memory chip in the palm of her other hand.

"Got your laptop handy, Edie?"

Curious at the spectacle taking place in the house, the men headed inside without finishing their drinks. They all huddled around the dining room table as Beth's fingers flew across the keyboard. Her memories returning faster than she could process. She attempted to access a number of the website links from the memory card. In almost every case she got similar results: it appeared the sites and databases she'd uncovered no longer existed, or their firewalls had been fortified.

She shrugged and turned to Edie. "No offense, Edie, but I could probably make more progress with my own equipment."

Edie smiled. "I think we can do better than that. This is my personal computer. My secure system is at home. I can't access sensitive information from this particular device. And the federal government frowns on my emailing pictures of Rosa over their so-called secure servers. Since we're closer to Maryland than California, I think I can arrange for you to play with the big boy toys at Fort Mead."

"The NSA? Now you're talking. Never been there physically, but I've spent a little time inside their databases." Beth looked at Catori and winked. "I've never tried your mode of transportation, although I've used the cloud from time-to-time."

Edie grabbed her phone. "I'll start things rolling. Make sure we get you the proper clearances."

Beth continued scanning through the data on the memory card and the returning synaptic messages barraged her consciousness. When Edie got off the phone, she joined Catori and Beth. Steve headed to the bedroom to pack and get Rosa ready for another trip. He made several calls of his own. DHS would have a helicopter waiting at the Morristown Airport.

He waited as the last call connected. "Mr. President? Ah, no... no. Not a problem. Edie appreciated the first lady and the rest of your family attending the funeral. When are you and Mike getting back from Tel Aviv? Great. I wanted to give you a heads-up. The Amber Alert project? I think it's about to pay off."

After briefing the president on the plan and asking him to drop a word with the agency, Steve finished packing and woke up Rosa. He signaled to Thomas who had volunteered to drive them to the airport. He dropped off the bags by the front door and caught part of the discussion from the dining room.

"I have no idea how much of this is fact or fiction. Once we find a way to access these organizations' databases, you can let the analysts dig through it. It's still coming back, but the connections you asked me about a few months ago? I'm sure I found solid links. Not only the terrorist ties to particular governments, but there are these peculiar links to this other group. It's still a little fuzzy, and my files aren't complete." Beth pointed to the screen. "Look at these names. Some prominent families involved in whatever this is."

Steve interrupted. "We should go, ladies. There will be a chopper waiting for us at the airport in about twenty minutes."

Edie arched her brows. "You trying to spoil me, Steve?"

"Oh my God!" Beth blurted out, preparing to shut down Edie's computer. "Sampson. Look at this."

Sampson peered over her shoulder and stared at the screen. He looked at Beth. "It's that bunch of rocks you wanted to take a look at. Wasn't it supposed to be the last stop on our magical mystical ghost tour?"

Beth nodded. "Yeah. I must've gotten the idea from searching one of those databases or websites." She shrugged. "Don't recall why though. The Georgia Guidestones. Let's make it the first stop on our honeymoon."

CHAPTER 55

STEVE'S PHONE RANG. HE CHECKED the caller ID before answering. "Hey, Dominick. It's been ages since we've talked. How are—"

"Steve, listen." Dominick Casella's voice sounded squeakier than usual. He was one of Steve's new-found relatives from New Jersey, and although they were close in age, Dominick appeared freeze-framed into the body of a gangly teenager still fighting the onset of puberty-driven, hormone-induced transformations. He was short, about five foot-five and as thin as a rail.

Dominick continued, "It's Uncle Vinnie. He's been stabbed. It happened right in the prison yard. He was in a bad way. Was on a respirator for a while, got a concussion—"

"Where is he now? Is he going to be okay?" Steve stood up and walked to the window of his hotel suite, looking out at the mammoth glass complex of the NSA headquarters at Fort Meade.

Dominick's voice settled down. "Yeah. They say he'll make a full recovery." He swallowed. "They're keeping him in the new hospital facility at the prison."

Steve checked his watch. He was waiting for Edie and Catori to return from the NSA. They'd finished getting Beth Dawson fixed up with a team of analysts and were about to catch a cab to take them to the airport. They were booked on a flight to San Francisco later this afternoon.

"I'm in Maryland, Dominick. I'll make arrangements for me and Edie to head up to Fairton. Probably can be there by early afternoon. I'll let you know the specifics after I make a few calls."

In the background, Rosa's complaints had escalated to a rock concert decibel level. Amber padded over to her with folded back ears. She changed her mind about interfering and loped into the bedroom, jumping on the bed, finding a cozy spot between the opened suitcases and piles of clothing.

"Thanks, Steve. It'll mean a lot to Uncle Vinnie to see you guys. Any chance you got the dog with you? I've shown Uncle Vinnie pictures of Amber. Says he had a dog like her when he was a kid. Can you pull some strings and bring Amber up to see him? Might put a smile on his face when he wakes up."

Steve grinned. "Yeah, I'll see what I can do." Amber had almost as much hospital time as Steve. Always a guest, not a patient. But never in a prison hospital.

As Steve ended the call, Edie and Catori walked through the door. Rosa immediately stopped crying. A big smile spread across her face. Her arms sprang out toward Edie.

Edie rushed over to pick her up. She turned to Steve, looking like she was about to scold him when she stopped at the serious expression on his face. He filled them in on Uncle Vinnie and then got to work canceling their flight and getting a rental car. Edie changed Rosa and finished packing. Catori insisted Steve cancel her flight as well. She'd join them and help take care of Rosa while they visited with Uncle Vinnie.

＊ ＊ ＊ ＊ ＊ ＊

The two-hour trip to the Fairton Federal Correctional Institution went without a hitch. Steve had called Dominick and he said he'd be at the hospital when they arrived. When they got to the prison, Catori jumped into the driver's seat to take Rosa to a nearby park. Steve figured that was a good idea. Even if they did let her inside—no sense trying to familiarize his daughter with the criminal justice system just yet. You never know if there were any recessive criminal genes floating around from Uncle Vinnie's generation. Catori offered to take Amber, but Steve explained his plan.

Edie looked at Steve. "You think they'll let you bring Amber in to see Uncle Vinnie?"

"Sure. Why not?" He attached Amber's lead, and they headed toward the building.

Fifteen minutes later, still in the lobby, Steve said, "Why don't you go ahead. Tell Uncle Vinnie and Dominick I'll be along shortly."

Edie smiled and patted him on the shoulder.

"We'll catch up as soon as the warden signs off on allowing a dog in the facility."

* * * * * *

Edie walked into the small hospital ward and saw Dominick sitting in a chair next to a patient who was hooked up to a multitude of monitors. She blinked away the familiar odors that reminded her of past encounters as a patient. The persistent beeps from the monitoring equipment echoed across the room.

Four of the six beds were occupied. Edie tried ignoring the two patients on the far side of the room who leered at her as she approached Uncle Vinnie's bed. The patient next to Uncle Vinnie lay on his side, facing away from her. He appeared to be either asleep or unconscious. Intravenous pumps with a barely audible hum pushed drugs into the man.

Before Edie reached Uncle Vinnie, Dominick looked up and smiled. He stood, and with an awkward movement stretched spaghetti-like arms around her. As thin as she last remembered, but at least he had replaced the vertical stripes for a less diminishing camouflage-patterned sweater.

Dominick released Edie and she stepped up closer to the bed. "How's he doing?"

Dominick motioned for her to take a seat. "Despite what we're seeing, the doctors say he's doing good. Took him off the respirator earlier today. By this evening they'll reduce the sedatives. Until then, he's pretty much out of it. He stirred earlier, but his words sounded slurred and incoherent." Dominick shrugged. "Probably having flashbacks of the old days. Mumbled about low-life thugs taking too many steps... something about no fun... and...." He raised his hands and waved them. "Like I said, he made no sense."

Edie stared at the strange expression on Dominick's face after he sputtered out those last words. "What's wrong, Dominick?"

He shivered a bit. "Nothing. Just got a weird vibe. So where's Steve?"

Edie had moved in closer to Uncle Vinnie, gently stroking the back of his hand. "He should be up in a little while. Getting a dog inside a prison hospital apparently is not the norm. They needed special permission from the warden."

"You sure it's the dog they're worried about? Every time I sign in, they get a funny look—like one Casella in this place is enough."

In the adjacent bed, still turned away from Vinnie Casella and his visitors, Anthony Funetti tried to listen to the conversation. He was fully awake and alert. He picked up a little of their words, but it was difficult to make out what the bitch was saying because the other two patients kept jeering and making obscene noises from the moment she'd walked into the room.

The normal debilitating effects from his intravenous chemotherapy treatment would not be a problem for him today. As soon as the nurse implanted the IV lines and started the drug infusion pumps, Funetti watched her walk away and then yanked out the needles, jamming them into the mattress.

He almost cursed out loud when the black bitch walked in by herself, but from what little he got out of the conversation, the other Casella would be coming soon. That made him feel good. If he was going out in a blaze of glory, it'd be good to off both meddling sonsofbitches along with the old man. The sniveling nerd would be icing on the cake.

Funetti smiled to himself. He had to admire the other old fart, Philip Lucchesi. Coming back from the grave: looking like the walking dead, but he still had connections. The assholes who worked in this damn prison were almost as corrupt as the inmates.

Not only did Lucchesi waltz in and out of the place pretending to be an attorney—with whatever fake ID and other papers he needed to show them he now represented Anthony Funetti—he fixed the hospital's schedule to make certain he was in this bed when the show started.

Funetti placed a hand under his pillow and double-checked the position of the knife left by one of the flunky guards. All he had to do now was wait for the younger Casella to stick his ass into the room.

He saw the picture come together in his head.

Steve Casella first. Then the black bitch. Pity there'd be no time to play with the merchandise before slitting her throat. He preferred the meaty Italian girls to a skinny little black girl, but this would be his last chance to clean his pipes.

He tried to refocus and stop with the fantasies. Too bad Vinnie was unconscious. Funetti had dreamed about getting back at that bastard for a long time. He would like nothing better than to be the last face Vinnie saw before his throat got sliced.

Funetti noticed a different sound coming from the hallway. Must be Casella. But there was something off about it, and a cold chill trickled down his spine. He shrugged it off as he sensed Vinnie's visitors turning toward the door. His mind became jumbled, and he made a last-minute adjustment to his plan.

He'd take care of the black bitch first, while she was looking toward the door. She'd be down and Steve Casella would be caught off balance. Funetti presumed he'd be finished before anybody reacted. He didn't think he had anything to worry about from the nerd. And, of course, Vinnie was already half dead.

The closest of the other two patients was mid-sentence in a seedy description of where and how often he wanted to stick it to the sexy little piece. The second patient had been busily jacking-off under the covers from the moment he had laid eyes on her.

Anthony Funetti grabbed under the pillow and latched onto the knife while yanking back the covers. For a sick, overweight has-been goon, he moved fast. Those thoughts almost made him laugh out loud.

The one patient stopped his incessant comments, but the other one kept on pumping. Funetti figured the guy hadn't gotten this close in quite some time, so nothing short of the electric chair could stop him now.

Funetti focused on his first target. His feet hit the floor between his and Vinnie's bed. He reached out to grab Edie's hair with his free hand and arched the knifed hand out, getting ready to slice it across her exposed neck.

Before that happened, Funetti's brain registered several distinct sounds.

From the side of the room away from the door, someone cried out as he released the motherlode all over the sweaty, soaked sheets.

At the same time, sharp screeching noises on the polished floor resounded from the doorway. Menacing growls erupted from a charging white locomotive. Amber dove over Vinnie's bed. Gripping jaws tearing at Funetti's hand. The knife clattered to the floor. Funetti's hospital gown torn from his body. Sharp teeth grasping the fleshy part of his ass as he scrambled for cover under the bed.

The sticky-handed patient moaned. A rare smile spreading over perspiring cheeks.

Edie looked at Steve. At Anthony Funetti's exposed ass. At Amber's snarling lips. A quick survey of the other two patients, but not wanting to linger on those scenes.

She turned back to Steve. "Did the warden give you any problems about bringing Amber in to see Uncle Vinnie?"

Steve rubbed his hand and glanced at the burns from the leash being sliced across his palm. He pursed his lips. "Said he'd make an exception, being Amber's a highly trained K9. But asked to keep things quiet—don't disturb the other patients."

Edie nodded.

Steve walked through the door. "How's Uncle Vinnie doing?"

"Sleeping like a baby." Then Edie added in a more serious tone. "He's gonna be fine, Steve."

Dominick snapped his fingers and slapped his knee. "It's Tony Two-Step. That's what Uncle Vinnie was trying to tell me."

CHAPTER 56

AS THEY NEARED THE FRENCH Quarter, the pace of the black and white taxi settled into an agonizing, slow crawl. The passenger loosened his tie and checked his watch. His tweed sport coat lay folded on top of the overnight bag squeezed behind the driver's seat. What passed for an air conditioning system did more to feed a pounding headache than cool the stale, tobacco-enriched atmosphere inside the cab.

It was only early March, but Fat Tuesday had targeted one of the hottest days of the year. With the humidity hovering near one hundred percent, the armpits on the man's wrinkled, white dress shirt were sopping wet. Rivulets of sweat had no trouble seeking a downward path to a sticky collar.

"What'd you say?" Agent Mike Finley leaned forward several inches, feeling the back of his shirt peel away from the grimy vinyl seatback. He couldn't make out a word the driver was saying, but he still wanted to keep his distance from the aura oozing from the man's whiskey-cured pores. Besides, it wasn't for any lack of volume—the man had all but screamed his words the entire trip.

What the hell language was this guy speaking?

"I sez, yawl needa ged oud right 'ere. Thiz'z faw as aw go."

When the words finally registered, Finley started to complain, but changed his mind and reached for his wallet instead.

"Yaw fust time in Nawlins?"

Finley got out of the cab, placed his bag on the ground, and handed over the cab fare with a generous tip. "No, I've visited New Orleans several times, but never during Mardi Gras season."

"Pshhh. Den thiz'z yaw fust time."

Finley nodded and took out a piece of paper. He was about to ask the driver to point him in the right direction, when the cab's engine coughed and rumbled, the tires squealing as the driver took advantage of a slight break in the traffic. Finley stood breathing in a cloud of fumes. The exhaust from the cab did a better job of cooling him off than the pathetic excuse for an air conditioner.

He had a rough idea of the location for his first stop, verified it on the map he fumbled with, and headed into the heart of the French Quarter. Raucous crowds, mesmerizing sounds of jazz, and malty aromas erased the stale taxi environs with a dynamic, raw mixture of excitement. The natives were restless, and Mike Finley was about to step into the pot.

It hadn't seemed like a big issue at the time he agreed to make this additional stop but lugging his bag in the sweltering heat and zigzagging his way through hungry mobs of drunken partygoers had him cursing out Olivia Davenport.

Her damn condo better be air-conditioned.

He fought his way along Decatur Street. He couldn't imagine the circus on Bourbon Street if the crowds along this peripheral route were so suffocating. When Finley spotted the Café Du Monde, he figured he was close. He checked the address and found the business about halfway up the block on the other side of the street.

Finley entered the store and asked the clerk if he had a package for Ms. Davenport.

Stepping back outside, Finley held the bundle at a distance, trying to keep it away from his overnight bag and sport coat. He looked to the western sky and thanked God the sun had begun to ease itself behind the taller structures in the Central Business District. A growing briny tang of seaweed encircled him, competing with the malty wafts hovering over the entire neighborhood.

With an added purpose in his stride, he turned onto the next cross street and headed toward Royal Street. His steps unconsciously keeping time to the riffs of combating saxophones. The roaring crowds reached a higher crescendo as he walked to the right on Royal, avoiding Mardi Gras ground zero by one block.

About a third of the way down Royal, Finley spotted the number of Olivia Davenport's condo. The three-story aged red brick building with white wood trim sported black wrought iron railings across second and third floor balconies. A bronze plaque next to the wide double entry doors stated the historic building was constructed in 1838.

Several strands of beads slapped to the ground at his feet. He looked up at the second story balcony to see a pair of oversized breasts bobbing under a raised T-shirt.

Olivia?

He couldn't see the face hidden behind the T-shirt. The breasts didn't look familiar either—not that he'd ever seen Olivia's. If those were hers, he wasn't sure he'd survive the evening. He entered the air-conditioned foyer and checked the number for Olivia's condo. Third floor. At least nobody had been flashing any body parts from her floor. With the sudden burst of dry, icy air, the sweat began evaporating from his body.

Finley exited the elevator on the third floor and rang the doorbell. The door opened and a tall, sturdy woman in her early forties stared at Finley. She had the strong, no-nonsense build of an athlete, but at the same time exuded an air of femininity in a body sculptured for contact sports under the covers. Her dark brown hair was wrapped in a tight bun.

Olivia Davenport had always scared the hell out of Mike Finley, and at his age he wasn't confident in testing the waters. Olivia smiled, and her face reminded Finley of a little girl who had just gotten her first taste of ice cream—not her first roll in the hay.

"Here's your damn oysters, Olivia."

"Hello to you too, Mike." Grabbing the bag, she stood back and gave him a onceover, her eyes lingering on his soaked shirt. "You dive into the Gulf and pick these yourself?" She stepped forward and poked him in the ribs. "Nah. You probably caught a glimpse of Angie's tits. She's been at it all day. The poor things are gonna get whiplash."

"I've heard yours are licensed as lethal weapons."

Olivia winked. "If you want to find out, we better wait till this mission's completed. You need to have all your wits about you—since you insisted on replacing my usual partner."

Finley sighed. "Okay. Enough foreplay. We should probably get to work."

Olivia stood aside, let Finley in, and closed the door. The aroma smacked him in the face. It was a pleasant blend of spices and tomato sauce steeping in a broth of

Cajun delicacies. Finley's stomach growled in protest as he inhaled.

Olivia's smile widened at his response to her culinary intonations. "It's my basic Creole stock, and the beginnings of a unique jambalaya recipe." She shook the sack of oysters Finley had handed to her. "Almost time for the finishing touches."

Finley licked his lips. "I am a bit hungry, but I was under the impression we needed to act on this lead right now."

"I'm afraid this meal's not for you, but if you behave, you can have a small taste before we leave."

Olivia made a quick phone call and then busied herself in the kitchen. "Grab a couple of Pepsis from the fridge and then bring over the stainless steel tray on the table. When you're done performing your duties for the evening, I'll buy you a real drink at Pat O'Brien's."

Finley wondered if she meant completing their mission, although she did look beguiling in the apron she'd just tied on. Kind of a domestic-erotic statement.

As if reading his mind, she turned slowly to meet his eyes. "I'd be wearing only the apron, but I'd have one less place to hide my pistol."

Quickly changing the subject, Finley said, "So how's this going down?" For the first time since he could remember, his face got hot. The Louisiana swamp furnace had nothing on Olivia's body.

Olivia bailed him out. "You get to wear one of these too." She pointed to the apron swung over the back of one of the chairs.

Finley walked over and picked it up. Thankful for the opportunity to turn his face away from her batting eyelashes. "*First String Catering?* You doing a little moonlighting?"

After shucking the oysters and cooking them for several minutes along with the simmering ingredients in the cast iron pot, Olivia spooned the finished oyster jambalaya into the warming tray and sealed the top.

As promised, she offered Finley a small bowl to taste. "The rest of the dishes have been packed in the van. It's parked in the alley. Have a bite and then we can go. I'll give you the details on the way."

CHAPTER 57

AS THEY EDGED THROUGH THE clogged backstreets of the French Quarter, Finley asked, "So this is a legitimate catering outfit?" The van certainly looked authentic. Bright, shiny lettering and logos splotched across the sides and back.

Olivia nodded. She braked to avoid hitting two drunks staggering across the road. "Anson borrowed this one. It had conveniently been scheduled for servicing yesterday."

"Anson? Anson Kostelecky? He's your partner, right?"

Olivia nodded.

"And where is Anson?"

"Since you decided to make an appearance, Anson's got our sixes tonight. He's been keeping an eye on the targets. Making sure they're staying put. Though we know for a fact they have no plans on leaving. Mr. Kravitz and your other friend—whoever he happens to be going by tonight—are relaxing over cocktails and waiting for Mr. Kravitz's favorite dish to be delivered from First String Catering."

The van emerged from the congested French Quarter tourist area and picked up speed along St. Charles Avenue, heading toward the Garden District. "Unfortunately for the real caterer, they believe Mr. Kravitz, at the last minute, canceled his order."

"Why didn't you simply buy the jambalaya from the same caterer?"

A sprawling smile appeared on Olivia, touching her eyes. "I got their recipe from a cookbook highlighting the premier chefs in New Orleans and thought I'd give it a shot."

"I've read real chefs leave out key ingredients so no one can duplicate their masterpieces."

"You're a shrewd one, Agent Finley, but it's not like our clients will be tasting this food. It's just got to smell authentic enough to lower their guard. Besides, you wanted to keep this operation under tight control. Once those two assholes disappear, the caterers might start thinking about coincidences and contact the local authorities."

Finley nodded. "Running an operation like this within the U.S. borders is still considered illegal, even if the president were to give his full approval."

"Then it's a good thing he knows nothing about this." She gave him a calculating look.

Finley didn't answer.

The catering van drove along St. Charles, and the houses began to get larger, separated by grander landscaping. Even the trees lining the wide thoroughfare seemed more majestic. Olivia turned left at a beautiful white cathedral and continued past a brick-walled cemetery with typical above-ground tombs. She made another left and approached their destination.

"Let me guess where Anson might be hanging out." He glanced over his shoulder. "Doesn't he realize cemeteries in this town can be dangerous?"

Olivia ignored Finley's comment. She slowed the van and it crept along next to an intricately laced wrought-iron fence topped with sharp, curved spears. Set far behind the fence and partially hidden by lush landscaping and copses of myrtle, sprawling oaks, and towering palms, the white colonial mansion dominated the entire neighborhood. As it had done for more than 150 years.

This was only one of many estate properties owned by Theodore R. Kravitz. At one time or another, most had been used to hold secret meetings between the world's most powerful and dangerous people. Under usual circumstances, Mr. Kravitz did not attend any of those meetings. Things had changed and, this evening, he and his only guest were desperate to regroup and salvage what they could.

Olivia and Finley passed the locked gates to the main entrance and continued down a narrow alley to the service road. Olivia stated their business into the remote intercom, and the gate swung aside, allowing the van access. She pulled up under the portico to the servant entrance.

"Follow my lead, Mike. Tonight, you work for me. I'm on top."

There was that damn wink again, Finley mused.

Olivia continued, "There's nobody else in the house. Only Kravitz and his guest. He's given the entire staff the weekend off to celebrate Mardi Gras."

They both got out of the van and loaded a portable serving cart with trays and containers. The door to the pantry entrance opened, and none other than the elusive Mr. Theodore R. Kravitz stood aside to let Olivia and Finley enter. Kravitz closed the door and led them into a service corridor next to the dining room. Standing to the side, dressed in a crisp white business suit, was a tall, elderly gentleman. Finley was surprised at how frail the man looked.

Kravitz stepped forward and pointed to the stainless steel tray labeled *main entrée*. "May I?"

As he lifted the top and took in the rich aroma, Olivia raised the lid from a smaller container on the second shelf and aimed the suppressed Glock. Two shots in the head to Kravitz; two shots in the head to his guest.

Finley opened his mouth but changed his mind, shrugging. Both men had fallen to the floor, face-up. He knelt down to confirm their identities before their faces became cloaked in blood. He'd seen Theodore Kravitz up close on several previous occasions, but this was his first encounter with Dunixi Sideris, also known as Mr. Clean. Finley looked up at Olivia. "So, this was your plan?"

"What? You wanted them to confess first?"

"Seems like you went to a lot of trouble preparing all this food."

Olivia reached into another container and pulled out two heavy vinyl sacks. "Okay, Mike, let's get the—" She stopped in mid-sentence and her head spun around.

"Oh-oh," she said in response to several distinct clicking sounds echoing throughout the house.

"Oh-oh?" Finley repeated.

Olivia dove at Kravitz's body, tearing open his shirt and glaring at the monitoring device strapped across his chest.

"Oops," she said.

"Oops?" Finley repeated. He hadn't paid much attention to the clicking sounds, but now he got a whiff of natural gas.

"Sonofabitch," Olivia said, unnecessarily. Before Finley parroted her phrase, she jumped to her feet and bounded to the door.

"Locked," she shouted. "All the windows are barred—even on the second floor. Those clicks came from a sophisticated deadbolt system on all the exterior doors. Triggered when his heart stopped beating. Pretty neat device he's wearing. We can't chance trying to shoot off the locks—probably wouldn't work anyway—besides—"

Finley finished for her. "Let me guess—we'll trigger the gas to explode. So, Olivia, you must have something else in mind."

This time, Olivia didn't wink. "At least Anson's prep work isn't going to waste. Follow me."

She charged through the dining room and into the grand foyer. They both ripped off their aprons but held on to them. Grabbing the ornately carved banister, she pulled herself around and up the wide, carpeted stairway. Finley was two or three steps behind and closing. His face was getting redder, but not from embarrassment. He followed her into the master bedroom and into a huge closet about the size of his apartment in D.C.

Olivia hopped onto a large cedar chest in the center of the closet and pushed aside a recessed panel in the ceiling. She latched on to the sides with both hands. Finley grabbed Olivia's ass and gave her a boost up and through the opening. She reached down and helped his frame into the attic space.

He could've imagined it, but thought he'd heard her whisper in his ear as she yanked him through the opening, *"Wait till later, I've got a lot more you can grab."*

Olivia switched on a small flashlight and carefully worked her way around boxes and crates. She found a small, dirt-encrusted window centered on the west gable. The sun had almost fully set, but enough ambient light filtered through the dense trees for them to see the steep roof sloping away from the attic window.

Finley nodded and stepped back. He raised a foot and kicked his heel through the mullioned glass. Shattered fragments sprinkled down the slate roof and disappeared over the edge. The pungent smell of the natural gas had worked its way into the musty attic.

From behind, Finley heard a loud clattering. He turned to see Olivia dumping out a large cardboard box and flattening it with her feet. She ran back to the window and pushed the cardboard through the opening, holding one of the flaps against the sill.

"Let's go." She climbed through the window and waited for Finley. She draped the apron on top of the cardboard and sat, keeping herself from sliding down the steep, slippery slope by grasping the edge of the window frame. Finley did the same and sat next to her.

She put one arm around his back. "You trust me, don't you?"

Before Finley responded, Olivia pushed away from the house with her other hand and the cardboard skidded down the roof at a frightening speed. As they reached the edge, the cardboard stuck in the galvanized gutter and a deafening blast filled the humidity-laden air, catapulting them over the edge. Arms and legs flailing like wings, but their bodies dropping like solid rocks, freefalling the entire thirty-foot height.

Blasts of flying concrete and burning wood from the raging inferno hurtled about them as they hit the kidney-shaped swimming pool and disappeared below the surface. Finley's shoulder skimmed against the edge of the diving board. Looking on the bright side, they had landed in the deep end. The muffled sounds of falling debris echoed mutely in the water. Above them, the burning house reflected off the surface.

Finley's body bumped against the bottom of the pool. He started kicking his legs and waving his arms to get to the surface, but when he looked to the left, in the remaining light he saw Olivia's body settling to the bottom. Her arms and legs limp; blood oozing from a gash on her temple. He switched course and swam to her side. With his arm wrapped around her chest he pumped his legs as hard as he could.

He fought for the surface and gratefully swallowed mouthfuls of hot, humid air as his head bobbed above the water line. At the same time, he struggled to bring Olivia over to the tiled coping. He hefted the woman over the side and rested her head on the two aprons he plucked from the pool. As he grasped her hair and pulled her head back and to the side, she coughed twice, spitting chlorine water in his face.

Olivia sat up and gazed at what remained of the once stately mansion. Finley ripped off a section of his shirt and wrapped it over the bleeding cut on her temple. He helped her to her feet and scooped up the aprons. "Can you walk?"

She nodded. "We need to see if the van survived—and get it and us the hell out of here before the authorities show up."

He dragged, pulled, and helped her back to the other side of the house. The portico had collapsed, the van nowhere in sight.

Olivia turned to Finley. "Anson must've come and got the van. That's why I had him wait in the shadows. He was supposed to drive it back to the shop as soon as we finished. He had orders not to hang around if things went bad." Olivia pointed toward the back alleyway. "He would've left his car parked around the corner—in case."

Finley drove and Olivia gave him directions. They weren't going back to the condo in the French Quarter. The place had already been wiped clean.

An hour from New Orleans, they exited the car and approached a tiny shanty at the edge of a deserted bayou. The front door slid open and Anson Kostelecky's short, wide frame filled the space.

He tipped his Saints cap and smiled. "Glad to see you folks are alive. I got your text. Transportation's waiting at the airport. There's a doctor on board, Olivia." He looked at Finley. "Are you coming too?"

Finley shook his head. "No, it's best we split up. Since we didn't dispose of the bodies as planned, I need to make a few calls. Most of the evidence has probably been destroyed by the blast and the fire, but someone's gotta lean on the locals a bit. Don't want them looking too hard at what happened. It's best for all concerned that those two gentlemen died as the result of a tragic accident." He shook his head. "The president isn't going to be happy about how things turned out tonight. Maybe at last he'll change his mind and accept my resignation."

Olivia signaled for Finley to lean closer and whispered in his ear. His eyes opened wide and he smiled. This time he was the one who winked.

"Tell me where and when."

CHAPTER 58

THEY MADE A HANDSOME COUPLE, blending in with the chic, early evening clientele. For the last thirty minutes Mike Finley and Olivia Davenport sat side-by-side at a small wrought-iron table at the street-side café.

Like the other couples seated around them, they watched the bustling crowds passing by. Some carrying bundles, others with baby strollers in tow, many holding hands. All enjoying the waning hours of an unusually mild and sunny late winter day. The first signs of spring touching the still dormant tree limbs lining Berlin's streets and parks.

Berliners, sallowed from short and dreary days, reveled in the chance to bask in the cathartic rays of a long-missed friend. The sun was about to relinquish its reign, and a crisp breeze dueled against the fading comfort it brought.

The Ku'damn, as the locals referred to the elegant shopping district along the broad Kufurstendamm, represented Berlin's global deportment to the world, although a growing younger element preferred the glitzy Potsdamer Platz as a reminder of the evolving nature of the centuries old city.

Finley watched Olivia slap down her third shot of schnapps on the table. He turned his head to the side and pretended to scratch his ear, his hand lingering for several seconds. Nodding at Olivia, he reached for his wallet. Olivia helped him root through the foreign currency to extract the correct bills. Her eyes appeared sharper than one would've expected after observing the three empty shot glasses lined up in front of her. During the same time period, Finley had nursed a single glass of pilsner and left at least a third of the brew when they got up to leave.

As she stood, Olivia stumbled slightly and Finley steadied her arm. She turned from the table with her foot gliding over a small pool of liquid dripping into the grooves of the stone flooring. Finley slipped into a lightweight jacket and helped Olivia drape a shawl over her bare shoulders. His fingers dawdled as they touched the soft flesh of her neck. He sensed her body react to the brief caress, filling him with images of last night and waking up in her arms this morning.

Finley guided her out to the street, and they strolled along the Ku'damn. In the distance, the war-damaged façade of the Kaiser Wilhelm Church loomed in the growing dusk. Olivia's stride appeared erratic, and she leaned in tighter to Finley. She was only an inch shorter than him. So when with moistened lips she whispered in his ear and gave a slight tug on his earlobe, anyone passing by would hardly have noticed the intimate act.

Finley kept an arm around Olivia's waist as they made their way along the crowded avenue. While they walked, Olivia's body swayed more, and she appeared to have a problem placing her feet in the proper position to maintain balance. Several times she tripped, avoiding a fall only because of Finley's assistance.

Those people approaching the couple on the busy sidewalk needed to be alert to avoid any possible collisions with the inebriated woman. Most were near misses, but she made contact with several pedestrians who hadn't sidestepped quickly enough. Finley, using his almost non-existent knowledge of the German language, stuttered out apologies.

An old man, shuffling along in their direction, barely kept himself erect, let alone watching out for anyone else. When he was two steps in front of Olivia, her left foot clumsily hooked to the right and her body pulled away from Finley's grip. She collided into the old man with a significant impact, her arms thrashing around his frail body for support.

Finley's reaction was swift. He spun around behind the old man as the momentum from Olivia's fall threatened to fling both her and the inattentive pedestrian to the pavement. Finley stabilized the startled old man and extracted the man's body from Olivia's clutches.

This time Finley made his apology in clear, precise English.

"I'm so sorry. You must excuse my friend. She's had a little too much to drink."

The old man nodded, muttering a few incoherent words in response.

"We'll be on our way," Finley said to the old man's back as he resumed his slow amble down the street. "I hope you'll have a pleasant evening, Mr. Lucchesi."

Mike Finley and Olivia Davenport continued to walk toward the old church, not looking back.

Philip Lucchesi took an additional six or seven steps before Finley's words registered. His eyes opened wide, but quickly squeezed tight as his trembling hands clutched his chest. He dropped to his knees, tottered for a second, and then flopped onto his back. Most people shifted their path around the stricken old man. Several stopped to gawk. One checked for a pulse but failed to find one.

Finley placed a finger against his ear again and nodded.

He straightened up and quickened his pace. Olivia mimicked his actions, no longer needing Finley's shoulder for support. At the next corner, they crossed onto the center divider and followed the masses of people through the turnstiles and headed down to the U-Bahn. Finley pulled out a map and struggled to determine the best route back to the hotel.

"This is one of the best first dates I've ever been on," Finley said after they hopped onto the next train.

"You really know how to show a girl a good time." She snuggled closer. "I could be wrong, but wasn't Lucchesi the last?"

Finley shrugged. "For now, but I'm sure there will be more to come. There's never a shortage of bad guys." He paused. "But not for me. I'm pulling the plug. As soon as we get back, I'm handing in my papers. Gonna relax for a while and eventually... maybe start something new."

"So, you'll have a lot of free time on your hands?"

He nodded.

Olivia pulled his head close to her mouth and whispered.

Finley smiled, cupped Olivia's chin, and kissed her lips.

CHAPTER 59

THE SUN HUNG LOW IN the western sky, and a distinct chill settled over the Sonoma Valley. Early autumn, and the shifting air currents channeled the bitter aromas birthed in the wine-crushing process over the deck in the once tiny A-frame cabin.

The entire deck had been ripped out and rebuilt when Steve and Edie tripled the square-footage of the original cabin. The expansive views across the Valley of the Moon and the southern vistas from the town of Sonoma to the San Francisco skyline remained the same. It was a clear night, and once the lingering glow of the sun surrendered to the shadows, the distant lights of the city would bracket the moon.

Steve and Edie sat across from each other at the same patio table that stood on the original deck the day Edie first showed up at Steve's doorstep.

Before picking up her glass of Chardonnay, Edie slid a hand over the smooth tabletop. "You did a great job refinishing this patio set. It's beautiful."

Steve waited for the punchline, but none came. He shrugged. "To me, it was always just something I found in a garage sale. Until the day I first gazed into your amber eyes while we sat at this table."

Edie twisted her head and narrowed her eyes: a playful smile spread across her face.

Steve shrugged again, returning the smile. "Well... excluding my first thoughts of wanting to toss you over the railing for coyote bait. But that was when I thought you were a journalist."

Edie clinked glasses with Steve and then placed hers back on the table. She leaned forward to kiss him. "For the record, we were still in the driveway when you first wanted to dispose of me, and I *am* a journalist."

Amber plodded over and plopped down under the table, resting her head on Edie's ankles and pressing her flank against Steve's legs. They both reached under the table and stroked the dog, encouraging her to roll over on her back. She was still in good shape, but the years and escapades had taken a toll. Monthly trips to the doggie chiropractor and daily supplements helped delay the inevitable failings of age.

Steve blinked back a tear, covering the action by raising his glass. Through the French doors to the great room, they listened to Rosa trying to boss around Amber's puppies, Max, Greta, and Sophie, who were now well beyond the age of Amber when she first burst into Steve's life. The dogs ignored Rosa's orders and lay bunched together on the leather sectional.

Steve and Edie stared at each other in a comfortable silence.

Then Steve snapped his fingers. "I almost forgot. Mike called earlier. He wants us to drop in for a barbecue this Sunday. He's smoking Almaco Jack fillets."

Edie opened her eyes wide. "Mike Finley lives in Key West. That's in Florida, if my journalistic instincts are still active. He does remember we're in California, doesn't he?"

"I'm sure he does. But I guess he's getting a little antsy. He's been retired now for over a month. Wants us to come on down and meet somebody."

"So, taxpayer-funded private jets are no longer at his beck and call?"

"Exactly why he suggested us flying down to see him." Steve pointed a thumb at his chest. "I'm still on the government payroll." He smiled.

Edie waved a finger. "Member of both local and federal unions. Which one do I bust first?"

"I told him not to forget his invitation for Thanksgiving dinner with us in Sonoma." Steve caught the shadow flutter across Edie's face. It was followed by a wan smile.

He continued, a hitch catching his words. "Be nice to see your family again. I remember the first Thanksgiving we spent together."

Edie nodded. "At Nana's house." She pouted her lips. "I thought you were going to propose to me that night."

"At least I got the words out before the next turkey dinner."

They sat again in silence, watching the moon toil to dominate the night sky.

Eventually, Edie looked into Steve's eyes.

"Do you think it's over?"

He caught her glancing into the great room, knowing her heart ached for the future of her family and the world.

Steve stood up and reached for Edie's hand. He helped her out of the seat and guided her to the railing. He pulled her tight. Her head rested against his chest.

"We both know it'll never be over. For now… we did the best we could. I'll never let down my guard, but I think the world's bought a little well-needed breathing time. We have a family to raise, Edie. One beautiful kid and a bunch of mangy mutts."

Amber raised her head from underneath the table and barked twice.

Edie's head turned up, amber eyes sparkling in the moonlight. "Speaking of beautiful children…."

She grabbed hold of Steve's hand and placed it on her belly.

THE END

Author's Notes

Amber Alert is the fifth book in
The Amber Restrained Series.

The series chronicles the escapades of two disparate individuals, Steve Casella and Edie Pauling, who surmount their differences and form an interminable bond that takes them on a journey to fight the injustices assailing the American dream. Together they challenge the seemingly unending barrage of incompetence and corruption that is ignored, facilitated, or orchestrated by the almost invincible power structure of an encroaching government. Along for the ride is Amber, a dog Steve has rescued from a fatal house fire. The sometimes disobedient canine companion is a constant source of frustration and amusement, but as part of their team, no one is more capable to assist when times get rough. As the nation and the world gather at the brink of extinction, Steve and Edie desperately try to gain traction against the slippery slope toward ultimate destruction.

<<ronvergona.net>>

Books by Ron Vergona

Opposition Reflex
Terrible Swift Sword
The Guarding State
Targeted Validation
Amber Alert